N_o S_{uch} A_{gency}

By

Eugene H. Eisman, M.D.

&

Diane Batshaw Eisman, M.D.

eeisman@bellsouth.net

ACKNOWLEGMENTS:

This book is the product of the efforts of more than the two authors. Nina L. Diamond contributed by showing us areas that would not be clear to the reader, and helped us create a first novel that would not read like a first novel.

To the Army for giving me all that wonderful experience in Viet Nam that I could draw upon for the novel's darker moments.

To Clem Alan, my dive instructor, who introduced me to all those interesting near death experiences.

The martial arts touch was gleaned from my Tae Kwon Do training with beloved Grand Master Young So Do and his family.

THE CAST OF CHARACTERS

Read Tolstoy and you will thank your lucky stars that there is a list of characters at the beginning.

How else could you keep from confusing the character Dimitrimsky Dompkkwskki with his friend Dromski Dopkswskkiire?

We don't read or write Russian, so the names we have chosen are short and simple. Our characters are not simple. They cheat, lie, and worst of all they change their names. Just try reading The Count of Monte Cristo without taking notes.

On the next page is a list of the characters in the order that they appear in the book. Try not to refer to it too often. We don't want to lose all the mystery. On the other hand, the authors have their own problem keeping everyone straight, and a little cheat sheet is useful.

Ombwe Nyuzu	A Major General of ?
Clara Weiss	Heroine cardiologist.
Jack Stanger	Hero type. Clara's boyfriend.
Georgii Aliyev	A starving scientist.
Lena Aliyeva	Georgii's daughter.
Sasha Aliyev	Georgii's son.
Eva Aliyeva	Georgii's wife.
Draco	Spy type. Military bearing. AKA Cliff. AKA Aaron.
The Director	Chief spy type.
Arthur Waldman	The Sidney Greenstreet (an old character actor) of spies. AKA Smith
Aaron Forsyth	See Draco
Sibyl Rosenthal	Spy type. AKA Cathy Slade
Cliff	See Draco
Jonathan Smith	See Arthur Waldman
Mark Sarasohn	Spy type
Arthur Waldman	See Smith

The

year

is

1975

CHAPTER I

"Out, out brief candle. Life is but a shadow…"

William Shakespeare

The odor of rotting flesh was over-powering. The body, stinking and decaying, was covered with giant blue flies. Forcing herself to move closer, she saw a row of bullet holes from automatic fire had ripped out guts, blood vessels, and brain.

Suddenly, the flies found a new feeding place. Swarming toward her, their feet sticky with gore from the body, they danced on her lips. Crawling over her tightly shut eyes, and into her nose, they bit wherever they explored. She wheeled and blindly ran back up the trail.

Retching, she ran in the soft sand. The ground sucked at her feet like quick sand. It seemed as if she was running in painful slow motion, when speed was absolutely imperative. At any moment a bullet from an M 16, a bullet traveling an amazing 3600 feet per second would tear through her back. As a physician, she knew what that bullet would do. The hole would be small, but the energy release would cook her tissues. Muscle, arteries, and gut would be changed to a pudding, and any bone within six inches of the bullet's path would be shattered.

Her shoes felt like fifty-pound weights. There was no ground cover, except for two-foot high palmetto plants growing two feet apart, their razor sharp, saw-like leaves cutting her legs to ribbons. There was no place to hide. The 120 degree heat on the bare little island was rapidly dehydrating her, and robbing her of what little energy she had left.

Several months earlier, Ombwe Nyuzu, resplendent in clanking medals and the robin blue uniform of a Major General, strode into a large sun drenched hotel lobby. He was an imposing man. Six feet two inches tall, with medals draped over the massive chest and belly of his three hundred pound frame.

"If I can only gain another six inches in height," he thought, "I wouldn't look so god-damn fat."

Taking a left past an immense urn, the fragile survivor of some ancient dynasty, he waded through the thick carpeting toward the door of his suite. Everything smelled musty-tropical. Years of hot, humid sun injected the carpet and draperies with an aura of sea, mold and heat that modern air-conditioning could not extinguish. The proprietors of the Ocean Club could well afford redecoration, but they figured that the mustiness, the sunlight, and the faded drapery all contributed to the 1990s nostalgic vision of 1930 colonial grandeur.

The lobby had its usual collection of tourists. Some were reading the *Wall Street Journal*; others were in the process of checking in, or sadly checking out. The vision of Nyuzu, this Technicolor manifestation of silver and brass, caused people to turn in his direction, and blink protectively as shafts of light reflected off his medals.

Fellow countrymen were mired in the pitiable poverty Nyuzu had escaped. Their per capita income was a miserable $275 a year. Only the hardy survived to adulthood. Most of the children had wasted limbs and big bellies. This was the hallmark of Kwashiorkor, the brother of death, a terrible disease of protein malnutrition. For the children that survived; adulthood was 20, toothless old age was 30, and death was 35.

Nyuzu's father was one of the few literate members of the tribe. This was not enough to lift his father from poverty, but it was enough to ensure that Nyuzu had opportunity. He remembered his little village.

The sewers were shallow ditches along the side of the street. Here and there, a wooden plank was laid across the foul stream allowing a street urchin to step across without walking in feces and urine. On each corner there was a little stone house set over the sewer. When nature called, you entered the enclosure, squatted over the stream, and did what you had to do. The odor of the village was burned into his mind, and even when he visited Washington, the lack of outhouse odor was a pleasant shock to his senses.

With tireless ambition, his father had convinced the right people that his son would be of great benefit to their nation if he could be properly educated. The small African government scraped its coffers to send Nyuzu to America. First, for a secondary education at which he excelled, and then to Harvard for pre-law and law. He appreciated the immense sacrifice, and responded with appropriate effort. His grade-point average even excelled the Oriental students in his class. Americans did not understand the Orientals. He understood them. Being first was a matter of family honor. Being second reflected as failure for the family. A failure of the living, and a lack of respect of your ancestors. It had been their shoulders that had brought him to his present opportunity.

He was now a Major General. Being a General in a little army top heavy with brass and a few illiterate soldiers, unable to write their names was no big deal. Their armament was a laugh. The common soldier carried the old US Army Springfield, a bolt action. An excellent soldier, using the bolt to feed individual rounds, would require a couple of seconds between shots. Nyuzu did not have excellent soldiers. They were painfully slow as they wrestled with the bolt between shots. Utilization of the front and rear sights was foreign to them. They merely pointed their rifle in the general direction of the target. He had two Maxim automatics; water cooled machine guns from the First World War. Their only artillery was a few mortars.

Nyuzu was special assistant to the President, and scheduled to attend a summit meeting of African states. The briefcase was chained to his wrist. He sat on the crapper with it chained to his wrist. He took a bath with his arm hanging over the tub – briefcase safely on the floor. He slept with that damn thing chained to his wrist. In that briefcase were the protocols for the meeting. There were other documents in that briefcase. But in spite of his top security clearance as a general officer, he did not know their contents. This must be bad stuff.

Carefully hanging his coat in the closet, Nyuzu stripped down to his under-shorts, and then lay back in the sprawling bed. This was a giant step up from the straw bed in his father's hut. This was a giant step up from the dormitory bed. The shoes he kicked off fell soundlessly into the plush carpet. He visualized his shoes falling through tall fibers, a jungle made of nylon fiber. Wouldn't it be ironic if he couldn't find his shoes in the morning, lost from sight in the deep carpet?

He was anxious to impress the other members at the meeting tomorrow. He went over his speech in his mind. It was well committed to memory. People who use cue cards do not impress their listeners. It takes a sharp mind to be a leader, and what better way to earn that reputation than by giving a twenty-minute speech without a note? Who knows, he could even be the next president. There were few in his country with the education to be serious contenders. He would be a strong president. He would change the import-export tariff policy the United States had foisted on the current leader. He would skillfully play the U.S. against China, until he extracted the best possible trade agreements for his country.

Nyuzu's reflections shifted abruptly to the bosomy white nurse he had met earlier that day on the plane. He had introduced himself to the young lady in the next seat with all the confidence and manner of a very important person. Still, he was surprised how easily the conversation flowed. She warmed up to him immediately, and soon they were exchanging itineraries, and making plans for later in the week. She called him "Om" rather than the cumbersome "Ombwe." It was a happy coincidence that they were sharing the same hotel, and he was sure that after a bit of rest he would have a sexually productive evening. Of course the briefcase on his wrist constrained his movement. She would have to understand. No matter, the three days of traveling took their toll, so he was asleep in minutes.

The hotel was small, but the guests were wealthy and demanding. Little men in white Bolero jackets flitted everywhere. The dining room had a staff of thirty-five, a large staff of featureless men. Not even the hotel manager would realize that tonight there were thirty-six men, rather than thirty-five. There were women in white, three maids for each floor. Most with black skin, but some were Oriental, and there was an occasional pale face. Were there the usual fifteen at work, or were there sixteen tonight? One of the pale faces was blond, and nicely endowed. She was pushing a cart of laundry down the hall.

A card, rather than a noisy key, opened each door. The machine for encoding the cards was kept in a locked administrative office. Not a real problem for somebody familiar with lock picks. The visitor walked soundlessly across the plush carpet. She placed a .22 caliber pistol gently between Nyuzu's eyes. There was no need for a silencer. Most of the gasses were expelled into the cranial cavity, and these gases are what create the noise of a pistol shot. A .22 short round is not that loud, anyway. The bullet has enough energy to penetrate the skull, but lacks the energy to exit to the rear. All it can do is lazily rattle around in the skull, turning the brain into a reddish soup.

South of Deadman's Cay

MARCH

CHAPTER II

"...a divinity that shapes our ends, rough-hew
them how we will"

William Shakespeare

The ancient Greeks believed that men make plans while the Gods laugh — or at the very least, smile indulgently. Lives are planned. They run smoothly on their tracks until a snag wrenches them to a standstill, or they careen in another direction. When things are idyllic, our inner darkness stirs. It warns us, "Such good fortune cannot last."

In the shallow sea of the Caribbean, waves can be so lazy that they pass unnoticed along the shore. What with blue skies and contented lovers, trouble comes only in the form of boredom. That is the way of the Bahamas. This is Paradise every day of the year. For two people this day was different. Paradise had turned to Hell.

Clara was choking on mouthfuls of saltwater, as she thrashed among the debris of Jack's boat. Fiberglass shards lacerated her skin. She was aware that kicking and twisting brought her battered skin into new contact with other pieces of broken boat, but panic engulfed her. Panic that forgot people drown when energy is wasted. Panic that doesn't care that blood draws sharks. Panic that kills.

Clara was not a stranger to the sea. She was an experienced SCUBA diver, and finally her training took over. She was sure that Jack was both alive, and mostly intact. As if on some distant, yellowed movie screen she visualized the events of the past hour. Flickering, in black and white, the film looped —an old silent movie, slowed to half speed, with the

contrast aged away. Is this all real? God, it can't be!
When she turned her head, Jack's boat would still be
there, whole, anchored, and gently rocking. A shard of
hull rammed into the side of Clara's head as a sudden
trough brought human and plastic together.

One hour ago the whole world was different—a
reasonable world.

Jack kept his eye on the echo sounder. After a
diligent search pattern, he was able to find the reef.
There are no street signs at sea, and finding a reef in a
featureless ocean is not an easy task. After two hours
of boring, zigzag patterns at almost idle speed, he set
his anchor carefully in sand so it wouldn't disturb the
living coral. Watched only by a gently warming sun,
Jack and Clara helped each other on with their tanks.
Then came the weight belts, and finally the fins that
made them look like two tall, clumsy frogs. In the
water, the fins gave them the power to swim
effortlessly, and even to fight up-current. On the boat,
the fins caused them to stumble about as they stepped
on each other's giant flippers. Together they struggled
to the port side bulwark, and made one last check of
each other's air pressure. Clara back rolled into the
water, and after making certain she was clear, Jack
made his back roll.

The reef was teeming with curious fish.
Underwater colors are bright, and sometimes
luminescent. Coral formations of unsurpassed artistry
appeared. It seemed to have been created to please the

human eye, an eye that was never intended to explore an under-sea reef. A curious clown darted from his crevice to study the giant with one eye and a sea of bubbles, while two gray angels, as big as serving platters, stood 5 feet off, majestically paired in a parallel array. Clara looked away, finding that Jack was nowhere in sight. After a few frantic moments, she caught him peeking over the edge of a giant tube sponge that engulfed his entire body. Jack joined her, and they continued their up-current swim. To Jack, it was a complete mystery that he would swim up-current, yet when it was time to return, he was always 100 yards away, and still had a difficult up-current swim to the boat. By the time he would reach the boat, he was exhausted from fighting the current all the way.

Cold water was the only thing spoiling this dive. For the third time in ten minutes, Clara checked the reading of her high pressure gauge. She was consuming air too quickly, but she was helpless to do anything except hyperventilate in the bone-chilling water. Although the year was too young for diving, enthusiastic followers of the sport found the weather a minor inconvenience. Her gloved fingers fumbled with the controls of the waterproof Ekalite case as she struggled to film dazzling sea worms clustered on Pillar Coral. Spirals of vivid red and white feathery gills covered the surface of the coral. These were the flowers of another world. Slowly Clara would creep up to a flower; finger poised over the shutter release, then just as she reached camera range, the flower would disappear. She would be left with a picture of featureless coral. In a tunnel too small to be seen, the worm had withdrawn itself and its plumage out of danger from the sea creature with the big glass eye.

Jack swam slowly ahead. Clara, always the conservative one, swam behind. The reef was fifty feet below the surface. An easy forty minutes of air was left in each tank, but they both knew that a large safety factor must be added to the Navy tables or they risked the bends from dissolved nitrogen. A plastic copy of the tables always accompanied sane divers. The ones with money to burn carried fancy underwater dive computers. By referring to the tables, they could tell how long they could stay down at their depth, without risking a hit. Certain limitations of the tables had to be kept in mind. The tables were designed for use in temperate water, and by divers in top physical condition. There was no safety factor built in. These tables were compiled for Navy Seals, in time of war when casualties were presumably acceptable to accomplish the mission. Clara and Jack were not athletes, and the water was cold. Both elements made the bends more likely.

Jack was in the lead, and with Clara's delay taking the photo, the gap was widening. She could see him disappearing into the dimness as he entered a channel between towering heads of crown coral. At this depth, togetherness was equated with security. Arching into a dolphin kick, she strained to catch up. Twenty-five minutes had passed, and her exertion had consumed tremendous amounts of precious air. Only eight hundred pounds per square inch of pressure remained in her tank. They would have to start back to stay out of trouble. She remembered last year when she had failed to check her gauge. Her partner had been thirty feet away with his back turned. He might as well have been thirty miles away. Clara had sucked the tank dry in an attempt to restrain her panic and return to the surface in a gradual, controlled manner. The choice then was simple. Either return to the surface slowly, with your body aching for one more breath of air, or shoot to the surface quickly, take your breath, and then die from the inevitable air embolism. After that harrowing experience, she swore she would never again get caught with low air.

She strained to catch up and show Jack her gauge. In the distance was another coral formation, and all she could see was the hazy outline of Jack's black flippers. She hoped he was planning to take one last hasty look and then let the current carry him effortlessly back beneath their boat.

A razor-sharp line separated one ocean stream from another as Clara passed into an even more frigid region.

Her struggle finally met with success, but as she approached Jack, she became aware of a mound just ahead of her partner. As the mound began to take on a shape, her interest was piqued. She forgot the cold, and forgot about the air. Half buried in the sand was the hull of a small naval vessel.

Nobody likes to admit it, but every diver dreams of discovering a Galleon laden with gold doubloons, and Pieces of Eight. Second best would be any old wreck, unspoiled, and full of artifacts.

A closer approach confirmed that the hull was steel. No name was visible. The numbers at the bow were barely discernible. Then she remembered that she was running out of air. Clara pointed to her gauge, and in response Jack showed her his pressure gauge. He was down to 700 psi. They both were carrying aluminum tanks and had started at 3000 psi. Their certification course had hammered into their heads: "Use one-third of the air going, one-third for returning, and reserve the last third for insurance." You could invade the last third only when you were safely under your boat. Seven hundred was hardly two thirds of 3000. Not even a nod in agreement was necessary as they reluctantly started back.

On reaching their small Sports Fisherman, Jack's tanks had less than fifty psi and Clara's gauge rested at zero. In the water, Clara slipped off the heavy scuba harness and passed her tank to Jack. Jack, with his strong legs, had entered the boat carrying a full load of equipment on his back.

On deck, Jack began rinsing the tanks with some of their fresh water supply. "Incredible," he beamed, too excited to be aware of the cold. "Doesn't look like anyone's been mucking things up around there—a virgin wreck!"

Clara's excitement was tempered by the cold. Tomorrow, with the sun at full heat, her enthusiasm for wreck exploration could be rekindled. For now, hot soup and warm towels.

She sat huddled and shivering, wrapped in a giant bath towel. The same towel you see everywhere in Miami Beach: emblazoned with a leaping sailfish and "FLORIDA across the top. Her long blond hair was a mass of cold dripping rope. A slender, large breasted woman, she was only 5'3" tall. Despite the lack of make -up and goose-pimple skin, she was still beautiful.

Jack began to wrap a towel around his shoulders, and then he paused and looked out over the sea. "You know, we could go back down." Sitting beside Clara, he put his arm around her. Thankfully she cuddled against the warmth of his body. But Jack spoiled the moment by saying, "It's early! What do you say we put on some full tanks?"

Burrowing further into her towel, Clara resembled a turtle with a fluffy, multicolored carapace. It took more than a minute before a word could escape her cyanotic lips.

"It'll be there tomorrow, I promise," she managed to croak between folds in her towel.

Shocked disbelief spread across Clara's face as Jack exclaimed, "Listen, I'm frozen' too. But if we leave we may not be able to locate that wreck again."

"The world would not end, nor would all the coral reefs disappear." Her nose emerged with a small speck of lint on it as she continued: "If you really

21

loved me, you would realize that what I need now is chicken soup, not frozen sea water. And yes, before you go any further, I am trying to lay a guilt trip on you."

"Okay, okay. But, while you're considering your comfort, consider also that we may very well be the first people to see that damn wreck." "And," he squeezed her, "wouldn't you like to have its ship's compass or sextant on your desk?"

Clara's fingers and toes were blue, and she knew that her red blood cells were tiny ice cubes clinking together, valiantly trying to squeeze through her capillaries. "And so," she shrieked as she ejected from her towel, "you're out of your mind! We've just about shot our limit down there. Have you ever seen a case of the bends? Well, I'm not looking for one." She suddenly realized that her cold, damp body was again exposed to the air. She recaptured her towel and continued, more softly. "You know, I can just see us, in a Lear jet, flying barely above the waves on our merry way to the nearest recompression chamber in Key Biscayne. Can you imagine the bill, or worse, can you imagine what it would be like to be paralyzed the rest of your life because you got a spinal hit?"

Smoothing the wet hair away from her face, Jack kissed her cheek. Clara hated feeling patronized. She felt childish as Jack reached into his dive pack for a large plastic card. The numbers ran together as sunlight reflected off the card. Using the edge of his logbook as a guide, Jack followed the rows across and the columns down. "You know, it's easier to read these things under water," he mumbled, squinting closer to the card. "If we wait two hours, the tables say we can take twenty minutes at sixty feet to explore without worrying about decompression."

"If we wait two hours, it's going to be even colder, and I'll end up hospitalized with hypothermia. Why didn't we bring our wet suit pants?" she moaned.

"Haven't you heard? The Gulf Stream is supposed to be a warm current. I thought we were silly bringing the wet suit jackets. Don't worry! I'll move the boat and anchor right over the wreck. We won't even have to swim."

Clara laid her head back against a life preserver. "Ah," she said, closing her eyes. Folding the towel around her, she said, "I am now in a toasty ski lodge. The pizza in the oven and the scent emerging from the kitchen tells me it's almost ready." Wriggling her toes, she continued, "My feet are near the fire, which of course, is not smoking, just crackling and glowing and warming the lodge. Through the picture windows I can see the last of the skiers coming down the slopes."

Jack paused while rinsing their equipment. "And where would I be?"

"You, my lover? You would be satisfying your whole macho-danger compulsion by skiing down some double black diamond icy precipice, thinking all the time how you would rush home to me and describe in infinite detail each muscle-twisting turn, every nuance of path angularity, all the breath-boggling scenery, the plethora of perfect photos that are now gone forever, and oh, the wonderful torture of it."

Laughing, Jack sat beside her. "Next morning, we'd ski together. You'd be thrilled because you conquered some advanced blue trail."

"Yeech!"

"Yeech?"

"You'd try to force me down some icy mountain, that was way above my level, and then I'd break all my legs and make your life miserable."

"All your legs?"

"Every single one of them."

"I think we'll need a service contract with an orthopedist before you go skiing."

"No, no. I will remain comfortable and warm in our lodge while you tackle the towering Alps. However," she added as she plucked a bit of seaweed from between her toes, "I shall remain useful. What will I be doing, you ask?"

"I hadn't, but I will if you want me to. What will you be doing? Consuming your quota of science fiction, solving the *London Times* crossword in twenty minutes, or four hundred and twelve pushups?"

"All of the above, plus, I will be keeping your cup of chocolate warm."

"Anything else you could keep warm?"

"That's entirely up to you."

Her arms slowly came out of the towel as she wrapped them around Jack's neck. As their lips were about to touch, Clara quickly bit Jack's nose.

Rubbing his nose, he commented, "Somehow, I don't think you're too romantic when you're soggy. Maybe the seaweed in your hair does something to you."

"I am sitting here, soul starved for a compliment, and you don't even notice my eyes, devoid of make-up, my lovely wet strands of hair, callused feet or unmanicured nails."

He held her head gently with both hands, and then slowly bent to kiss her nose. "Clara," he whispered, "some day you will look into a mirror, and you'll take your time. You won't focus on some nonexistent pimple. You'll just look deeply into your own eyes, and you'll really see that person."

Clara held Jack's hand and kissed a ragged fingernail. "You really *do* love me."

"A very perceptive woman."

"Of course, why else would you sit through all those foreign films you hate?"

"I don't hate them all, just the profound ones in Japanese, with Italian directors, French cinematographers, a script in German. Oh, yes! They always put the white subtitles against the light background and the black subtitles in the shadows."

Clara stood up, holding a hand out to Jack. "Let's get these wet suits off. I'm beginning to feel clammy."

The sun warmed her glistening body as Jack peeled her neoprene suit away. These things were tough to put on a dry body, even with the help of baby powder. They were almost impossible to peel off a damp body without help. Clara's suit was one of those short, legless, half-sleeve jobs. It was a suit intended for summer diving when the water was only a bit cool. Neoprene protected a diver's back against the chafing of the tanks, and straps, but gave only minimal protection from cold. Not many divers in the Caribbean used full wet suits because the water was usually warm, and having rubber enclosing your arms and legs felt like you were wearing a giant spring; sport divers complained of a loss of freedom, and the feel of hard-hat diving, like a commercial diver. What fun was that? You hardly get wet.

As abbreviated as the suit was, removal was most unromantic. Neoprene clung to skin like it was glue. Clara wrapped one arm around a guy wire, as Jack struggled to peel away her suit. Then they changed places and Clara helped Jack out of his wet suit. Each one had the same thought: "What would happen if I was out diving alone? Would I be doomed to wear this clinging sheath of neoprene until I reached land?"

Freed of the clammy garment, Clara began happily scratching her waist and shoulders. "I think I'm getting a new wet suit. Kate Robbins has one in a beautiful blue floral print."

"You think blue is less scratchy?"

"Of course, the better you look in your wet suit, the less you itch."

"And then, only your dermatologist would know for sure. You should keep in mind that sharks in the Caribbean are attracted to bright colors. Bright colored divers look too much like their food," he added, as he came over, wrapping his arms around her.

The sun warmed them as they stood close to each other without moving. The boat, at anchor, gently rocked.

"Better than being alone in front of your fireplace at that lodge in your mind?"

"That lodge I built a few minutes ago was only okay because you were on your way over, Jack."

"I still want to take you skiing with me."

"I still say, 'yeech!'"

Jack traced lazy patterns on her back. "I can't imagine enjoying something without sharing it with you. Even if it's just being in a darkroom watching a photo develop."

Like a butterfly, Clara kissed his neck, saying, "if only we could stop the clock right now, Jack."

Still in each others' arms, they sank down to the deck. Clara began collecting cushions and propped them against the hard wood. Jack grabbed Clara cuddling her. .

"You must have had a teddy bear," she sighed.

"I did."

"I feel very lovable when you hold me."

He kissed her as he began to slip the straps of her bathing suit down her shoulders.

"Jack! We're in the open."

"There's no boat for a hundred miles, and the nearest land is way over the horizon. We're really alone."

Her arms circled his back as they came together.

"Airplanes," she managed to whisper.

"We'll hear them before they see us."

A few giggles and Jack felt her muscles became more pliant and relaxed under his hands.

Coaxed by the sun into a breezy sleep, they lay in each other's arms. Clara's dream-merging thought was about how wonderful it was to feel as tall as Jack. Her shoulders were as high and wide, and her nose met his exactly. His eyelashes fluttered against hers. They now shared one giant lash. One part of her consciousness believed it was really the wing of some bird creating staccato patterns in the air.

Later, they lay side by side on the deck.

"We only have another hour of good light." Jack commented, his lips brushing Clara's nipples.

"Jack! Here we are, two lovers, rocking away on a boat in the Caribbean. Isn't it time for wine, or after play, or something? That was not a romantic thing to whisper into a girl's ear."

"But, honey, if we wait much longer, it'll be too dark to spot the wreck."

Smiling, she moved her hand down the angles of his face. She knew Jack. He could he so one-tracked. Never in a way that went roughshod over another person, but when his curiosity was piqued, he had to continue. If a picture wasn't right, he analyzed and experimented until it was. He could never let a problem remain unsolved.

"Okay, my love. But, before we dive, let's get some bearings. We might want to find the wreck again some other time," she suggested.

"I just got one of those fancy gadgets that uses the satellite. It's supposed to give you your position, accurate to a few yards. I can't wait to put it to the test. Especially since I paid 400 bucks for it."

The sun was close to touching the horizon when they dove again. Clara had been right. The water was even colder. Yet the presence of the wreck, perhaps one that was never plundered, was irresistible. Jack had used his Fish Finder sonar to locate the site. The dive began only yards from the wreck.

In the dimming amber light of dusk, an extraordinary changing-of-the guard was playing out. Fish swam into shadowy crevices of coral to hang motionless as if asleep. Night creatures crawled out of adjacent tunnels. Large moray eels slithered freely along the sandy bottom. Clara paused to stroke a queen triggerfish. The fish was oblivious to her. Coming from nowhere black sea urchins suddenly covered the coral. Urchin spines are needle sharp, and 12 inches long. They can easily pass through the thick rubber of a boot.

Swimming toward the wreck, they noticed that the bow had buried itself in the sand to a depth of several feet. The stern, with its twin screws, was now totally exposed. The angle of the sun allowed a little light to penetrate, and their visibility was no more than twenty feet. As they moved along the boat, they were able to estimate its length as seventy feet.

They swam back in order to examine the strangest find of all: Just forward of the cabin was a *deck gun,* eight feet long with a muzzle three inches in diameter. The gun's various wheels and gears were obviously designed to change its elevation and azimuth. The cabin proved to be a bridge complete with communicators for signaling the engine room, and both port and starboard railings held *mounted machine guns.* Recalling his army days, Jack determined that they were fifty calibers. Getting inside the wreck would be easy, not just through a hatchway, but through a gaping hole on the hull's port side.

Their exploration had begun in waning light. Jack and Clara now found themselves in almost complete darkness. Neither of them was experienced in wreck diving, and so they didn't have the foresight to carry necessary equipment from their boat. They had neither safety lines nor submersible lights. Time was running out, and because of the cold water, an additional safety factor had to be allowed.

Returning to their boat, Jack swung himself aboard wearing all of his equipment. He was then able to help Clara lift off her tank while she was in the water.

Before he could remove his tank, Jack noticed a boat approaching. "Uh-oh! It looks like we're about to be checked out."

A Haitian police vessel came alongside. A uniformed man, probably the captain, hailed them with a bullhorn.

"Hey mon, I hope you not be using SCUBA and catchin' lobster. You in fo' big fine if you do."

"Wouldn't think of being such bad sports. We're just sightseeing, but we found something interesting. It looks like maybe one of your patrol boats sank right here."

There was a pause while two men on the bridge appeared to argue. A few words of Jamaican Creole drifted across the water. The man with less braid on his cap yelled, "You drink too much Pina Colada. No way we lose boat here. You see old fishing boat. Hey! You drink and dive, mon, and you don't be back."

"What would a fishing boat be doing with a three-inch deck gun, and a pair of fifty-caliber machine guns?" Jack shouted.

The officials didn't answer. Their engine roared at open throttle, as the police boat backed off. Cutting their engines down abruptly, they dipped into an enormous trough about fifty yards away. Suddenly the recoil of a loud explosion rocked the police boat, and a thirty foot column of water shot up five feet short of Clara and Jack's port side.

"Jesus! Jump, Clara!"

Once more they jumped into the frigid water, their boat only a few yards away from them. Each was still wearing their diver's weight belt, taking them down more than ten feet before they could begin to fight for the surface. With lungs bursting, they saw their boat listing helplessly. Pieces of fiberglass flew, while round after round from light cannon tore through the hull accompanied by the rat-tat-tat of automatic weapons.

"Jack, they're destroying your beautiful boat," Clara said with disbelief. "What is wrong with them? Are they insane?"

"Insane or not. They're trying to kill us. Try to keep our boat in front of you. If they see that we jumped ship, those bastards will hunt us down in the water."

"What're we going to do when there's nothing left to hide us?"

"My tank's still on," Jack said. "We can go underwater, and maybe they'll figure we went down with the boat."

"How much air do you have left?"

"The gauge reads 1300 pounds. We can stretch it to fifteen minutes for both of us if we stay shallow and breathe carefully."

At the last moment, just as the sea swallowed the final wreckage of their boat, they released the air from their buoyancy compensators, sinking below the surface. Safely out of sight, Jack took two deep breaths from his regulator and passed it to Clara. She took her turn at air then handed the regulator to him. Motionless, in order to conserve air, they remained below for fifteen minutes. Breathing became more difficult and they realized that they were sucking the tank empty. Finally, they heard the roar of engines, as the patrol boat left the scene. When Clara and Jack reached the surface, gray horizon met black water in every direction.

"Thank God," she sighed.

After a few silent minutes, getting in tune with a normal rhythm of breathing, Clara's body began to shake. Jack paddled closer to her. She was sobbing, her legs frantically pumping up and down in the water.

"I was afraid," she gasped, "they'd be here when we came up."

"It's all right, honey," he soothed.

Her words were coming in explosive puffs of fury and terror. "We're still miles from land, and it's getting dark."

As the erratic quality in Clara's words and movements began to increase, Jack acted quickly. Reaching over, he pulled the lanyard on her vest, and the punctured CO_2 cartridge filled her buoyancy compensator with gas. The noise of the inrushing carbon dioxide began to calm her and the garment's flotation stilled the convulsive kicking of her legs.

Clara was terrified. No matter what she did, her body shook. Intellectually, she knew this was not the way to survive. Right now, her intellectual level was like Saran Wrap covering all other layers of her consciousness. Those other strata were roiling with primitive fears. She had to take control. "Breathing! That's a key. Slow and even. Just concentrate on each breath." Soon, her body relaxed as she rested in her buoyancy compensator. More for Jack than for herself, she said, "A boat's bound to come by sooner or later."

Hours passed. A slow leak forced them to blow air into Clara's buoyancy compensator every twenty minutes in order to keep her head a few inches above the water. The first time she tried this, she made the mistake of inhaling a bit of the gas left in her B.C. The carbon dioxide that remained in the compensator burned her lungs. For fifteen minutes, she hacked and coughed. Her chest felt tight, and she couldn't seem to get enough air. In time, the burning and wheezing stopped, and she was able to breathe easily again.

They were denied the refuge of pretending that this was a placid lake. Lifted by massive swells, they rose to dizzying heights, and then were dropped into deep valleys. The continuous lurching made them nauseous. The water's salinity increased beyond endurance. At first the sea had tasted faintly briny. Now it was solid crystalline salt. The sourness set their tongues on fire, and neither diver could keep from repeatedly gagging and retching. There was no freedom from the intense thirst. A fog enveloped Jack's mind, and as a phrase spun through his head, the naiveté of his thought made him fight to suppress an insane giggle. "Water, water everywhere..."

Clara was trying to think of anything except the numbing cold, when something brushed her leg. "Jack! Something bumped me." She strained to control her voice.

"Stay calm. Sharks aren't going to bother us unless we splash around like injured fish."

"I didn't say 'shark,' Jack." Her mouth stayed partially open while her eyes slowly dilated with fear. "There are sharks out here, aren't there?"

"There are always sharks around when we dive, but you know they're not interested in people."

"Don't hand me intellectual crap when I'm floating in ice water. There are too many reliable stories that say people can get arms, legs and heads chewed off."

"Those are only people splashing in the water — people who are drowning anyway."

"We're drowning anyway."

"Oh, honey," Jack whispered, brushing salt flakes from around Clara's mouth, "you know sharks interpret splashing as struggling fish. You never hear about divers being eaten, just some poor soul who was splashing on the surface."

Clara grabbed his shoulders, unable any longer to control her voice. "It's so absolutely black, I can't see my hand. Anything can be swimming within a foot of me and I wouldn't see it."

"Clara, when we were diving before, you let everything approach you. You were feeding those creatures with bread from your hand. You knew then that nothing would bite you. Last year a Green Moray Eel ate out of your hand. There's no difference now except that you can't see them."

"I've never fed a shark and I'm scared, Jack. I mean scared!"

Clara lost control as she shrieked, "The damn thing just bumped me again."

"Clara," Jack soothed. "You know we're going to be OK. Look, we've already been through worse. We survived that attack on our boat. We just wouldn't have survived that if we were not meant to make it now. These are busy waters. Lots of pleasure boats, good weather. We'll be picked up. We'll be stuck here until its light enough for us to be seen. Just try to conserve energy."

"I'll tie us together by hooking up the straps of our B.C.s. We won't drift apart even if we doze at the same time. Besides, we'll look like too big a mouthful if we stick together," he added with a weak laugh.

Icy water circulated about their unprotected legs causing spasms of violent shivering. Nightmarish visions of hammerheads, great whites, and things with giant tentacles drifted across Clara's mind.

Jack and Clara clung together, their legs entwined, trying to conserve body heat. The constant struggle in the water led, inevitably, to dehydration. After two hours an unbearable thirst competed with the cold. The briny taste of the sea continued to bring waves of nausea, and their hunger for fresh water was ever present in their minds.

Years of training to become a physician had shaped Clara's responses to emergency situations. She learned to act with competence, and used humor to lighten a horrendous predicament. Jack's weak attempts at comfort did nothing to alleviate her anguish. It annoyed her. Their only option was to continue floating helplessly in an inky blackness. In the dark water, more primitive emotions and thoughts began to emerge. She wanted to disconnect all functions of her brain. Let this male take charge. Let him handle things and make them better.

Jack floated in silence.

"Damn!" he thought. "I could cry. Why is the man always supposed to be the strong one? With all her training, she's better equipped than I am to handle emergencies. I've never been in such a miserable mess in my life." Deep within his mind he sighed with helplessness, frustration, and fear.

She felt Jack's arm around her shoulders, pulling her closer. His gentle, salty kiss started tears down her cheeks. "It'll be OK, trust me. Try to sleep." Pushing the wet hair out of her eyes, he said, "If we survived my navigation out here, we'll survive tonight.

It's getting lighter already. When you wake up, it'll be morning, and we'll be picked up."

His arms tightened about her both to reassure her, and to conserve their heat.

As she drifted, half asleep in his arms, she remembered their first meeting three years ago.

Near the end of a particularly grueling Friday morning, knowing that Dr. Ben Fishberg would cover for her, Clara looked ahead to a peaceful weekend away from her cardiology practice. A good novel, sleeping-in on Saturday, and then a Sunday dive at Elliott Key.

Casey entered the office. Searching at first for a clear patch of desk to land a chart, she changed her tactics to making neat piles out of chaos. Clara finally volunteered, "Okay, I'll stay ten minutes later tonight and get my desk cleared."

"Ten minutes!" Casey's voice boomed from the hall. "Don't bother, Doc. I've already called in a few wrecker services for estimates."

Casey shook her thick golden hair. "It's really incredible. I remember when we moved a desk into this room a couple of years ago. I know it's under there somewhere."

"I can still find the telephone so it can't be that bad."

Clara walked into the lab for a cup of coffee and cookies, her afternoon fortification. Munching away, she asked, "Who's my next patient?"

"A Mr. Stanger, for one of the scuba physicals. Ann did his chest film, but it's not developed yet."

"He's gorgeous," Casey broke in. "I don't think there's an ounce of fat on his sinewy body. He's got beautiful, black hair, and I told him you were single."

"Great, Casey." Clara tried to give her office manager a nasty look, but she could never manage it with Casey. The cardiologist was five feet three in her stocking feet, and that included several layers of jogger's calluses. Her most comfortable heels stretched her only up to five four and a half. Casey was six feet tall, unshod.

"Look, Doc, you are extremely single. The weekend is here. It should not be spent two thousand leagues under the sea cuddling up to a sting ray."

"Casey is right," Ann said, as she brushed cookie crumbs from Clara's white lab coat. "You should go places where you'll meet young men."

"I don't believe it," Clara groaned. "I can't figure out what I've done in my previous incarnations to earn so many Jewish mothers in this one."

"And Casey and I pray you should only *be* one some day."

Casey was a remarkable office manager. Her compassion soothed the sick and frightened. With firmness, and some help from her imposing height, she extracted money from those patients who, although able to pay, were reluctant to honor their debts. It was a warm, relaxed office, with Casey's wit transforming the hysterical into the humorous.

The office banter hit a tender spot for Clara. She was far from happy over evenings filled with hospital meetings, emergencies, and medical journals. In a profession filled with men, she rarely met someone uninvolved and attractive who wasn't turned off at trysting with a woman doctor. Those seductive offers from her colleagues only came from the married ones.

Sensing Clara's irritation, Casey deftly pulled Anna out of the lab.

"She's growling," Casey said. "It'll be a twelve-cookie afternoon. She'll gain a pound and be impossible Monday."

Clara gulped the hot coffee, managing to splash some on her blouse.

Changing into a fresh lab coat, she studied herself in the bathroom mirror.

Blond hair fell to her shoulders, gently curling under; the soft bangs framed her slightly rounded face. Despite countless dive trips, and hours crewing on sailboats, sun screen had kept her skin fair and unfreckled.

The large eyes returning her gaze displeased her — they were "no color." Applying for things like a driver's license caused her pen to hover aimlessly above the line that said, "Eyes." Actually they were chameleon, changing from deep gray to blue-green. Under certain lights, reflecting certain colors, they were even tinged with violet. Her eyes were, of course, her most startlingly beautiful feature. She didn't know this. Clara's physical self-image was embryonic. Entering college at fifteen had robbed her of the self discovery girls normally acquire during this period. No time for hours in front of mirrors, piling her hair in different ways, experimenting with eye make-up, followed by a presentation to her friends for a serious critique. To Clara, a perfect circle of a face peered back unbroken by any artful symmetry. Her fair, clear skin seemed bland. Full breasts with slim hips and firm, slender legs—the reward accruing to a serious runner—she dismissed as "top-heavy."

Casey referred to Clara's social life as "icky." It was actually nonexistent. Doctors were just not "In" as dates this season. Flight attendants, always; but a lady doctor was a conversation-stopper to an attractive man. Perhaps it was the fear that she knew more about his physiology than he did. "She knows how I work. *I* don't even know how I work." The only thing worse would be dating a woman physician who specialized in psychiatry. "She not only knows *how* I work, she knows what I'm *thinking*."

"Casey, you can show the next patient into my office."

"Comb your hair first," shrieked Casey.

"It *is* combed," Clara fired back.

In her office, Clara noticed that all the disorder on her desk had been organized into piles. 'Casey's touch," she sighed.

Clara's desk was a huge, teak "L" shape. The mammoth desk was meant to hold all of Clara's paraphernalia with neatness and organization. Of course, it didn't. Clara suspected that she had some sort of learning disability, or maybe the brain area that helped you to organize had been shorted out at birth. As far back as she could remember her room was always a mess. Probably her nursery turned itself into chaos as soon as her mother closed the door. Her father once framed a cartoon he found, possibly from the old *Saturday Evening Post*. It showed a meticulously groomed teenager greeting her date, not a hair out of place, departing from a bedroom that King Kong must have swung through.

Ann had selected the rug, lush heavy pile in comforting earth tones brightened by flecks of orange. A small orange sofa (to create a sunny feeling and warm her office, according to Ann) occupied a corner of the room. Clara found it great for sacking out between patients. Two chairs faced her desk, the wall behind her loaded with certificates. Matching teak bookcases covered the wall to her left, and to her right, richly wood-paneled in shining oak was a display of needlepoints made for her by Ann. Clara's two favorites were a huge monarch butterfly, and a large oval filled with flowers on a black background. Ann maintained that her masterpiece was a large rectangular "no smoking" sign she had done for the waiting room. Daisies fell haphazardly against the letters, as if to soften the blow for those die-hard nicotine addicts.

On the most unobtrusive wall, behind the chairs for patients, hanging almost shyly, were a few of Clara's own photos taken with her old Nikon FTN.

Grabbing the chart from the door, Clara entered exam room #1. Holding out her hand, she said, "Mr Stanger, welcome to our office. I'm Dr. Weiss."

"Well," he smiled, staring at Clara. "I'm impressed. When I heard the doctor was a woman, I imagined an older lady with glasses."

Uncomfortably, Clara smiled back. All she could manage was a "yes." When people qualified "doctor" with "woman" she felt twinges of irritation. Why? She knew one of the reasons she went into medicine was to prove something. With that title surrounding her name, she didn't have to deal with her insecurities. She could just throw out, "I'm Doctor Weiss," and she'd made quite a statement. Call her "Miss" or "woman-doctor," and she was shaky and angry.

Going through the usual introductions, hand-shaking, chair scraping, Clara's saw a tall, lean, confident-looking man. The usual garbage about "shocked to see you're a doctor," didn't nettle her. He seemed so nice.

Protectively pulling her white coat around her, she said, "I understand you're here for a scuba physical, Mr. Stanger."

"That's right. Al Clemson's my instructor. Some of us don't have regular doctors to do our physicals, and he recommended a couple of doctors who are divers. You were only a couple of blocks from my apartment. You know, I haven't been to a doctor in years," he said smiling. "I'm really overdue for a physical."

For a millisecond, Clara's eyes glazed over. My! All those iridescent teeth in that tan face. He was really gorgeous with a sleek, kind of jungle look.

Jack smiled at her, talking about the scuba course he had just finished. She sat back, lost in a swirling daydream of this man. Clara disliked long hair on men, but his black hair just looked carefree.

Taking control of the interview, she began to deal on the professional level for which she was trained.

"In scuba, we're most concerned with disorders of the ears, sinuses, lungs, and cardiovascular system. Of course, we wouldn't want to clear somebody with a seizure disorder. You said you haven't been to a doctor recently?"

"Actually, not since Vietnam."

"Vietnam? That must have been frightening."

"Thinking about it is worse than being there. It was just one day at a time, and then finally, you DEROS. Then you start thinking about how lucky you are to have all your arms and legs."

"DEROS?" Clara leaned forward. A crossword puzzle addict, this was a nugget to store in her brain.

"Typical army fog for your *estimated date of departure* from Vietnam. When you arrive, the whole year stretching out in front of you boggles the mind, but you just plod through, thinking that each day is only one day. Most of us kept maps of Vietnam divided into 365 little fake counties. Each day we would color in one of our counties, and when the whole map was colored, we went home to the real world."

"Were you infantry? "Asked Clara."

"Well, I figured, if I have to go I want to be challenged. Let me tell you, Special Forces was some challenge."

"Well, since you haven't had any regular medical care for a long long time, we should do a complete history and physical."

"You go over me from stem to stern, huh?"

"That's right. I think we have enough time today. First of all, how do you feel in general?"

"Fine."

"We'll just start at the top and work down."

Making rapid notes Clara asked. "Have you ever had any ear infections, or pain, or discharge from your ears?"

"No."

"Headaches?"

"Rarely."

On a table, in a baggy, green paper gown, Jack felt naked and ill at ease. She, however, was on her own terrain.

Checking Jack's blood pressure, she happily clucked, "Beautiful! 110/60."

As she entered the figure in his chart, he said, "I've been running five miles a day for several years. I've heard running really lowers your blood pressure. When I first went into the army, it was 140 over 80, and I was younger, of course."

"Why, I run, too."

Serious runners share a special bond. Behind that simple statement "I run" are episodes of painful tendonitis, muscle cramps, and other tortures until you find your running style. Dragging yourself out of bed early in the morning, or away from an evening party to run; self-discipline to continue when you're tired, or the weather is not postcard-perfect; watching what you eat the hours before you run, no matter how delectable, so you won't get those awful cramps; running when you would like to go to a movie, or party with your friends. Then there's your own set of mystical pre- and post-run stretching.

"I'm only up to three-and-a-half miles a day," Clara continued. "If you're interested, I can give you some information on the Miami Runners Club. We've had some terrific speakers and films at our meetings, and I've just gotten into the weekend fun runs."

Probing his ear canals with her otoscope, she commented, "Some old scars on your ear drums—just means you must have had some ear infections as a kid. That shouldn't be a problem. Now, do you have any trouble clearing your ears when you go under?"

"None at all," Jack answered.

Listening carefully to his back, while Jack inhaled and exhaled deeply, she said, "Your lungs are nice and clear. Ordinarily, in a non-smoker in such good health, I wouldn't bother with a chest x-ray, but since you're going to be diving, and haven't had one in several years, I think we made the right decision to do one today."

Jack nodded his head in agreement.

She continued, listening to his heart, palpating his abdomen. Then she insisted on performing a rectal exam. It took some explaining to show him how important this part of the exam was. Men were so shy. Women have been going to male gynecologists for years. Nobody likes being up in stirrups in that terribly vulnerable position, but women recognize the importance of the PAP smear, and readily subject themselves to this indignity. Men can be so impossible!

When she was finished, she paused at the door and said, "After I look at your chest film, Casey will bring you back to my office. I should have your scuba form ready by then."

Seated in her office, Jack scrutinized the photos on her walls while she completed his paperwork.

"I'll tell you something, doctor, the photos in your examining room are all pretty damn good, and the macro of the mushroom behind me is really unusual. Where did all the prints come from?"

"They're mine," she smiled. "Including the developing. I crammed an enlarger next to my x-ray processor."

She hesitated before continuing. "Your information form says you're a professional photographer."

"Yeah, I'm a freelancer."

Behavioral science and interviewing courses cautioned against bringing personal experience and fancies into an interview situation. Fleetingly, Clara realized she should be in charge of leading into a discussion of Jack's physical findings and lab work. Shouldn't be aimlessly chatting now. New patient. Must establish proper doctor-patient relationship. She looked down at her pen as she retraced her signature, and said, "Do you really think the photos are good?"

Jack leaned on Clara's desk, looking straight into her eyes. Then he grinned as she tried to look elsewhere. "Doc, you've got some very fine underwater shots on these walls. What do you shoot with?"

How the hell did women do it? Let a man know they were available/dateable? What do you do? Bat your false eyelashes? Drop your stethoscope at his feet? Run him over with your car, and then follow with a romantic rendezvous in the emergency room? Shit! Anna will be at that awful buzzer soon. I'm taking too long.

Clara tried to cover her discomfort by talking.

"The mushroom was shot with a one-0-five millimeter Nikor on a bellows. The other print in back of you…" While she chattered on about her camera, Jack mused about how a woman could be at the top of her profession, and yet be insecure. The idea made him smile as she moved out of her chair and went to the wall behind him. He turned as she indicated a print.

"This one is something I took in Caesarea — in Israel."

"I know. I once had a *Vogue* assignment there in an artists' colony."

"I think this photo's my favorite," she continued.

Clara turned toward him, expecting some sort of comment. A huge, barren, gray-brown tree, with its few branches in an intricate, yet mournful pattern, held foreground interest. In the background ancient ruins melted with the shadow of the tree, and the cloudless sky shone clear and bright blue.

Remembering a psychiatry professor who discussed closing up space when greater intimacy is desired, she sat in the chair next to Jack.

"It is a good photo," he said gently. "You've been shooting long?"

She nodded her head. "I started diving in high school, and then took up photography so I could bring back something from the reefs." She began to chuckle as she remembered all those early underwater photographic disasters, which still occurred too frequently.

"What's so funny?"

"My first undersea photographs."

"From what I gather," he smiled, "It's unusual for the equipment to work. I hear a lot of yapping about the moray eel that got away because the damn strobe didn't go off"

"Or just kept going off, and destroyed its batteries," Clara added.

She jammed her hands in her lab coat pocket and began mutilating the prescription pad as she tried to think of something moderately flirtatious. "I looked at your chest x-ray, and its okay."

With reluctance, she arose from her chair and crossed to her desk. As she handed him the scuba paper saying he was cleared for dive class, she asked, "Would you like to see what your chest x-ray looks like?"

"Fine."

As she showed him down the long corridor to the darkroom area, Casey and Ann grinned over their departing backs. Casey opened the sliding window, and perused the patients piling up in the waiting room. "I'm terribly sorry," she announced, "but Doctor's had an emergency, and will be an hour late. You can wait, or I'll re-book you for the first thing Monday morning."

Casey muttered to herself, "Thank God no one's got chest pain."

Casey, fastest dialer in Miami, was already on the phone canceling the rest of Clara's morning.

Following Clara down the hall, Jack remembered those ancient darkroom jokes. Too bad he was past sixteen, and a little old for ass grabbing. He had to be more sophisticated. Too bad!

Clara pointed to the film on the view box. "That structure in the middle is your heart. It's nice and small."

"What if it's big?"

"Usually, that would indicate heart disease. Basically, the heart is just a pump, and as it loses efficiency, it becomes big and boggy."

"Well, beautiful as it may look to you, I don't think I'd want it framed in my den."

Clara laughed appreciatively.

"What's that?" Jack pointed to something below the heart shadow.

"Stomach bubble."

"Doctor Weiss, I know you're gonna think I led you into that one, but I'm starving, and I need someone to show me a nice restaurant around here."

"Oh," escaped softly from Clara. She knew she couldn't say yes because she had other patients to see.

Watching her, Jack thought, "When she can't hide behind a stethoscope, or view box, this is not a very poised woman. She obviously likes me. Why is it so hard for her to say yes, I'd like to spend some time with you?"

"Or maybe, dinner tonight would be better for you." He wanted her to smile again. "Don't worry about me. I'll just starve until tonight."

"That would be lovely," Clara said. "I mean dinner," she laughed, "not your starving."

As they walked past the desk, Casey said quite loudly, "All your morning patients have canceled, Doctor. Since it's your afternoon off, you can run down to the planetarium and see that show. You know, you'll never have a better chance. If you wait for the weekend, who knows what emergencies the fates may have planned."

Turning to Jack, she queried, "Have you ever been to the planetarium down here? Yerkes Observatory quivers each time Miami mounts a new show. Doctor's been anxious to see this one. You really shouldn't miss it. It's in your field. Holographic photography."

Jack knew the next line in Casey's script.

"Well, since Doctor Weiss is free this afternoon, we ought to run down together."

An embarrassed Clara retreated down the other end of the hall, toward the lab. Jack called out to her, "Why don't we leave as soon as I pay my bill? Then we'll have time for lunch at the marina."

Casey's expression brightened.

Walking to Jack's car, Clara felt skittish. Actually, it was similar to what she experienced in the first few minutes of a school play. She'd walk out on stage, feeling as if she were at the top of a roller coaster, without any control. Yet, her body did all the appropriate things on its own while she could hear her voice off in the distance, saying all the right lines. Somehow, the real Clara hovered around and observed this performing Clara. Her feet moved in unison with Jack's toward his vintage 240-Z. Her voice automatically filled any conversational gaps with the usual cluck about Miami's weather. She was annoyed with this woman who was discomfited by an attractive man.

Nearly all her dates were blind arrangements via the wives of colleagues who managed to dredge up Cousin Hymie who was doing well in investments, or some primate who would spend the evening bragging about himself; as enticing as a palmetto bug. Clara was able to feel safe chatting sociably, remaining uninvolved.

She could keep those painful areas of self-worth, and self knowledge securely cocooned away from her awareness. This worked until she found herself confronted with a man who was physically attractive, confident within himself, with a sense of bravery about him. A man she liked.

Taking her arm Jack steered her around to the passenger seat.

Clara managed to trip as she entered the car, falling across the gear shift, her rear end up in the air. With the choke poking her stomach, she heard Jack laughing gently as his hands encircled her waist pulling her up.

"You hurt?"

"No, we klutzes of the world develop some kind of protective immunity so we no longer feel our bruises."

Lunch at the marina dissolved into the Sangria, which turned the harbor into a Monet-like vista. Then, they walked hand in hand throughout the planetarium, discussing the practical applications of holography. With Jack's arm around her waist, contentment filtered through her mind. Even her beeper cooperated by remaining silent. No nurse called wanting to know what Mr. Ackman could have for his constipation, or if Mrs. Kemmelman should increase her insulin because she had chocolate cake for lunch. Back in Jack's car, she gave him her address, invited him to dinner, and promptly fell asleep.

Jack glanced at the sleeping woman as often as safety permitted. Faint shadows crept under her eyes. Cardiologists probably didn't have many uninterrupted nights' sleep. Vulnerable, that's how she looked.

He pulled up in the lot of Clara's building. As the heavy engine rumbled to a stop, the stillness awakened her.

"God, you have great air-conditioning," she said. "That vent was blowing right on my face. Loved it."

"You'd like the wind in your face on a sailboat, if you could manage to find a baby sitter for your friend." Jack pointed an accusing finger at the beeper hanging from the shoulder strap of her bag. "We could spend a day sailing."

"Sounds great. I'll ask Casey if she'll make us some of her great chocolate chip cookies, and I'll bring some Piesporter."

"Cookies and white wine?" Jack asked, as he helped her out of the car. He did this very carefully, so she wouldn't trip. He was beginning to know her well.

Fishing in her huge bag for the apartment key, Clara muttered, "It's a good combination. Red wine usually overpowers anything but ginger snaps."

Watching her struggle, he said, "Why don't you let me hold your purse while you hunt around? That monster looks too heavy for you to support with one hand."

"I can't find it. I know it was here."

"Why don't you look in one of the zippered side things?"

"I never put it there," she protested, unzipping the compartment anyway so he wouldn't think she ignored his suggestion. She came up with her key. Feeling foolish, she mumbled something about maybe putting it there so it would be accessible, and not in the dark reaches of her bag, and then forgetting she had made the change. Jack smiled. He had the insane desire to straighten up her bag, and organize everything neatly for her. With Clara, it would probably be a career. He was imagining what her apartment must look like. Clothes piled all over her bed, and she'd be self-conscious about her messiness. He pictured her place as clean, but with the furniture and floor totally obscured by clothes, books, and papers.

On the way up in the elevator, Clara thought, thank God, the housekeeper came today. At least the bed was made, kitchen cleaned, and all her assorted junk in neat piles. It always looked better; the same amount of crap in the same space, but when Lois finished piling it up, it just looked like part of the decor. Clara was a real marshmallow, never having the guts to ask her housekeeper to hang things up, or straighten cabinets. The closets were filled with junk anyway, so where could things be put?

Watching her fumble with her key, Jack shook his head. Finally he suggested, "Turn it the other way," and the door opened. Clara looked at him forlornly. "You wouldn't believe I'm the fastest cardiologist north of the Pekoes at inserting a right heart catheter, would you?"

"I would," he said sincerely.

It was neat. Jack was shocked. "Bet she had someone in to clean," he thought wryly. To their left was a small kitchen. Clara took some packets out of the refrigerator, and put them on a drain board. "Casey's dad has a boat and loves fishing. He's one of those unusual fishermen, who catch more than they can eat, so he gives it away. This is some dolphin. I just dumped it in the refrigerator when I brought it home from the office yesterday. It's a good thing I forgot to put it in the freezer."

Jack grinned as he thought, "We're lucky you even remembered to put it in the refrigerator, let alone bring it home from the office. I bet sometimes you forget, and leave it in your car. The Florida sun must do wonders with that." He was beginning to know Clara very, very well.

As Clara began to unwrap the tinfoil covering the packets of fish, she said, "I've got some wine stored in the closet right next to the kitchen. Why don't you pick something for dinner?"

"In a closet?"

"Uh-huh," Clara mumbled as she began ransacking the refrigerator for fresh limes. "Don't worry. They're not upright."

He poked his head into her small kitchen. "That is not why I approach your closet door with a hint of anxiety," he thought. Gingerly, he opened the door, stepping nimbly to the side. A few tennis balls rolled out at his feet. The bottom of the closet was a wealth of rackets in various states of disease and stringing. These began to topple as the tennis balls, which had precariously propped them up, went into the living room.

As jack scrambled along the carpet, accumulating the balls, Clara shouted out to him. "It's a good thing I cleaned out that closet last week to store my wine. The only mess is on the bottom."

Stretched on his stomach, his long arm finally made contact with a ball hidden beneath the couch. "Wonderful!" he muttered.

Walking back to the kitchen, he watched Clara for a few minutes, enjoying the picture of her shapely rear as she hunted in the bottom shelf of the refrigerator.

"I can't find them," she said irritably.

"What?"

As she emerged from the vegetable crisper, Jack held his breath, feeling sure she'd manage to bump her head on something. When she straightened up, unscathed, he allowed himself to exhale.

Standing there, in her tiny kitchen, his arms cradling a slew of tennis balls, he asked, "What are you looking for?"

"Fresh limes. They're great on fish. I had a dozen here yesterday."

Staring at the large bowl of limes on top of her refrigerator, he indicated, "Up there."

"Oh, I forgot. Thanks! Must be great to be six-two."

As Clara reached up for the limes, he quickly said, "Don't! Just show me to your garbage and I'll get rid of these dead balls. Then, I'll get down the bowl for you."

As Clara began squeezing limes over the fish, he returned to her closet and gathered up the most decrepit of the rackets. They arrived quickly in the trash. Then, while Clara set the table, he neatly arranged the few usable items on the bottom. He arose and selected a Cote D'Rhone from the shelf.

"How come a red wine?"

"Just as good with fish. I don't think we have time to chill anything," he answered.

It was a simple but excellent meal. At least she could cook. What do you mean; "at least," Jack berated himself. "She's brilliant, beautiful, and charming. That touch of disorganization is very appealing," he tried to convince himself.

The fish had been broiled with tomatoes, onions, and mushrooms; lime adding just enough tang, but not overpowering it. A crisp green salad, plain sliced, sautéed potatoes, and she wasn't afraid to leave the skins on the potatoes.

Jack had begun life as a serious artist, but the exigencies of providing food, shelter, attachments for his camera, and time to enjoy life, made him begin photography in earnest. The ingenuity of his photo layouts placed him in high demand by the fashion industry. His painter's eye for color and composition resulted in unusual spreads, and occasional award-winning ads. He commonly found his lens focused on super slender models, rather than Playboy centerfolds. He found more pleasure in the shapeliness of a background tree than the lovely, but too-thin (for him) women he worked with. It was a lucrative living, and more enjoyable than a commercial art desk job. He took a great deal of pride in the photographer part of his life. There were other parts to his past in which he was not too comfortable. It was best that that aspect of his life should remain a closed book to Clara. Clara possessed the beauty that was a pleasure for him to paint, and he felt concern that she not only downplayed her attractiveness, but obviously held negative feelings about herself.

They cleared the table, then brought fruit and cheese out to Clara's terrace. Most Miami apartments come with terraces. Unfortunately, Clara's overlooked

a busy street, but it was on the seventh floor, and at
least the traffic noises were softened.

Jack had expected a cardiologist to have a more
sumptuous home, and was surprised at the shabby, flat-
patterned beige rug in the living-room, and the motel-
chain sofas and chairs. Later, he learned Clara had
spent years paying off medical school obligations, and
then incurred more debt opening her office. Her big
luxuries, besides scuba, were what Jack expected;
compact discs, stereo, books, camera, and computer.

"It's more sensible to buy some sort of house,"
Jack suggested. "Then your monthly payments would
at least give you a tax benefit."

"I suppose so, but I wouldn't like living alone
in a house. The condominiums are an unattractive way
to live. Everybody sees you walk through the lobby,
there's no privacy, and if they found out I was a doctor,
my door would have a steady barrage of rashes, and
questions because they don't want to bother their own
doctor. It happens a bit here, but in a condo, I'd feel
permanent. Here, I keep thinking, 'I'll get out just as
soon as....'"

"As soon as what?"

She speared a piece of cheddar as she said, "as
soon as I get enough money, as soon as I get time to
look for a place, as soon as I feel like packing; you
know, as soon as..."

"A procrastinator too, huh?"

Leaning back in his chair, Jack studied Clara, framed by the yellow lights of her terrace. "It's great to be out of New York."

"Even with this magnificent unencumbered view of Miami traffic jams?"

Jack nodded.

"Mmm. This cheese is great," said Clara, slathering cream cheese onto a cracker which she covered with another piece of cheddar, topped by a second cream cheese-laden cracker.

Jack stared numbly at the entire process. "Why?"

"Why? Well, I have this problem where I put on weight because I love to eat."

"Then, why don't you just have a slice of that apple, and eat it very slowly."

"This woman really needs looking after," he thought. Deftly, he sliced the apple and handed a sliver to Clara as he held his other hand out to receive the two hundred-calorie snack she was about to devour. As he did so, he managed to slide his chair closer to hers. Before she could put apple to lips, his left arm encircled her shoulder and he tilted her face up with his right hand. His kiss was gentle and lingering. When her arms came around him he knew he had to get them out of these romance-defying canvas chairs. Managing to stand up, he slipped his arms around Clara, hauling her out of her chair. Kissing her again, Jack opened her mouth with his own. With each expiration, he tasted the sweetness of her breath, and felt the soft heaviness of her breasts against him. The phone, a nagging petitioner intruded. Her body lost its pliancy. Emotionally, her universe was already connected to the phone.

"Look, you're on beeper. If it's your service, they'll just beep if they want you."

"I guess you're right."

As he reached for her, she eluded him, saying, "I really have to go to sleep now. I have to get up at six tomorrow."

They said their goodnights, a few more soft kisses, and they parted. Jack didn't have to make any definite date. They both knew he'd call.

He was about to enter the elevator when he heard a door click open. Turning, he saw Clara flying down the corridor. With great anticipation he hurried toward her, happily expecting an invitation to spend the night. She came closer. "My car! It's still at the office!"

A jellyfish sting forced Clara to let out a piercing scream. The pain wasn't agony, but the surprise jolted her from her pleasant reverie.

"I'm sorry, Jack, I know you're frightened enough without some silly twit shrieking every time she hits a jellyfish."

"Damn, I thought something had taken a leg off. You scared the hell out of me, and I thought all along that I was at the highest plateau of being scared shitless. You just raised me two more levels."

Now the cold, the thirst, and the burning jellyfish stings formed a symphony of pain that prevented her from leaving the present, and returning to past happier times. Hours passed, and blessed fog overcame her mind, blotting out the discomfort, and allowing her to pass to a state of delirium where once more she and Jack were falling in love.

He had called her at the office the next morning. Casey did not have to be told to put him through immediately.

They made a date for dinner. Jack wanted to create a meal for Clara in his own home. He envisioned an unhurried evening, offering a haven, yet he knew she would feel uncomfortable accepting an invitation to his apartment.

Jack made a bakery run for a chocolate chip cake. He planned to take Clara to Michael's for dinner in their back room. Lots of good wine, then dessert at his place. Feed Clara and you had her attention. The models liked liquor. It had to be a fashionable bar where they could be highly visible, drinking the lowest calorie booze possible, and sitting there for hours. Boredom forced him to drink with them, and the alcohol often made him impotent by the time he got them home—or just too sleepy to care.

Clara glowed around the office. Casey had visions of rearranging the appointment book, and obtaining coverage for a honeymoon.

At day's end, Clara rushed home to don an emerald green dress, bought on sale last year. The deep 'V' revealed more of her breasts than she felt comfortable showing, but she had forgotten to have the neck raised by the seamstress. Now she didn't have enough time. The wide belt was tight around her trim waist (despite occasional cookie binges) and the soft material clung to her hips. Rummaging for her green and black heels, she came up with one Etonic jogging shoe and her old Adidas trainer. She finally retrieved the appropriate pair of shoes from two different closets, and even had time to touch up make-up and hair. A few minutes before Jack was due, she picked up the phone. "Hello, service?"

"Hello there, Doc."

"For the next couple of hours, emergencies only. Don't hesitate to beep me if you really need me."

"Heavy date, huh, Doc?" The voice seemed to wink.

"Actually, yes."

"Well, have a nice time. I'll try to screen the calls, and may all your patients be healthy tonight."

Clara dumped the jeans from the hook over her full-length mirror, and stared at herself. That neckline! She hadn't realized how exposed she was. She raced to her desk looking for a safety pin to shore up her plunging top.

The downstairs buzzer caught her halfway across the room. Another frantic dash to the kitchen, and she spoke into the box, releasing the outer door lock when Jack answered.

Black lace stole! A grateful patient had brought it back from Spain. Where was it? Almost hysterically, she began foraging again through the dark abyss of her closet. Not here! Where could she have put it? She'd never worn it. Was it still at the office? Couldn't be. That was eight months ago. She couldn't have forgotten to bring it home every single night for the past eight months. Maybe it's on the dresser. Yanking open the bottom drawer, she pawed through a mess of scarves. Something was caught at the back. In frenzy, she pulled the drawer out further, dropping it on her toe. Her screams were obscured by Jack's buzzing at her apartment door. Hobbling into the living room, her hair now out of place, some of her lipstick bitten off, she caught sight of herself in the mirror. Wanting to cry, she answered the door.

Jack was in a cream-colored, impeccably tailored casual suit over an open-necked, silky dark brown shirt.

Taking her hands, he held her away from him, "You are really lovely. What a pleasure; taking out a lady in a dress, instead of jeans."

The pain in her toe stopped. The stole was forgotten.

Talking across a small candle-lit table, they became close friends.

For the past two hours, facing Clara's décolletage, Jack thought often of sex, but not just for tonight. He wouldn't mind waking up next to her in the morning. Her clothes would be scattered all over the bedroom floor. It didn"t matter. He had more time to pick up things than she did. Organization came easily to him. That was the only way to keep camera equipment, or a darkroom, neat and organized. In the office, her staff must keep everything in its place in those examining rooms so Clara could lay a quick hand on instruments. They had their hands full keeping after her. He recalled that even when she had examined him, the reflex hammer had not gone back to its designated slot in the drawer. Unknowingly, it had been placed in her pocket. The otoscope had not been replaced on charge. Her stethoscope was left haphazardly on the examining table. It could have easily been thrown away with the disposable gown and sheet, but he knew Casey and Ann would never let that happen. He grinned as she continued to talk about underwater photography. No wonder she kept stethoscopes all over, with two in her purse. There was one in her car seat, and another dangling from her glove compartment. No room to stuff one in her bra, he thought, with infantile amusement.

When the waiter brought around the pastry cart, Clara became rhapsodic, but Jack told her about the special cake and the cappuccino machine he had brought back from Italy. After he solemnly promised to top her cappuccino with gobs of whipped cream, she agreed to go to his apartment for dessert. Just dessert, because she had to go home. Tomorrow was Friday, and a working day, etcetera, etceteras.

At his apartment he wouldn't let her help him. He knew she had put in a more than full workday. She plomped down into his loveseat, and he tenderly removed her shoes. After turning on the stereo, Jack started the cappuccino machine and while it buzzed away, he went into the kitchen. He soon returned, bearing a magnificent cake. Dishes and cutlery had been placed on the coffee table before he had left. His apartment was not much more personal than Clara's. It belonged to a journalist friend who was on assignment in Asia for a few months. So Jack sublet it. This gave him time to look around for a little house.

They ate their cake, and enjoyed each other's company.

Jack put his arm around Clara, drawing her closer. He began to kiss the whipped cream off her face. Laughing to himself, Jack imagined that future kisses would often taste of chocolate or whipped cream.

Clara curled up in Jack's arms, her head buried in his chest. He held her, conscious only of their breathing. A monotonous dissonance intruded. It was several seconds before they realized it was her beeper insisting on attention. Left attached to her purse in the kitchen, it sounded faintly muffled, but its staccato whines seemed more emphatic after midnight.

Clara looked forlorn. "You'll have to get me to the nearest phone."

Making sure she avoided the coffee table, he extricated her from the loveseat, and then led her into the kitchen. The bright lights, reflecting on gleaming yellow and chrome, dealt a final blow to the mood Jack had created. After a few seconds, their pupils were constricted enough for Jack to locate the phone.

As Clara dialed, he found his hand instinctively smoothing her hair. Grabbing a dishcloth, he cleaned the chocolate and smeared lipstick from her face.

"This is Dr. Weiss. You beeped?"

After listening for a few seconds, she replaced the receiver, and rapidly punched out another number. As Jack listened to the questions Clara fired at an emergency room nurse, he felt displaced. He was hearing some strange foreign tongue. No wonder medical school took so long. It must take them at least a year to learn the language.

"Jack...."

"I know! I know! Where are we going?"

"I'll take a cab. I could be there for hours. I may have to put in a Swan-Ganz right heart catheter, and...."

"Look, whatever it is, I'm going to take you there. Anyway," he continued, as he pulled her close to him, "you only gave me that cab shit because it was the socially acceptable thing to say. You really want me to take you to your kinky party."

She hugged him as she reached for her purse.

There are few places less romantic than an emergency room lobby. As Clara flowed through the inner sanctum, Jack settled himself in a chair, and grabbed the nearest two-year-old copy of *Time*.

A half-hour of people watching and page-turning, and Clara emerged without a single hair in place.

"Listen, Jack, it's going to be at least another hour. I have to go to the Special Procedures Room and insert a pacemaker."

"I'll wait."

"I know."

She held his hands. "But afterwards, I'll have to go home, and go right to sleep. I'm really tired."

"I know," he sighed.

In the Intensive Care Unit, Clara carefully prepped the patient, going through the procedure of inserting a temporary cardiac pacemaker. During the procedure, she thought about her life, not without some bitterness. She had never minded the physical labor, or scholarship involved with medicine. It was the loneliness, always there.

"Doctor Weiss, what size introducer? Is 8 OK?"

"That's fine! I'll use a 7 *French* wire."

After the pacemaker was in place, she watched the faultless capture played out on the monitor screen. Simple and perfect. First, the artifact showing the stimulation of the pacemaker, and then the patient's own heart beat, dutifully following the pacemaker spike. The sweet pairing of pacemaker and cardiac impulse. Symmetrical and perfect. Hypnotic in its simplicity. She broke away from the eloquence of the images before her, and scrutinized the patient. Good pulses indicating good peripheral circulation. At her firm touch, the patient stirred and opened his eyes.

"Hi, Doc. Looks like we made it."

"We certainly did, Mr. House."

Leaving the concealment of the dim fluoroscopy room, the glare of the nursing area assaulted her. Lighting so bright and clear, it was unreal. Robotic clicking of the monitors and the occasional rustle of paper as one of the cardiac machines decided to roll out a strip, showing off its work. The sudden feeling of exposure made Clara scurry to a corner to do what she detested most. Create organization out of the artistry she had just completed. Put on paper everything she had done. This was the chore of documentation, the recording of all the details. A ritual of medicine that stripped away much of the joy and creativity of caring for a patient.

Placing the dictating monster back on its little hook, Clara looked up as Jack appeared.

"Just don't ask me how I got here. Trade secret. I am so good at this that there is no celebrity bash I cannot crash; no inner sanctum I can't con my way into."

He carefully placed a container of hot coffee in front of her.

"It's all in the technique. In fact, I could probably even trespass my way into the executive john at Microsoft."

As Clara began to struggle with the lid, Jack reached over and nimbly removed it.

Looking up over the rim of the plastic cup, Clara said, "You are so terrific that I'm almost afraid to blink my eyes. You might disappear, you know."

"That's one thing I don't think I'd be too good at."

Clara's eyes were misty as she pushed back her chair. Carefully keeping her face averted from Jack, she clumsily gathered together her paraphernalia.

In the car, Jack paused, his key in the ignition.

"I don't want to say good night to you. Look, I'll take you anywhere you want. Do you want music, more food? Anything! I just don't want us to be separated."

"I'm so glad."

She was silent as he reached over and wiped her sweaty bangs off her face.

"You know, twenty minutes ago I was exhausted. Then you walked into the unit, and I just wasn't tired anymore."

He took her hands, contemplating the reflections in her eyes. "What shall it be? A night flight to Paris? Rent a sailboat to take you out into the bay? Or, I've got a friend with a helicopter that does some wicked tricks?"

"Oh, Jack," she laughed as she hugged him.

The pressure of the beeper, attached to her skirt, dug into his skin. "I forgot about your friend," he groaned. "Are you on call all weekend?"

"Mmmm."

"You'll have to translate. What is 'mmmmm,' Paris, or the helicopter?"

"'Mmmm' is I alternate weekends with a friend, and, so, when I'm on call, I make rounds on Ben's patients too. This means that I have to see about a dozen patients tomorrow at three different hospitals."

"I don't think I like 'mmmm.'"

He started the car, wishing he wasn't driving his antique 240-Z with a gear shift between himself and his passenger.

He followed Clara into her apartment.

"I have wonderful Tokay," she trailed off, tossing her purse toward the coffee table. Jack reflexively retrieved it from the carpet. He lit the candles near her couch, and then dimmed the living room lights.

After Clara brought in the wine, they curled up together in the candlelight. As his kisses became more sensuous, Clara held back a moment. "I just don't know how I feel, Jack."

"I know how I feel. I want to make love to you."

"Are you trying to flirt with me?"

"You probably flunked that in high school and never caught up with the rest of the girls," he laughed. "What did you do, take Chemical Thermodynamics in place of Coquetry 101?"

"No, it was an advanced course in How to Mess Up Personal Relationships You Really Care About."

Pulling away, she grabbed a napkin and held it to her eyes.

"What's wrong?"

"I don't know."

Pulling her back into his arms, he cradled her head on his chest. "You do know."

The candles flickered as Clara's breathing came down to normal.

"I'll never push you."

Her voice was barely audible. "It's just so stupid. I was afraid that if I made things too easy for you, I wouldn't see you again. I'm such a child!"

He caressed her hair as he felt her body relax. In a few minutes he realized she was asleep.

Smiling to himself, he carried her into the bedroom, gently placing her on the spread. He removed her shoes, found a blanket, and then tucked it around her. Quietly moving through the living-room, he extinguished the candles and let himself out the door.

On an out-of-town assignment the next week, Jack found himself more anxious to get to the phone at night than to reach the darkroom after the day's session.

For his first night home, Clara had arranged a night dive at Frenchman's Reef in the Florida Keys.

"Where's Frenchman's Reef?" he had asked.

"About a thousand yards northeast of Molasses Reef, if you must know. I think Molasses has more life per cubic foot than the Red Sea and the Great Barrier Reef combined."

"Then why aren't we going to Molasses?"

"It's just that I've been snorkeling there so many times, that I've got to try some place else. Even the fish know me. Last time I didn't bring food and they were angry. I even found one Yellowtail rooting around in the pocket of my buoyancy compensator. When I tried to get him out, he actually snapped at me."

Jack laughed, "Maybe that's why they belong to the Snapper family."

"One more like that, and I'll leave you with the fish."

Jack had just completed a six-week diving course. Twelve hours was lecture, twenty-four hours in a pool, and only two ocean dives. He was aware of his limitations. He could grab his camera, and in an instant his fingers would find the controls. Knowing the rule of fifteen, he often did not bother with the light meter. *F*-stop, shutter speed, and focus would be perfect, and he'd get the shot that any amateur would miss. Not true of his diving gear. He'd release his belt when he meant to release his tank. Minutes would be wasted as he fumbled for the controls on his buoyancy compensator. Instead of dumping air from his BC, he would add air, and float helplessly to the surface. He knew that in a jam he might panic, or even do the wrong things without panic. The ocean was unforgiving, and that wrong thing—that uncontrolled ascent— could mean air embolism to the brain, and death. Uncertain of his skills in the open water, he was even more uncertain of himself in the darkness. He felt like a small boy desperately walking a picket fence to impress that cute little girl with all the answers to the test, and a pocket full of potato chips.

Leaving Miami at eight, they drove to John Pennekamp Park. This is the strangest state park in existence. Strange because it is invisible to the uninitiated. The park begins at the water's edge, and extends along the ocean bottom for miles out to sea. It's not a park to walk through, but a park to explore with mask, flippers, and tank. A preserve. We do not attack the fish, and the sharks and barracuda, in turn, swim peacefully about us.

Jack, like any typical male, had to show he could make the arrangements for the dive.

"Where were you able to round up a boat at this hour?"

"A friend of mine is letting me use his. He's leaving it tied to the dock," Jack answered.

At ten, Clara and Jack arrived at the pier. With the next day promising a new moon, a hair fine crescent now saved them from total darkness.

"I don't see any boat, Jack. I think your friend reneged."

"What do you think this is, right down at your feet?"

"I give up, what is it?"

"A Zodiac."

"It's a raft, a little rubber life raft. You're kidding!"

"Oh, it's not so little, Clara. It's a good ten feet long."

"We'd have to be crazy to go out in that. This isn't a little pond. It's a big ocean with big waves. It's also very deep and very dark out there."

"These rubber boats are safer than a lot of the big ones. There is no way this thing is going to sink. I've been on three night dives on this boat, and Clem, who happens to be the owner, is a dive instructor at the Y."

"Jack," Clara said seriously, "you've been shopping for a boat. Why don't we just call it quits for a day or so, and wait until you get it? It'll be comfortable, with a cabin, and bunks, and a head."

Jack looked forlorn. Like someone who had put together an elaborate surprise party to which the guest of honor never showed up.

So Clara listened patiently as he told her of harrowing rides his safety belt hooked to the "D" ring in the deck, so that he could hang out of a chopper in Nam, and photographic stints in the Andes that he thought he'd never survive. Night diving from a Zodiac in Pennekamp Park looked benign to him, as long as he was with an experienced diver, which, Clara certainly was.

She took a line from the little craft, and looked back to find him staring at her in amazement. Holding her hand out to him, she said, "Come on, we'll be late for all those flashy night fish." Grunting, she inelegantly sat down on the dock, and cautiously lowered her legs into the boat. "Oh, dreck," she thought, "if I could only have leaped into this thing gracefully like those long-legged, athletic things I see playing tennis, but when you're klutzy..." she sighed to herself.

The run out to sea was uncomfortable. At first the boat planed over the surface of the water, but after a while, the waves grew higher, and buffeted the small craft, crashing over the bow, and drenching its occupants. A high wave would first smash against the bottom of the thin deck. This would be followed by a period of weightlessness, as the boat fell into a deep valley to end with another gut-wrenching jolt. The combination of water and wind was chilling, and they took turns at the helm while each donned a wet suit.

"It's black out here. How do you know where we are?"

"By the shore lights and the lighted buoys. Relax; we'll be there in about thirty minutes."

Finally, at what seemed a totally arbitrary point in the continuum of space and time, Jack cut the outboard and announced, "We're here!"

"We're where?"

"Over Frenchman's Reef."

As far as Clara could see, waves were blending into darkness. Nothing differentiated this from any other patch of ocean. Clara and Jack helped each other on with their tanks as the boat bucked to free itself from its anchor line.

"We'll both back-roll simultaneously," Clara said. "I'll meet you at the anchor line. Then let's check to make sure the anchor's fast. I'll leave the strobe light on the bow, and I'll tie my spare light on the anchor line."

"Yeah! It might be nice to find the Zodiac again."

As Jack back-rolled into the water, he felt a short period of disorientation until his head struck the hull of the boat. At least he now knew which way was up. They met at the anchor line, and slowly pulled themselves down, stopping momentarily to exhale against pinched nostrils to equalize air pressure in their ears and sinuses. At the bottom, Clara took Jack's hand, and with their narrow light beams pointing the way, they swam into the darkness.

The beam from Clara's light was suddenly reflected off a wall of solid fish. The grouper had to weigh over four hundred pounds. Before Jack could stop her, Clara swam to the giant, and began to pat it on the nose. The fish hung motionless, oblivious to her attentions. Jack swung his light about. Everywhere he saw fish that appeared asleep. He swam to a File Fish, and touched it lightly. It made no move to avoid him. Next he explored the wall of coral with his light. There, staring back at him, were the beady eyes of a Spiny Lobster. Jack lunged at the lobster, but the big bug easily evaded his grasp and backed into a hole. Jack quickly suppressed the urge to reach in after him when he saw, protruding from an adjacent tunnel, the head and gaping jaws of a Spotted Moray.

Turning toward Clara, he saw her light go out. Illuminating her in his beam, he saw her signal to extinguish his own light. The expected blackness never came. Now each motion of hand or flipper was followed by a streak of phosphorescence. This bioluminescence came about because they had disturbed the dinoflagellates, the microscopic marine algae sharing the ocean with them. With lights on, they continued to explore this eerie world until their pressure gauges told them that it would be wise to return to the world of the air breather.

Once on board, with their tanks safely stored, they began to peel off their wet suits. Clara sat for a few exhausted seconds while Jack removed his. Then, as Clara rose and began to struggle with the zipper, Jack helped her. The ebony neoprene peeled away, letting his fingers linger over her bare, damp skin. When her suit was stripped off, she began to shiver. Quickly, he put his arms around her, cradling her body against his. At first, her lips were salty and cool.

"I'll keep you warm."

She clung to him as his warmth began to diffuse through her. Waves gently lapped at the boat, rocking them as they embraced.

"We'd better get back, or we'll freeze out here."

Jack fumbled with the ignition key, fingers numbed by the cold. "You wouldn't think it would get so cold in Florida. How about freeing up the anchor? I'll start the engine."

"Shit!"

"What's wrong?"

"The key broke in the ignition."

"I don't suppose you have a spare key, or a spare radio."

Jack responded in a voice straining to remain calm. "On this little boat? You must be kidding."

"OK, Clara, let me set the anchor again. It'll give us time to think."

Men are expected to be resourceful while immersed in this technology of super-specialization. Clara's next question reflected an expectation of unlimited power, of omnipotence in the average male. "Can you hot-wire an engine?"

"Clara, all the anchor line's out, and I've not touched bottom."

"I guess we've drifted off the reef into deep water. You'd better get to work on that engine."

Jack carefully investigated the control panel. "You know, this panel is steel plate, obviously made so that nobody can jump the motor and steal the boat without some fancy tools. See if you can find a tool box."

"There's a box buried under a bunch of stuff up forward. I'll check it out."

After much struggling to keep her balance on her knees in a choppy sea, Clara finally pulled an old dented tool box from beneath a pile of line, spare anchor, and life vests and opened the lid. "I see a spare spark plug, and an old rusty socket wrench. Not too promising, is it?"

"Let's forget about the engine, and start waving our lights. There are plenty of sports fishermen around here."

Fifteen dark, cold minutes passed.

"Great, Jack, people sure are friendly. We wave our lights, and they wave back. They must think we're just being sociable. Let's try flashing an SOS, and hope somebody out there knows Morse code."

In less than an hour Jack and Clara had succeeded in attracting the attention of a small cruiser.

"Ahoy! Having difficulty?"

"We've lost our power. Can you tow us in?"

"Hate to screw up a good fishing trip, but I'll see what I can do. I'll give the Coast Guard a call for you."

Twenty minutes later, the cruiser returned.

"Ahoy again! Because of this holiday week-end, the Coast Guard has all of its boats tied up in rescue missions. They said that as long as you're in no danger, they would come by for you in about four hours, but I can't see leaving you out here for four hours so throw me your line."

An hour later, they were in Jack's car, and leaving Key Largo.

"Clara, we're wet and cold. Your apartment is a good thirty minutes further than mine. Let's stop at my place and dry off."

Jack's temporary quarters consisted of two small rooms. There was a bedroom and a living room that had a closet-like space with an accordion door. This concealed a stove and a bar-sized refrigerator. The furnishings were Spartan. Next to the waterbed was a stereo. One pair of speakers guarded each side of the bed, with a second pair high on the wall in the living room. The only comfortable place to sit, a small brown love-seat occupied the center of the living-room, where Jack had served her cappuccino and cake on their first dinner date. A small kitchen table and two folding straight-back chairs occupied a corner. The bathroom was hardly a bathroom any longer. Its sole window had been made light tight with several layers of aluminum foil. Black felt lined the door and frame. Over the bathtub was a fold-up shelf supporting an enlarger and developing trays.

Jack pointed Clara toward the bathroom. "Go on in and take a hot shower. I'll get the enlarger down first, and then I'll get you some towels and a robe."

The diving gear had been arranged on the lawn, and washed down earlier with the hose. With that

chore out of the way, Clara felt she deserved her turn.
Standing in the hot shower, she began massaging
herself with a washcloth heavily laden with soap. The
sticky, salty brine and the chill of the long night in the
unsheltered Zodiac quickly left her. She kneaded rich
suds into her hair, luxuriating in the warm jets of
water. Jack's bathroom was amiable and comfortable.
Gracious plants, a sunny watercolor, and a pristinely
folded stack of towels, contrasted with a few bottles of
fixer, and developer stashed in a corner. The mirror on
the medicine cabinet was unsmudged. Her inquisitive
hand touched the cabinet and hesitated. Damn it! She
had to look. Suspicious that orderly people created
hidden clutter, she hopefully opened the door a few
more tentative inches. Clean shelves with a scattering
of necessary items were arranged to patiently await
their owner's use.

Sighing, she gently closed the door.
Tomorrow, she'd organize. Start with just one room.
Maybe she'd pick half a room. Grimacing at the vision
of clutter that occupied just half her bedroom, she
began to enfold herself in Jack's white terry robe.
Feeling indulgently clean and comfortable, she reached
for Jack's hair dryer. Of course it was neatly placed in
its own wall rack. How could anyone maintain a
bathrobe in such an unstained, alabaster condition?
Drying her hair, she thought about her own apartment.
Maybe a drawer at a time would be a logical way to
start organizing. Then work her way up to her closet.

Warm and clean, Clara emerged into the muted
lighting and subdued stereo sound lingering over
Jack's apartment. Jack was adding whipped cream to

two mugs that had been place on a free form, wood coffee table. The only seating arrangement was a small ash-brown suede love seat. She squeezed in next to Jack.

He handed her a mug.

"Hot chocolate made from scratch with melted Kron's chocolate. Though the Creme de Cacao is my improvement on Kron."

"And the whipped cream," she added.

"What about those rich, dark chocolate shavings I slaved over while you puttered around the shower like some princess?"

"If this is princess-hood, I'll give up medicine any time."

Smoothing her hair back behind her ears, he turned Clara's face toward him.

"You know, I really care about you," he whispered."

"I know."

"I think about you a lot. I wonder if you're getting enough sleep, or it you ever got your mess of an apartment straightened out. If you didn't, wouldn't you feel better if it was less chaotic? Then I wonder if you've eaten anything but chocolate chip cookies all day, or which lunatic is disturbing you with a dripping nose he's had for the last six days?"

"The next thing you know, you'll be making me chicken soup."

"Not a bad idea."

"I think about you a lot too, but I don't worry about you. I just want to be with you. I think about what you said the last time we were together, or remember what your kiss was like."

"Memories are faulty at best," he said as he kissed her.

Putting her arms around him, she buried her face in his neck. "Much better than I remembered it. You neck is so warm and soft."

"Hey, I'm supposed to say that to you, and tell you your neck smells good."

"Does it?"

"I don't know," he murmured almost indistinctly, "but it is warm and soft."

He kissed her neck tenderly as he began to undo the cord of her robe.

Her hand caught his. "It's not just for tonight."

"You don't have to tell me that, Clara."

He kissed her gently. Then staring at the remaining whipped cream on her nose, he said, "after all, I'm not some guy you can just pick up and expect to get right into bed."

She giggled as he wiped the cream off. "I like you."

Holding her face in his hands, he said, "What's wrong with love? A perfectly good word. Should be used a lot. Why don't you try it? I love you."

"I love you too, Jack." She cuddled against his chest. "I guess I was afraid to tell you."

"Why?"

"Because then you'd know I liked you."

"Of course," he said stroking her hair. "That's very logical."

"You know, one of the games you're supposed to play. Can't let the man know you like him, because then he'll take advantage of you, and so on."

"I don't like that game. In fact, I won't play."

"Never expected you to," Clara managed to whisper as Jack's mouth pressed against hers.

*　　*　　*

The raw pain of a jellyfish sting cruelly tore Clara away from that night in Jack's apartment. Each time she drifted off into a daydream, waves of pitiless cold would awaken her. They'd never get out of this. Who could possibly find them? They were fish food.

Gradually, the surface changed from a light chop to five-foot rolling swells. In spite of their fully inflated buoyancy compensators, the waves broke over their heads. In these seas, their snorkels were of little benefit as they choked on mouthfuls of water.

"Jack! A fishing boat! It's coming in this direction."

"They may not see us. Wave something at them."

"Wave what? Oh, maybe my yellow bathing suit bottom will attract them."

"Anything! Hurry!"

"The damn swells are so high, I can't see the boat most of the time, "Clara said. "I'm sure they can't see us."

"You're right. They'll be passing us, and only about fifty yards off. They would only be able to catch sight of us while we were on a peak."

"Shit! It's raining. What little visibility we had is being shot to hell."

"Jack, let's yell like crazy."

"Save your breath. They couldn't hear us over the sound of their engines even if we were right on top of them."

"Oh Jack, they're passing us. They're going away."

Clara was startled by a shattering scream. "What is it, Jack, what...."

"God! A Man-O-War. Its tentacles are all over my left arm. The pain's killing me. Don't touch, Clara. Just pull away the air-sail. Careful! Don't get stung."

The jellyfish was hanging by its long stream of tentacles, its nematocysts firing poison into Jack's arm. Clara cautiously grasped the balloon-shaped sail, and lifted it from his arm. With the sail came the tentacles as they peeled from his skin. In their place were bright red stripes as if he had been struck with a Cat-O-Nine Tails. She flung the sail from him, being careful not to come in contact with the stinging tentacles, and then back-paddled away. Jack was hanging limp in his B-C, unconscious.

The next couple of hours were spent making sure that Jack was floating with his face out of the water. The sleeveless wet suit had given him some protection, but across his arm the giant red welts continued to increase in size.

It is undoubtedly the strong, treacherous currents of the Devil's Triangle that supply some of the energy for its reputation. Just such a strong current gathered up its two prisoners, and sent them miles from where pleasure craft plied. As the hours passed, they drifted to the southern tip of Florida, and the beginning of the Everglades. Perhaps they too, would become another tale among many, of another plane or boat lost in the Triangle.

It was now a bright, cloudless day and the steady hack-hack-hack of a helicopter could be heard in the distance.

Uralsk, Kazakhstan

March, the year before.

CHAPTER III

The heavy hanging chains shall fall,

The walls shall crumble at the word,

And Freedom greet you with the light

And brothers give you back the sword.

Pushkin

"Eva! Where is Lena?"

"You know where she is, Georgii. Don't go asking me. You want a fight? I'll give you a fight." Eva turned from the kitchen sink, and glared at her husband. After the laundry, the dishes, the floors, and the children, she was tired, and not really in the mood for a fight.

"That whore belongs at home. I don't want my daughter whoring around," Georgii shouted as he threw the five-pound sack of potatoes to the floor.

The apartment was part of an Uralsk slum, exceeding the depths of degradation commonly seen in the New York Bronx. Your eye naturally moves to the ceiling where water drips on your head. Probably a leaky drain from the floor above. Most likely, their toilet, but you try not to think about it. Some of the water drips down the wall where the old moldy paper has peeled away, revealing cracks. In turn the cracks reveal rotted and broken lath. Of course the floor is wet. Some dripped from the ceiling, but some from the leaky pipes in the wall, as it oozed out of decayed baseboard, joining wall with floor.

The gloom is accentuated by the lighting, a single 40-watt bulb hanging by its cord from the ceiling. The frayed cord periodically emits a bit of extra light from sparks as the ceiling, and cord vibrates with passing locomotives.

Eva Aliyeva was standing at the only sink in the house. It was a large stone sink, more commonly seen in a laundry room, than a kitchen. It served the kitchen, the post toilet ablutions, and as the family bathtub.

Once, Eva had been a beautiful woman. She'd made a painful choice among several suitors before picking Georgii a as her husband. He was an excellent catch at the time. Only twenty-six years old, and a Ph.D. in physics. His major interest was neutron interactions in the Actinide series. Already, he had a job. It wasn't the university post he had hoped for, because a weapons plant paid a better salary. Too bad he had to schlep 250 km to Kubyshev. The high and mighty Soviet Federative Socialist Republic had great trust in Kazakhstan, but not quite the kind of trust that puts a weapons plant in Uralsk.

Every Sunday evening, Georgii would show his travel papers to the guards at the RSFSR border, work and sleep at the plant until Friday, and then show his travel papers again as he came home. The perks were wonderful, however. What other family in Uralsk had their own one bedroom apartment, and their own private bathroom? Then, every year, they got 2 weeks at the dacha at Feodosiya. He was considered one of the elite. His wife was not obliged stand in long lines only to reach a counter in front of a wall of empty shelves. Georgii's papers allowed him to shop in the same stores as Yeltsen. What's more, he had the money to pay for nice things for his family.

Now, times have changed. Her beauty is gone. Gone down with the dirty dishwater in the sink. Gone down with the dirty water from the dirty cloths. Rubbed away as she rubbed the floors. The skin gone badly with bad food, bad work, and bad sleep. Georgii never touched her anymore.

Eva stared into the dirty, soapy water thinking, "Who wants to touch an old hag? Besides, how can he think of sex? The dacha is gone along with the job and the money. All my Georgii can think of is how he can feed his family. I scream at Georgii. I can't help being a nag. What a terrible life. Now he is drinking. Just one more way to spend our little money. He screams hateful things at Lena, but I know he really hates himself."

The less information he had, the better, but she had to talk about something. "Lena is out with Petrov." She felt like biting her tongue, but as a little girl she was trained not to keep secrets—especially from her husband.

"Petrov! You know who that son-of-a-bitch is? He is a pimp. He lost his job at the GUM. Now he is selling little girls to the tourists. You'll see, your daughter will bring home some terrible disease. Eva, when I get hold of Lena I'm going to beat the shit out of her, and then I'm going to lock her in the closet."

With a cry of exasperation, Georgii threw himself on the bed in corner of the room. It was hardly a bed. It was a thin, lumpy mattress lying on an old door. The door, in turn, was supported by four stacks of old books.

"Georgii, you can't blame the girl. Try to understand. It's better to be a whore with a full stomach than starve to death in the apartment."

"When she gets AIDS you'll think otherwise. Then you will think, 'better she should have starved to death.'"

Georgii angrily rolled on his side toward the wall, and thought: "How can women be so practical? His wife was doing the neighbor's laundry for a few kopecks, and his daughter was debasing herself in the streets. It wasn't his fault. That damn Yeltsin, and his democracy. The country is falling to pieces with their stinking democracy. Under Communism there was no freedom, but there was always work. Now there is freedom to starve. Kazakhstan has its beloved independence from the RSFSR. Independence to fall into the dark ages. Mother Russia has no need for weapons. You don't need weapons when you're already dead. Kazakhstan, Estonia, Lithuania, Ukraine, Turkmenistan, and all the other states; just abandoning the empire. My factory sits there, quiet, empty. I and the other workers have all gone home to live like vermin."

Georgii Aliyev was a squat little man, hardly measuring 165 cm in height. Athletics could not be his forte, although his short stature did not keep him from excelling in weight lifting, and wrestling. He was not a violent man. He chose weight lifting and marshal arts because they separated competitors by weight class. He tried Tae Kwon Do, and enjoyed its art. Self-defense was never a thought. He was not one to get into barroom brawls, and took pride in avoiding anything but intellectual confrontations. Others found that his small size limited his reach. He did not fight with his hands. His kick well compensated for the limited reach of his arms. However, his flexibility also was limited. There

was no way that he could kick a tall opponent in the face.
Through years of perseverance he finally made first
degree black belt, but then dropped out of class.
Excellence in most sports depends a great deal on size.
Intellectual excellence was not related to one's bulk, and
so Georgii applied himself to his studies.

He made top grades in his early schooling. When
it was time to enter advanced education, Moscow State
University accepted him. The tuition was free to those
who made the grade. He stayed through undergraduate
training, made top ten percent in his class, and then went
on for his Ph.D. The years were joyful. Work was hard,
but the university sat on the Sparrow Hills in Moscow,
and for the first time in his life he enjoyed the fruits of a
cosmopolitan center.

Crouched on the edge of the bed, Georgii thought,
"Well, I don't have to starve. I can feed my family, but
there are limits to what a man does even to save his own
life. That damn Iraqi, Musaff. He can take his millions,
and go to hell. I don't feed my family so I can watch the
world turn into a giant fireball."

Saturday, he finally got the contact he was looking
for. He was sitting in the park, burning time (he knew
that search for work was hopeless), when a young slender
black male sat next to him.

"Mr. Aluyev, my name is Michael Areata. How
would you like to make a suitcase full of rubles?"

"I'm not in the counterfeiting business, Mr.
Areata."

"Very funny, and please call me Michael. I know who you are —or were. We can use you, and it will be worth lots of money. Listen carefully, and your hard times are over."

"I don't have money for a lottery ticket," Georgii responded. He knew what this was really about, but he didn't want to seem "easy."

"No down payment is needed. You don't even need easy terms. I just want to borrow your special skills."

"OK! Enough kidding around. What do you want of me?"

"We know that you have certain knowledge. You were involved in designing nuclear warheads. Am I right? Yes, of course I'm right. That knowledge is cheap these days. It's only worth a small part of a suitcase. More important, you had access to plutonium, and weapons grade uranium. Am I right? Of course, I'm always right."

Georgii bent forward, his face in his hands, and thought, "Last year, it would have been unthinkable to be approached like this. Not only would it be an affront to his honor, it would be impossible to obtain the material. You did not leave the plant without walking through a scintillation chamber. Even the minutest spec of plutonium would be detected. This was as much for the worker's safety as it was for security. At the end of the day, every bit of Uranium, and Plutonium was audited by weights accurate to the milligram. Once a month the

101

auditor came from Moscow. He would weigh the metals himself, and then review the books. Inconsistencies were unacceptable."

"Now, nobody can afford this kind of security. The factory is closed, anyway. Uranium and plutonium are divided into small aliquots, each carefully separated in its lead pig. The pigs are secure behind the thick steel door of a bank safe. There are no audits any longer. There are guards, but economics has even thinned their ranks. Formerly, the safe combination was changed weekly. That is no longer bothered with. Last year's combination is this year's combination. I have the combination."

Georgii looked up at Areata. "I will not lie to you, I am a desperate man. The money is tempting, but for me to put atomic weapons into the hands of a bunch of insane terrorists, I would have to be an insane animal myself."

"These are not terrorists. I cannot tell you who I work for, but I will tell you this much. My country is in West Africa. It is small, but its government is stable. It is being threatened by its large neighbors. We do not want to use nuclear weapons. Everyone knows that is craziness. We want to say, 'See, I have an atomic bomb. Leave us alone, and let us live in peace.' When we have an atomic bomb, nobody will bother us, and we do not wish to make war on our neighbors. Do any of its neighbors seriously threaten Isreal?"

Georgii did not have the luxury of analyzing Michael's argument. A rich man can afford to be thoroughly moral. A starving man must make some compromises.

"It can be done. Let's talk money."

*   *   *

The travel papers were outdated, but with the dissolution of the Russian Soviet Federative Republic, the police organization was chaotic. Lawlessness was the rule. Nobody cared to look at papers. There were more important things to deal with. The world order was coming to an end.

The more difficult problem was explaining to Eva why he had to be gone for a few days. It just took a loosely concocted story about a promising job in Pugachev to get him off the hook. In a way they were a bit relieved. It gave Lena a bit more freedom to get money for groceries. He was becoming a pain-in-the-neck to them.

He took a late train in order to arrive after dark. He was not well known in Kuybyshev, but there was no need to take chances. He avoided the bus, and walked the ten kilometers. He avoided the main thoroughfare, and walked the dimly lit side streets. It was bad enough that he had to show his identity card when he bought the train ticket, he did not need additional exposure.

A high, galvanized, chain-link fence surrounded the factory. Barbed wire rolled in accordion fashion topped the fence. This was a minor inconvenience. The motion sensors had long since failed from lack of attention, and he didn't expect to see a guard. Every movement had been planned in detail.

He said to himself, "Imagine coming hundreds of kilometers to find that you forgot a critical tool. You couldn't show your face at a hardware store. After all the risk, I would have to turn around and return home empty-handed."

Even though it was only fall, and the real snows hadn't started, he had worn his heavy winter coat—the one with the deep, roomy pockets. The pockets were heavy with tools. He would like to have brought bolt cutters, but there were limits to what he could carry. He chose his heavy wire cutters, and began to work on the fence.

The wire cutters were not meant for this kind of work. It took twenty minutes of bending the nicked wire with pliers before he could slide through the narrow opening. The wire cutters were dull, and twisted. After carefully wiping away fingerprints, he threw the useless cutters into some nearby brush.

Georgii had the security of a new moon. A fine drizzle of rain accompanied him, and only a few stars were visible. There was no light anywhere. That meant an unoccupied guardhouse.

Georgii swore to himself, "Imagine having enough nuclear material to destroy a good part of mankind, and yet being so irresponsible that you did not post a single guard." The irony was not lost to him: He found himself complaining about a factor in this equation that would make his work child's play.

No moon. He recognized Orion's belt just at the horizon as the only stars visible. The blackness was so complete that he could not see the ground he was walking on. Georgii carried a small flashlight, but to use it now, in the open, would be insane. If there were a guard, a light in an open field would warn him an intruder was present.

Georgii had worked in the plant for three years. When the weather would allow, he would take his lunch, and sit in the field between the fence and the plant. He was blind because of the darkness now, but like a blind man trained to his surroundings' he knew his way. He carefully set his back so that he was facing ninety degrees from the fence, and noted that Orion's Belt was over his right shoulder. Without that guide, he would be walking in circles as soon as he left the fence. Traversing the field was not as simple as he had thought. The factory had been closed for six months. No longer were its grounds manicured like a golf course. It was overgrown with tall grass, and weeds. Now and then he would blunder into a thorny bush, and have to carefully make his way around it. Trash was strewn about, and at one point his shin made painful contact with an old engine block. He kept his face always looking toward Orion. To look ahead was pointless. The blackness was so complete that he made contact with the factory wall with his outstretched arms well before he could see it.

He knew that the main entrance was toward his right hand, but it would be of no avail to work his way to the front door. Even if there were no guards, they certainly would have locked the door. They did not give keys to Junior Physicists, and lock smithing was never covered in any of the courses at MSU. After moving along the wall for about ten feet, he came to a first floor window. It was protected by steel bars, and appeared formidable to the casual observer, but he knew from his walks about the grounds, that the bars were of hollow steel. This had become obvious. The bars hadn't been painted for years, and here and there, rust had corroded away the steel to show its insubstantial structure.

Georgii carried three hacksaw blades in his pocket. He knew he would break at least one, and that having a couple of spares was prudent. He hardly needed the saw blades. It was obvious that the welder did not understand metals: He had used dissimilar metal rods for the welds, a common mistake. The resulting electrolysis had greatly accelerated corrosion where the bars had joined. It was hard to believe his luck. First, there were no guards to be seen, and now the corrosion. His training with weights, together with the corrosion, enabled him to use brute force to bend the bars.

The weakness in his plan was the noise the glass made, as he shattered the pane to reach the latch, but knowing that the area was deserted put his mind at ease. He was inside the dark room in a matter of minutes.

He congratulated himself on how easy the whole thing was. Just a matter of careful planning. He went over each move, step-by-step, being careful to lay aside

the proper tools. Now, at last, it was safe to turn on his
flashlight.

A sliver of light illuminated the wall before him.
By moving the beam about, he determined that he was in
a small storage room. Boxes were piled to the ceiling.
Many cartons were torn, and their contents of ledger paper
spilled out upon the floor. This represented years of
paperwork: recording this shipment to Minsk, or that
shipment from Pinsk. Moisture from a leaky roof had
invaded the room. The smell of mold swirled around him.
Hours of labor rotting away into an illegible mush. Labor
that was never of value to anyone anyway, but served to
justify salaries to hundreds of secretaries and accountants
in a monstrous bureaucracy.

Opposite the broken window was a door. With
trepidation, He reached for it. What a disappointment to
have gotten this far only to meet a locked door. But the
handle turned easily, and he directed his light down the
long hallway. Two meters from him he found a pair of
eyes, staring accusingly at him.

"Who are you?" said this voice of authority.

In a flash he saw the end of all his hopes; his wife,
and daughter starving in their apartment, while he was
sent to the Gulag, never to be heard from again. His
action was instantaneous and without thought. Two years
of training in Tae Kwon Do evoked an automatic response
to a threat. Georgii left the ground springing with one leg,
while the other shot out a sidekick. The man eyes
reflected his screams of pain as a knee cracked in two.
Without support, the eyes fell forward, toward their

assailant, and Georgii drove his fingers through those eyes, through the thin orbital surface of sphenoid bone, and into the brainstem – the center for respiration and consciousness. It was lights out for his opponent. All was done in silence, and accomplished in a couple of seconds.

Georgii collapsed against the near wall. Wiping his hand against his trousers, he left a trail of blood and brain tissue. In a few seconds he recovered some composure, and explored his victim with the flashlight. This was not the uniform of a guard, but the ragged clothing of a transient.

"What have I done? He's just a poor bum using the factory as a home. I have killed a man who's starving just as I am. I wouldn't go hunting with my friends. I wouldn't kill an animal for food, and now I've killed a man. I wonder how many other men are going to die over my stupid greed."

Georgii thought of turning around, climbing through the window, finding his way back to the fence and returning home. Too much had happened. Too much effort had been committed. He had to continue.

The transient would not be living here if there were any guards. He walked down the hallway knowing nobody of consequence would challenge him. He took a flight of stairs down. The metals were stored in the basement. This eliminated the problem of protecting the floor below from radiation. Finding the massive safe door, he began working the combination. If they were smart, they would have changed the combination before abandoning the building. But they were not smart people. Worse, they had little sense of responsibility. He heard the welcome clicks of the tumblers, and then he turned the giant wheel. The door was massive, but well balanced. Except for the inertia of several tons of steel, it swung open easily.

What he sought was in the floor. He was now walking over 50 by 50-cm square metal plates. Each plate bore the universal radiation caution sign, and at the corner of each plate was a large finger hole.

He lifted a plate at random. This revealed a chamber holding a large lead pig with a label on its cover. "Uranium 235, grade A2." That would not be a wise choice. It takes 16 kilograms of 80% enriched Uranium to make one critical mass. The American's crude Little Boy required 2.8 critical masses. That would be 42 Kilograms of this enriched Uranium to make one bomb. That does not include the lead pigs. This would be a poor choice. Arnold Schwarzenegger couldn't lug it very far. He would need special equipment to remove it from the factory, and a truck to transport it home.

One by one he lifted and then replaced the plates. Anybody doing research stored their isotopes here. There was not only uranium, but also other radioactive materials such as Cobalt 60. Finally, in a corner of the floor, he found the label he was looking for, "Pu^{239}, 3.0 kg." He removed the pig, and lifted the adjacent cover to reveal a second 3 kg ingot of Plutonium. Six kilograms would not be much to carry, but it would lead to certain death if he did not carry the Plutonium in their heavy lead pigs. Five kilograms made one critical mass. Carrying six kg in one pig was out of the question. He needed both hands to lift either pig. Carrying both home will be extremely difficult, but not impossible.

Weight was only one factor influencing his choice in favor of Plutonium. He was about to hand over to strangers material for the most awful weapon ever developed. Any little group of terrorists can manufacture a Uranium bomb. All they needed was a six-foot long gun. A sub-critical mass of Uranium on one end would be fired into a set of surrounding rings also made of Uranium. The rings plus the bullet would yield 2.8 critical masses, and an atomic explosion. A very simple bomb. The problem was the separation of U^{235} from U^{238}. It had taken the USSR years, even with our knowledge of American technology to separate these chemically identical substances.

The Plutonium bomb was a different story. Producing Plutonium was easy. The Uranium in the pile is completely different from its product—the Plutonium—and separation is simple. The bomb is another matter. Fire two blocks of plutonium together, and before they touch, the fast neutrons trigger the explosion—a dud of an explosion. Five kilograms of Plutonium would yield the explosive power of five kilograms of dynamite. An extremely expensive, and not a very practical bomb.

The Americans were the first to solve the problem. A hollow sphere of Plutonium, the size of a small orange, was surrounded by explosive. This compressed the Plutonium into a solid sphere that exceeded critical mass, and you had your atomic explosion. There was just one little problem. In the early trials, the explosion would result in a deformed lump of metal, not a sphere. It took years to develop the necessary complex geometry needed. Finally, they developed a series of complex shaped blocks of explosive. Some of the blocks consisted of a high brisance explosive, and some blocks of a slower burning variety. This complex combination of shapes and explosives produced a uniform shock wave that reduced the hollow orange into a small solid ball. The Americans began to work on both problems at the same time. Accumulating enough enriched Uranium for one bomb took the same number of years as the solution for their geometry problem.

"When I give them their Plutonium," Georgii wondered, "what are they going to be able to do with it? Only a large nation, with a lot of time, and a lot of money, is going to solve this problem in solid geometry."

With his conscience somewhat assuaged, he unrolled his knapsack from his pocket. The thin canvas would never hold the weight of the heavy pigs without tearing, but he was prepared as usual. He had lined the inside of the knapsack with two layers of 1.5 mil Mylar. The sack would be strong enough. The question was whether *he* would be strong enough.

Laying the open sack on the floor he carefully placed the pigs side by side. After tying the sack securely closed, he sat on the floor with his back to it. He slipped the straps over his shoulders. These, too, he had reinforced. Standing up was a major problem. He made it to his knees, and then using the wall for support, slowly stood.

If he made it home, all they would get is one bomb. That was all he could carry, and that was all he had promised. For their purpose though, this was enough. Then all they had to do was to solve a very difficult problem in how to get a sphere of critical mass. Several different kinds of explosives needed to be arranged so one shock wave would not cancel or augment an adjacent shock wave. If successful, they would explode one bomb. That would show their neighbors that they were a nuclear power. Only a few would know that it was their only bomb. They would gain the respect they needed, and the threat to the rest of the world was minimal.

Back at the stairs, he held the light in his teeth as he pulled himself up to the ground floor by the bannister. From the inside, there was no problem leaving through the front door. This time he was careful to keep Orion over his left shoulder, but at the fence it took him twenty valuable minutes to find the hole he had made. Then he had to sit, remove the knapsack, crawl through the opening, and pull the knapsack through after him. Again he sat with his back to the knapsack, put his arms through the straps, and finally used the chain link to help him stand again.

It was a different ten kilometers on the way back. Every few minutes he stopped at a nearby tree, leaning back to relieve the weight of his knapsack, and allow his legs to regain some strength. Years of weight training with leg presses made the ten kilometers possible, but not easy.

He must not look like he is carrying a heavy load when he enters the train. Everyone must think these are groceries in his sack. He must make it look easy, even if he feels like dying from the strain.

At the station he was careful not to sit down. There was no way he could rise from a sitting position with ease. He stood leaning against a supporting pole of the roof. His timing had to be good. He could not stand there forever. Not with his limited strength.

The train came, and he walked toward the steps to the passenger car. He tried to use an easy, ambling gait, even though his knees were killing him. With effort he placed his left leg on the high step to the train, and at the same time grasped the handle near the door. Horrors, he could not get on. He could not lift his weight with that one leg.

"Can I give you a lift, old man?"

The voice was that of the conductor behind him as he pushed from under his right arm pit. A passenger from the car grasped his right hand and pulled him aboard.

"Thanks, I didn't realize how bad my arthritis has been acting up. You are both lifesavers."

He took his seat carefully next to a pole, joining ceiling with floor. He would need that pole when he wanted to stand again. The rest on the long train ride was welcomed. He took a deep breath, and looked up. A stifled gasp escaped his lips. There in front of him were the eyes. The eyes in the flashlight beam. It seemed that everyone in the car was staring at him.

He was staring at his reflection in the window. Those eyes were his. In a few moments the other passengers returned to their papers, or their daydreams. Just another crazy one. Probably dozed and had a nightmare or some crazy thought had entered his deranged mind. He *did* look strange, with that sack straining at his shoulders, and that terribly pained look in his eyes.

"They're no longer staring," he thought. "They don't want me to know that they see the blood on my pants. Christ! They must smell the blood and brains. They surely have radioed ahead for the police."

He arrived in Uralsk at 5 a.m. Surprised to see that the police were not swarming all over the station, he began the long walk home.

It was still dark, and anybody seeing him lurch down the street would think he was drunk from a night of bingeing. Quietly entering his apartment, he stored the knapsack in back of the closet, and then covered it with old clothes they had planned to give away to someone even more unfortunate than they were.

When he was finished, he slid his aching body into bed beside Eva.

Michael would be at the park bench every Monday. He would do this for one month. If he did not make the meeting within the month, Michael would start looking for another supplier. It was Friday, and Georgii had three days before their meeting. He used this time to prepare for the other half of their bargain. He carefully drew diagrams, and described in detail what kind of device it would take to detonate a bomb. Every schoolboy knew that explosives were used to implode the plutonium into a critical mass. The kind of explosive, the amount of explosive, the geometry, and the trigger were another matter. The technology was formidable. Just because you had plutonium, and all of the specifications, didn't mean you could make a bomb. He would do his job to the letter, but he had doubts that a little country could follow his plans faithfully. Their bomb would probably be a big dud, but there would be enough explosion and radioactivity to convince their neighbors that this country was on its way to being a nuclear power. That was all that was necessary.

Sunday, he had a sleepless night. The meeting on Monday was for two p.m., but he was in his place at one.

"Ah, Georgii, you have come. Then I trust you were able to fulfill your part of the bargain? You will not be sorry."

"I have everything. I have the plans and the material. The lead makes everything quite heavy. How do we make the exchange?'

"Here are two keys to adjacent lockers at the station. I have copies of the keys. In the first locker you will find a small suitcase full of gold Kruggerands. Take the suitcase out, then place your package inside the locker. You have two lockers just in case you need the room. Be careful and lock up."

"But I thought I would be paid in rubles!"

"If I paid you in rubles, I would have to rent *five* lockers! We have to economize in some way. Listen, I know where you and your family live. Do this right, and you will be secure in your old age. I don't have to tell you what will happen if that package is not there."

"I will do as you say, but I must take two trips. The package is too heavy for me, and I will divide it in two. Don't come to the locker until I have made my second trip."

Georgii had no intention of cheating. He had seen enough Western movies to understand what happens when somebody tries to cheat the gang. This was more than a gang. It was a country, and they would not brook being short-changed.

He took his assignment seriously. This time, carrying only half the load, the trips were easy. On the first trip he waited until the area was clear of passengers, and then he opened the suitcase. There they were; piles of gold coins. On the second trip, he locked the last compartment, and took his gold home.

CHAPTER IV

Corporations have neither bodies to be kicked,

nor souls to be damned.

Anonymous

"I believe we can get to him easily."

"What do you have so far, Draco?"

Draco was the younger man. His well-tailored suit did not conceal his wiry lean muscled body, and close-cropped hair gave away his military origin. Draco leafed through a folder in his lap, and brought forth an eight by ten photo. He passed it across the desk to the well-groomed man in his fifties. An anachronism of style with a silk double-breasted suit perfectly tailored over his vest. Across the front of the vest, from buttonhole to pocket, hung a fine gold chain. It was undoubtedly anchored to a pocket watch. He was a bit on the heavy side. He was not "fat" heavy, but more like "line backer" heavy. He colleagues referred to him as "the director," and to his face as "sir." They never referred to him by name. Perhaps this is because when you first met, he was introduced to you as the director, and somehow, you were never given a name. Perhaps his mother never gave him a name. His colleagues assumed that his mother also addressed him as "sir," or when speaking about him to others, referred to him as the director, or occasionally as Mr. D.

The Director smiled as he looked at the familiar face in the photo. "He looks even more arrogant than he did three years ago at that conference on Third *World Countries and Population Control.* I must say, his taste in women has improved, Draco. This one looks less vapid than his usual twit."

"She should. Sibyl's one of ours. We arranged for her to be seated next to him on his plane to the Bahamas."

A frown appeared on the Director's usually poker face. "I assume she's not making the hit. Any new face will be suspect, and this operation is not of such priority as to risk exposing the existence of the organization."

"Of course not! Sibyl merely compiled a complete dossier on the Power's movements."

"'The Power!!' That code name fits his ego perfectly."

The room in which the two men talked was spacious. It was a good 20x20 with fine oak paneling. One wall was lined with bookcases. Two of the other walls were occupied by a weapons collection carefully arranged in chronological order. Beginning on the east wall with the broad swords of 400 AD or King Arthur's time, it gradually advanced to short swords containing hidden pistols. This was a time when men did not have full confidence in gunpowder. By the time one's eyes traversed to the North wall, it was evident that we were in the modern age. Here we began with the .45 caliber Tommy gun of the thirties –a favorite of the Chicago Mob, passed through some laser-sighted weapons, and ended with the high velocity, fully automatic M-16. On the desk were strewn parts of several semi-automatic pistols.

The director stared admiringly at the M-16. How could it take so long for the US Army to discover a principle of physics that every high school boy knows? They wanted a man stopper. A bullet that would stop a berserk man loaded on drugs, and bent on killing regardless of his own death. So they picked a nice heavy bullet, the .45. From the days of Newton, we have known $E = \frac{1}{2} MV^2$. The weight of the bullet is of little consequence when measured against its velocity which is squared. The M16 has a tiny bullet, little more than a .22, but what a wallop. The muzzle velocity was 3650 feet per second, and at 100 yards was still traveling faster than 3000 feet per seconds. Its energy at impact at 100 yards was 800 foot pounds. You didn't have to hit a vital organ with that bullet. The energy would destroy tissue many inches from its path. Bone that was nowhere near the path of the bullet would shatter. What a magnificent weapon.

"How hard is your information, Draco?"

"Several independent sources yield the same data. The meeting is set for May 23, at North latitude 25 degrees, ten minutes, longitude 77 degrees, and thirty minutes. They're planning a mini summit conference with few staff in order to allow frank discussion."

The Director leaned back, gazing at the intricacies of the Durer prints on the fourth wall. He was a bit disgusted with himself. Once he had been quite physically fit. He'd even played some college football, but time, sloth, and those administrative dinner meetings had taken their toll. He thought of himself as rather round now, and only a few hairs made a last ditch stand on his balding head. In his mind he was no longer James Bond, but was now M. M did not have the capability to ski down 60-degree slopes, or rappel down cliffs, but he had control. He had the control of many 007s, and was the more deadly for it.

"They're certainly security conscious," he said, as he tore his thoughts from their pleasant reverie.

"With good reason, wouldn't you say?" Draco added. "The problem is that we have an extremely short timetable in which to do everything with the precision it requires."

"By the way, just how reliable is this stuff from Sibyl? She's been around for some time, hasn't she?"

Draco paused a moment before answering. "Our history goes back a long way. All the way back to Viet Nam. Remember that problem with Westmoreland's Staff Sergeant? He was leaving Viet Nam, and about to tell the world about our illegal adventure into Cambodia before it was a *fait accompli*. Sibyl managed to delay his departure by several weeks, and she did this before she'd had any training in the service. She's been a superb operative ever since. We can have confidence in Sibyl's skills."

"I'm afraid this will have to do, Draco. He will not be outside his country again until the elections. By that time he will firmly be on home turf, and quite secure. If we procrastinate, the window of opportunity will not reappear, and we will be faced with a situation like the United States has with Cuba, where all they can do is grin and bear it. Please schedule his accident for May 23."

The director idly wiped some Cosmoline from the dismantled breech of the Glock. "Who has the assignment?"

It was 0500 hours, and wake-up time. Sibyl no longer used a clock. Her regimen was the same seven days a week, and her body had a well-trained internal clock. First, out of bed, then empty bladder, then onto the bathroom scale. The scale, accurate to 1/4 lb, would tell the tale. Did last night's calories really count? There was a further critical examination in the mirror. Her reflection revealed hard, lean muscle.

The morning run would have to be five, rather than four miles. That extra half pound could not be tolerated. Later, she would go to the gym for her weight training, and Martial Arts lessons. She favored Tae Kwon Do. As a woman, she knew that all the weight training in the world would not make her a match for a Tyson type. Her legs were as strong as anyone's. After all, she walked on them all day. Tae Kwon Do trained her to fight with her legs. She had snapped a three-inch pine for her first Dan; she could easily break a femur with a well-placed kick.

Sybil had begun to hate her job this past year. Her work required youth. She had to have the beauty, and the agility of youth. Without beauty she couldn't do her work. Without strength, and agility, she might not stay alive. She was forty now, and it took constant training to hold back the clock. What was worse, she was beginning to question the importance of her work. A few years ago, when nations faced each other with nuclear arsenals, the whole thing made some sense. Now, with the dissolution of the USSR, there was little chance of a worldwide conflagration.

Her boss was still finding assignments for her. Some were utter nonsense. It was getting obvious that her boss was trying desperately to justify the continued existence of the agency.

Twenty years ago she felt quite differently. Early in life, she developed a syndrome common to many young girls. This Florence Nightingale triad consisted of a vision in which the heroine is, one, covered with glory, two, surrounded by handsome, single doctors, and three, saves lives daily.

Perhaps there is just enough truth in the story to keep the legend alive and to attract unsuspecting maidens. In the early years of her nursing training, Sibyl learned about the less advertised aspects of her profession: enemas, bedpans, and excrement covering incontinent patients. Two years on the wards at a county hospital and she also learned of the endless charting and the endless routine. Most nurses entered their profession with enough maturity to understand that life cannot be a constant excitement of change and challenge. Sibyl Rosenthal had entered graduate nursing at the age of fifteen. An extraordinarily high IQ enabled her to skip many years of grade school and high school. She had the intelligence for her curriculum, but not the maturity to cope with reality.

After two years on the wards, bored with nursing, Sibyl was seeking an out to her daily drudgery. The army promised a life of excitement, and far-off places as a nurse in a combat zone.

Sibyl spent six weeks at Fort Sam Houston learning to be an officer and a gentlewoman, and was then sent off to Viet Nam. Her tour was not what she had expected. Cam Rahn Bay was a convalescent center, far from the fighting zones. The casualties here were gunshot wounds well on the mend, malaria, and hepatitis— all waiting to heal and return to duty. If the routine was a bit different, it was also a bit more boring. The daily temperature hovered around ninety to one hundred and twenty degrees. Not a blade of grass grew. Sand was everywhere. It was on the beach, of course, but it was also on the ward. Forever sweeping it out of your hooch, brushing it out of your hair, and sleeping in it in your bed. There was an Army Officers' Club for the nightly sixteen-millimeter movie and drinks, but that was the extent of the entertainment. Oh, yes, there was that rare visit by some comedian surrounded by half-naked bouncing blondes. Just what our fighting boys needed. That little bit of stimulation made her life impossible with her patients for at least two weeks following the show.

The ratio of men to women had its advantages. Sibyl was short, but reed-like. She had jet-black hair and pointed little breasts. Her youthful face made you want to hold and protect her from the harsh surroundings of a theater of war. There was never any lack of attention. The doctors were all married, but marriage had meaning only in the "real world." There were also the helicopter pilots as they stopped in on their way to their base at Ban-Me Thout.

Cliff was craggy. He was a cross between the Stars and Stripes version of a helicopter pilot, and Dick Tracy. You couldn't get craggier. That should be enough to make a man stand out in a crowd, and Cliff was like neon. He never wore a uniform.

One of Sibyl's girlfriends pointed him out. "Do you know what he does?"

"No, do you?"

"I don't know him, but you can't help but notice that he's the only one in civvies. He's got to be CID."

"I'm new here. What's CID?"

"Intelligence. You know, spies and that sort of thing. They all dress like civilians so no one will know who they are. The trouble is, it's pretty obvious because no one in a combat theater dresses like a civilian unless he's got some sort of secret mission."

Sibyl's experience with intelligence agents was based on Ian Fleming's novels, so Cliff now had the aura of 007. Other men faded into the background. In the informality of an overseas base, it was not difficult to meet him. She planted herself on the folding chair next to him at the Officers' Club as they were showing *Sixty Seconds over Tokyo*. Conversation was easy between reels.

As the last of film slapped its way around the take-up reel, Cliff turned to her and said, "It's already black as pitch outside. How about if I walk you back to your hooch?"

"I've been here a couple of months, and I still get lost when I step out in the dark," she confided. "Last week I walked straight when the path turned. I ended up rolling down a ravine."

She laughed heartily, and then touched Cliff's shoulder as if to steady herself. "It took a couple of guys from engineering to cut me away from the accordion wire, and the doctor spent a lot of time patching me up."

"You sound like you need a guardian."

"I'm okay in daylight, but when it's dark, I lose all sense of direction."

Cliff smiled at her. "I know. This place has the darkest nights I've ever seen. You got much time left?

"Cliff, from midnight, I've got two hundred and thirty-eight more days to DEROS."

"That's a long time to spend here," he reflected. "I really wish I could invite you somewhere quiet for a drink and some music, but even a walk along the beach is out at this hour."

"Yeah, I don't feel like ambling through a free fire zone. We'd be in season for the Viet Cong, the North Viet regulars, the RVNS, the Koreans, and not to say the least, our own guys."

"When are you on duty?"

"I work days, eight to eight."

The conversation continued with the usual periods of silence. He learned about her life as an RN. She learned what she recognized as his cover. He was an engineer for a civilian contractor. Sibyl discovered very little regarding the type of work this contractor did.

Courtship in Viet Nam presented several problems. One soon became bored with eating at the same Officers' Clubs, watching the same club acts, and the old sixteen-millimeter films. At times Sibyl would find herself with a day off, and then she and Cliff took his jeep and explored the countryside. He carried his M-16 automatic rifle, and Sibyl would check a .45 out of the armory. The heavy semi-automatic would slip over her hips, pulling down her fatigue slacks, and she frequently stopped to hike up her pants and tighten the gun belt.

Cam Rahn Bay was not a combat zone in the sense of infantry advancing along a front, but like most other quiet areas of Viet Nam, the occasional sniper fired from a roof or a tree. The eight-year-old boy riding past you on his motor bike might drop a grenade in your lap. Occasionally, sappers, with their packages of explosives, would try to penetrate your perimeter at night. Across the road from Sibyl's quarters was a concrete slab, twenty-foot wide by forty-foot long. It had been the foundation of a nurses' quarters. It was now a monument to false security before the sappers came. Last month, the bird colonel lost his jeep. An ingenious soul had bound down a grenade lever with a rubber band, pulled the pin, and then dropped the grenade into the gas tank. Lucky for the colonel, he wasn't riding in the jeep when the gasoline dissolved the rubber band.

This is not the kind of place to take a girl for a drive, but boredom pushes people to madness.

Cliff occasionally took Sibyl on his trips into Cam Rahn City.

"Cliff, what's in those boxes in the back seat?"

"I'm taking them into the city for a friend of mine. The big box is a Sony TC 760 tape recorder, and the other two are Pioneer receivers. I also have three Nikon FTN's back there."

"How come all that valuable stuff? We must be on top of a fortune."

"My friend bought this stuff from the PX, and also from the overseas catalogue. There are a few rich Vietnamese who are willing to pay for these little goodies."

"Listen! That's black market and we're going to have to go through a checkpoint to get into the city. They'll put us in the stockade and leave us there after everybody's gone home."

"No sweat. I have a special pass. Nothing in this jeep gets searched. Some day, I'll explain it to you. Meanwhile, just relax and enjoy the ride. My cut is fifty percent of the profits. I'm going to live real well when this war is over," chortled the black knight on his olive drab steed.

"So, what good is all this money? You can't spend Piasters in the States. If you convert them to Military Payment Certificates, they're worthless except in Viet Nam."

"Listen, Honey," Cliff said. "I've got a few friends involved with banking. I also have friends that fly Med-

Evac missions to Japan and the States. So, all those problems are trivial."

"Next time we go on a date, leave all the loot behind, okay? I've got better things to do with my life than spend it in Sing-Sing. You're not into narcotics too, are you?"

"I never deal in shit. It's bad news for a lot of guys out here. They're admitting junkies to the Sixth Convalescent Center at the rate of thirty to fifty a day."

Sibyl exploded in paroxysms of coughing as the jeep kicked up dust and sand along the crude road. The road snaked along a valley. On one side rolling sand dunes hid the bay. On the other, hills of broken rock were surmounted by barbed wire interspersed with machine-gun emplacements. Now and then a sign over a wooden gate would announce that some engineering battalion made their home there.

The jeep skidded into a turn, and they suddenly found themselves in deep sand. To one side was a sign reading, "PLEASE DO NOT WALK ON THE GRASS." There was not a blade of grass for miles. Cliff deftly shifted into four-wheel drive, and held it there until they were on firm ground again.

The process of passing from Cam Rahn Army Base to Cam Rahn City was nerve-wracking for Sibyl. Any moment, one of the MPs with their big .45s could step from the gatehouse and demand that he be allowed to inspect the jeep. Then the terrifying ordeal of court-martial would begin. After being stripped of her

129

commission, and thrown into the crude stockade, she would then be sent to the States, under guard, to continue as a convict in Leavenworth.

Sibyl felt her face redden, and sweat poured down her brow, stinging her eyes. She was aware of the MP staring at her, and hoped that the heat of the one hundred and ten-degree day was adequate excuse for her appearance. To her surprise, he waved them on past his gate, and into the city of Cam Rahn.

The next leg of the journey took them down a side street in the city. Even though it was one of the larger streets, it was barely wide enough for the jeep to pass between the buildings. No little white picket fences here. Instead, each house was surrounded by its own form of densely woven barbed wire mesh, and over each window there was more cris-crossing strands of the same wire. Finally the jeep stopped at a store.

"Stay in the jeep, Sibyl. I'll be right back."

Cliff was in the store for ten minutes when an emaciated little oriental man came out and began carrying the boxes inside. A moment later Cliff emerged, stuffing a wad of bills into his pocket.

"OK, let's go explore a bit of the countryside."

In the coming weeks, Sibyl found herself more relaxed as they rode past the checkpoints. More than once Cliff remarked how cool she had become under a situation that had been so stressful earlier. Several times, he had invited her to invest in his little business, and after refusing, she began to bring a few of her own purchases across the checkpoint to be sold at an obscene profit.

One month after their first meeting, Cliff drove her over to ARCO Contractors, and introduced her to his boss.

Incongruity is common place in war. While men were living and dying buried in mud and vermin, others lived in luxury. There were Olympic-sized pools, fancy officers' clubs, and PXs. Cliff led Sibyl to an unpainted frame shack. In this land in which the United States had erected so many well-constructed "temporary" edifices, the main office of ARCO Contractors had actually achieved a true "temporary" look.

Sibyl was anxious to enter anything that promised good old-fashioned American air-conditioning. She knew how Lawrence must have felt as he traversed the anvil of the Arabian Desert. It was a typical day in the Cam Ranh Peninsula, and they had traveled for too many miles in 120-degree heat.

As they crossed the threshold, the only improvement was the fact that the hot air now circulated. A man was seated behind a roll-top desk, sucking noisily at some iced drink while he thumbed through a manila folder. He was a large man, wearing a white Panama suit. The slow-moving ceiling fan was the only "air-conditioner" in the room. Sweat rolled down his face, staining his collar, and soaking his armpits.

Sibyl was annoyed with herself. She should never have allowed Cliff to push her into this visit to socialize at

the contractor's office. She looked on with disbelief at
this character who had just stepped out of a Humphrey
Bogart movie. Here he was Sydney Greenstreet
resurrected from the dead. She felt the sweat sting as it
rolled into her eyes. Languidly rubbing it away, she was
thankful she had long ago given up wearing mascara in
the sweltering heat of Viet Nam.

"Hello, Sibyl. Let me apologize for the weather in
here. Our air-conditioner is being repaired. In a theater of
war I'm afraid replacements are impossible to come by.
Let me introduce myself: Smith. Why don't you sit
down?" He indicated two archaic folding chairs.

"Cliff, before you get comfortable, there's a
thermos of Tom Collins, and some glasses in the cooler.
Please get some for yourself and the young lady."

Turning to Sibyl, Smith said, "I'm sorry I have
nothing more elegant to offer you, my dear, but the French
influence did not go as far as leaving a few of their finer
wines buried in the sand."

Gratefully replenishing the fluids she had sweated
away, Sibyl felt perplexed. Why would Cliff take her to
the hottest part of Viet Nam she had ever endured, and
allow her to sit and swelter in this miserable room? They
could have been at the beach at Cam Ranh right now.

Mr. Smith rapidly drained his glass. "It must be
more difficult for a young woman to be in Viet Nam."

Feeling irritable, Sibyl drank greedily at her
Collins. Obviously Cliff wanted her to captivate his boss,
but with her khaki pants sticking to the sweat accumulated

on her legs, and her hair falling in limp strands around her shoulders, she felt unsociable and uncharming.

Ignoring her silence, Smith continued, "I've enjoyed a delightful youth, and now, if I spend a few months here, supervising a construction crew in a war zone, it's an exciting adventure to relate to my friends at home." He leaned forward, smiling gently at Sibyl, "but it is difficult for you, my dear, with nothing but rain to break up the tedium, and committed for a year."

His empathy drained away some of her morose feelings.

The phone on the large man's desk rang. Picking it up on the first ring, as he listened, he beamed, "That's absolutely delightful. You're a gem!"

With startling agility, he rose from his chair and took Sibyl's arm. Cliff followed as Sibyl was steered to the door. "We do have a few amenities here, Sibyl, and because they are so few, we appreciate them all the more. We are blessed with an itinerant air-conditioned trailer which just arrived from the wharf. Luncheon awaits us."

As soon as Sibyl crossed the threshold, the cold air evaporated much of her annoyance. After a quick look at her surroundings, she was tempted to step outside again to make certain this was really a trailer. The polished hardwood floor had been sectioned into areas by rich oriental rugs. The farthest area held a dark desk; obviously an antique, but its exact period was a mystery to Sibyl's untrained eye. As Sibyl's hand reached for the nearest wall to steady herself, she encountered the nubby texture of raw silk covering. The exterior door had been nondescript, but its inner aspect was opulent mahogany. Exquisite prints were scattered over the walls. On close examination, she recognized that these were numbered, and bore the signatures of Dali and Picasso. She had barely made herself comfortable in an overstuffed easy chair when she became aware of a tantalizing aroma. Smith was approaching her, his out-stretched hands majestically bearing a crystal dish laden with cheese puffs. As her teeth broke the golden crust and mingled cheeses filled her mouth, the hot jeep ride became very distant. Mr. Smith then presented her with a goblet containing a golden liquid. Although Kir Gallique may not have been the sommelier-approved choice, it was appropriately refreshing.

"These are really fantastic," Sibyl extolled as she reached for another puff.

"I'm delighted that you appreciate them, Sibyl," Smith patted his extensive waistline, as someone else would treat a favored pet, "but I'm afraid I've overindulged myself on too many occasions."

"Oh, Mr. Smith," with her mouth engulfing a cheese puff, she could afford to be charitable; "I guess I'm just lucky. I've never had to watch my weight. I can eat as much as I want."

"Your girlfriends must have hated you," said Cliff.

Sibyl laughed as she licked crumbs from her fingers.

A serving man brought cold soup to the table. Mr. Smith rose, and graceously helped Sibyl with her seat. As they ate their gazpacho, Sibyl paused long enough to demolish half a crisp loaf of French bread. Cliff shook his head in amazement. "It's got to be your thyroid, Honey."

"I'm afraid to have it checked," she laughed. "It's probably off the scale. If I ever got treated, I'd have to eat like an ordinary mortal, and I don't think I could stand it."

Smith smiled as he gently chided Cliff. "I should think Sibyl would like to get away from shop talk. Sibyl, please, I'm Jonathan. That 'Mr. Smith' is such a chauvinistic affectation." Between delicate mouthfuls of soup he continued, "What are your plans when your year here is up?"

Sibyl shrugged her shoulders.

"You ETS when you leave Vietnam, don't you?" Cliff asked.

Looking at Smith, she explained, "That would mean I'm out of the Army. Unfortunately, I still owe them another year."

"I'm familiar with the jargon, Sibyl. Do you intend to enlist for another term?"

"Oh, no!" Sibyl answered quickly. "I'd never re-up; I'll just serve my last year in the real world."

Nodding sympathetically, Smith said, "I can understand how a tour of duty in Viet Nam can sour a young woman on an army life."

"I felt this way before Viet Nam. It's not the danger. That's the only part I can tolerate. It's not even the heat, but the boredom, the chain of command, knowing what you'll be doing, wearing, who you'll be with, reports in triplicate if you're lucky, but it's usually six copies of everything, even the toilet paper. Then there's always the idiocy." As the soup made dark dribbles down the front of her blouse, she watched it, muttering, "Even my underwear is khaki."

"I can understand that an imaginative person would find this life stifling," Smith clucked.

Her zest for the food momentarily deserted her as Sibyl put down her spoon, and thought aloud. "I don't know what I'm going to do when I get out, but it certainly will include great lingerie."

Cliff laughed, while Jonathan redirected the conversation. "You're a nurse. You shouldn't have any trouble finding a job."

Sibyl went on for the next half-hour, through the salad and entrée, telling them and herself about the boredom of nursing, almost as bad as army khaki, worse than the boredom of Viet Nam. "At least in a combat zone a nurse could do a lot of stuff that only doctors are allowed to do at home. Now I'm over-trained," she lamented. "If I put in a central line, or a chest tube in the states, they would have my license."

Ever since a high-ranking political figure, recovering from an elective herniorrhaphy, had first observed her sharp intellect and lurking dissatisfaction, extensive research had begun on Sibyl's background. Probing continued with psychological profiles, the subtle equivalence of Minnesota Multiphasic Personality Inventory, and scrutiny by carefully trained personnel. Now as Sibyl's tirade of displeasure with her profession chugged on, the men who called themselves Cliff and Mr. Smith became more certain of their terrain. Cliff, in Viet Nam for other purposes, had decided to personally observe Sibyl. With the evolution of a minor assignment in the area, he concluded that the time was right for an approach. This is so much cleaner than bringing an agent in. After all, Sibyl was already in place.

At a surreptitious signal from Cliff, Mr. Smith's probing became more obvious as he discussed other lifestyles, ways of feverishly escaping ennui by the assumption of a multitude of successive identities. He spoke of foreign travel, and saw lights go on behind her eyes. When he shifted into patriotism, Sibyl's face glowed. After painting his picture of intrigue and excitement, he paused. It was time for Sibyl to pick up her cue.

She was speechless, her mouth a trifle agape.

His smile disappeared, and with hardened eyes he broke the stillness in a few cold, carefully articulated words. "Actually, we know a great deal about you, Sibyl."

It took a few seconds for Sibyl to become aware that Smith's charm had dropped to the floor, and shattered like a porcelain mask. Sibyl's mind began to click back in place and she realized that Cliff's silence during most of the afternoon had been calculated to allow him a study of her responses while Smith directed the conversation.

"Now you're about to tell me why Cliff brought me here, aren't you?"

Gauging her mood as holding some hostility toward Cliff, Smith continued, "...but I do think it's important for you to know that Cliff began keeping company with you before we made the final decision about selecting you for our group."

Cliff held her hand gently, as he gazed into her eyes and lied, "That's right, Sibyl."

Imperceptibly, Cliff nodded to Mr. Smith to resume.

"I'll be brief. We represent a federal organization, but before we can go any further, I must have you sign a paper agreeing that everything we say here will be kept in strict confidence whether you agree to join us or not. If you break your promise, you'll be violating the Official Secrets Act, and can be prosecuted. Do you understand?"

"I'm not sure, but my curiosity is whetted. Where's that paper?"

After Sibyl had digested and signed the document, Smith continued, "We represent an international organization that is under the combined auspices of NATO and SEATO, and originated as a branch of NSA. Our mission is to work behind the scenes, so to speak, to counter espionage originating from Chinese, Soviet, and certain hostile Third World blocks. We are far removed from NSA's original mission."

Leaning back, Sybil tilted her chair as much as safety permitted. "So you're a bunch of multinational spies. Tell me something," she whispered, as she now leaned closer to the fat man, "are you good guys, or am I in the midst of the baddies?"

"Actually," Cliff grinned, "we just do a lot of dirty laundry as cleanly as possible."

"Without getting caught," Sibyl mused aloud.

As the daughter of a naval commander and one of the first female survival instructors, Sibyl's legacy included rational behavior under stress, and the ability to present an unflappable exterior. So, although off-balance inwardly, she was able to take in the last few minutes with a calm facade. Another person might not have accepted the situation without pangs of disbelief, but Sibyl felt only a sense of displacement. Her childhood, devoid of religious beliefs, had been strong on service to one's country. Although her upbringing had taught her to question the existence of a deity, those involved in covert operations were her super-heroes. As she studied the two solid faces at the table, her sense of unreality faded. It was soon replaced by elation. My God! She was being invited into spydom.

Sibyl looked up at Cliff, "but I don't understand. Who are you? Is this the NSA?"

"We refer to ourselves quite simply as The Department of National Safety."

"I never heard of your organization," responded Sybil.

"Well, I will give you a little history, Mr. Smith responded with a sardonic grin spread across his face. Real secrecy is impossible. Politicians and their ilk leak like sieves. It serves them to leak items to the press when it serves their careers. We had to find a solution to this. We had to develop an organization divorced from congressional oversight. We wanted an organization that would not have to deal with leaks. We…"

"Why are you telling me all of this stuff?" Sibyl sat with shock across her face.

"Oh, yes! You are wondering how we could trust you. Think back to your nursing board exam. Do you remember all those questions that delved into your psychological make-up?"

"Oh, I remember. I remember remarking to one of the other nurses of the total gall of those questions. They queried me about my most personal life, what I would do under the most ridiculous situations, my basic likes and dislikes, and other questions that had nothing to do with nursing and was none of their damn business. The funny thing was, when I asked one of the other nurses about these questions, they looked at me as if I was crazy – that they had taken an entirely different test."

"You did take an entirely different test, Sybil" said Mr. Smith with this broad grin painted on his face. "My dear, you have been thoroughly vetted. We know who we can trust.

"So let me go on with my tale. A group of us at the NSA decided we needed a solution to this security problem. We decided to form our own little organization, but retain our credentials with NSA. There are people at NSA that know only one thing (they really don't want to know any more.), and that is that we exist. So we get our salaries and a little money from the kitty that is for top secret stuff, but otherwise we do not exist. We retain enough of a connection with the old organization to utilize their resources etc. In addition, not existing means that we cannot utilize the judicial system. Anybody who strays, threatens our security, leaks information etc, is treated extra judicially. They conveniently have an accident, and that is that. As they say, the wages of sin are death.

"No, Sibyl. We're just what I said we are. A group who does intelligence gathering, and performs other related functions, but composed of many non-Communist nations.

"Although, my dear," continued Smith, while arranging his features to project a certain paternal understanding, "on occasion we do trade resources with our friends in the Company, and aid each other's operatives."

With unusual slowness, Sibyl added cream and sugar to the coffee that was now before her. She stirred and sipped, focusing all her interest on the exquisite Delft cup in her hand. So many questions, but if she asked...perhaps they'd find her foolish and reconsider. Ridiculous! Obviously she had been carefully vetted or she would never have been contacted.

Mentally, she took a deep breath and plunged. "Of course I'm interested, Jonathan. You knew I would be or you never would have suggested I might be suitable for your group. What is it called?"

Since, in deference to age and size Smith appeared to be the leader, she looked searchingly into his eyes as she asked, "What would I be doing?"

As Sibyl re-stirred the already dissolved sugar, Jonathan Smith continued to reel in his catch. "My dear, you must realize that I'm not trying to hedge when I say that I can't give you specifics as to every assignment you could conceivably get."

"Jonathan, you have to remember that however unhappy I may be with nursing, I've still been trained in medicine, and will always hold certain obligations to my profession."

Years of association had left scars between the two men. Cliff had judiciously negated many of Smith's choicest plans. Yet, Smith had still managed to be Cliff's *bête noire*. So, with great relish, Cliff placed Jonathan Smith on the spot. "Sibyl will always have a nurse's ethical code, Jonathan, and I think she's trying to ask you if she'll have to kill."

Smith glared at his colleague. This was something to which certain types, such as Sibyl, could become gradually hardened, and then serve quite well. It was not to be brought out in the clear, unprepared air. Artfully creating his sincere look, careful not to smile too much, Smith answered, "You always have the option to refuse a certain number of assignments. We would never want one of our people acting against their conscience."

Cliff rejected the thought of telling her how many assignments she could turn down and still remain operative.

Subconsciously, Sibyl's decision had been made in her teens. Her first lover had been an attractive house-guest who did "something" diplomatic in the State Department. Later, snatches of hushed parental conversation revealed him as someone with incredible panache—a young man involved with "covert operations." No movie star or football player could have made the same impact.

"Should you decide to join us," Jonathan continued, "your initial stipend would be $10,000 more per year than your present Army pay. We would also see to it that you continued to collect your hazardous duty pay. As you have been so vociferous in your critique against continuing as a nurse, it will not be at all surprising when you elect to join the State Department."

Sibyl choked back a giggle.

Jonathan slogged on through his discourse. "Rigorous physical training will, of course, be necessary. You will learn the art of...."

Interrupted by a bored Cliff, "Sibyl, for now you should know that there is going to be a lot of training and testing involved."

"And in the end, I might not make the club."

"I must remind you, Clifford, that Sibyl has not formally stated she would accept our proposal."

Smiling at Sibyl, he answered, "I doubt if she's had any better offers this week."

"Well, since no publisher has offered me an advance on my memoirs, and no major studio is wining and dining me with contracts, this does look almost terrific. In fact, I haven't even been suggested for a Playboy centerfold."

"That's only because you're hiding in Viet Nam," Cliff grinned appreciatively.

As Sibyl eyed her aperitif, Cliff impatiently signaled Smith to speed up his delivery.

Clearing his throat for attention, the corpulent man proceeded. "Fortunately for you, we must alter our usual means of recruitment slightly since we have a very pressing assignment. You my dear can have a trial run as an agent in place. The skills that will be required of you are those we'd expect of any novice, no more."

"Do I get to use a code name, or do I just get a number?"

"Please don't interrupt, Sibyl. There will be time for questions later."

She rolled her eyes at Cliff, having lost her awe of Smith several sentences ago. God, this ponderous man!

"An operative has no need to know the details of 'why' on an assignment, but rather merely 'what' is expected. This is the situation: There's a Staff Sergeant who is part of Westmoreland's staff at headquarters. He is privy to some top-secret material. We know, however, that he's a double or possibly triple agent in place. We don't have enough hard evidence to arrest him, mind you. He is about to DEROS home tomorrow and he will be debriefed by hostile sources. We want to delay his departure by seven days. After that, his information will be stale, and he'll be harmless."

"How can I help hold up his departure? I'm a nurse, not a transportation officer."

"My dear, you have no concept of the enormous power doctors and nurses have in the military. This sergeant, like all other soldiers, must present a urine sample before leaving Viet Nam. As you know, anyone found with heroin by-products in his urine must be incarcerated at the Sixth Convalescent Center until the urine is clear. Since all urine is examined at your laboratory at the center, you will see to it that a little opioid will find its way into the sergeant's sample. We'll show you how that will be managed. Thus, for the next seven days, his urine sample will be found to contain heroin."

"You understand that what you're asking me to do is far from ethical nursing. This episode will become part of his permanent record. You can imagine that he will never earn another stripe."

"Tut! Tut! An attack of principles hardly becomes you, my dear. I know about your little business dealings with the black market. You're not quite as pristine as your uniform. Remember also, we know this man is a traitor."

Sibyl found the task to be surprisingly simple. As a nurse at the Sixth Convalescent Center, she had access to the laboratory, which was off limits to other personnel. Each week the staff at the center was required to present the lab with a sample of their own urine to establish that they were not on narcotics. Once a week she would pass the line of doctors who were standing in a field and urinating into bottles in full view of everyone. This was done to prevent any switching of samples. Much to the consternation of the men, the females were allowed the privacy of a bathroom.

As Sibyl placed her sample bottle on the table, her hand passed over Staff Sergeant Wrigley's bottle, into which she released a small quantity of white powder. The heroin was the easiest part of the assignment. Every roadside stand seemed to have some in stock.

Watching MPs drag off the bewildered sergeant, Sybil felt a stab of guilt. But, this was soon replaced by a sense of pride. The next six mornings she visited the lab, having developed a sudden interest in the various detection methods. She questioned the technicians regarding the advantages of gas chromatography over thin layer chromatography, and the problems of quinine and methadone interfering with the determinations. As she would leave, she would hear the lab techs discussing the day's sample from the sergeant.

"That guy's urine is still loaded. He's gotta be getting it from inside somewhere. Well, if he loves Viet Nam this much, we'll oblige him."

On the seventh day, the sergeant's urine was negative. By this time his mental state was one of blind anger, and his DEROS home was further delayed by a court-martial for striking an officer, a major who was the hospital's Chief of Professional Services.

Sibyl often reflected on her start in the organization. After her initiation and training, she never saw Cliff again. Her boss had been right. The passage of time hardened her, and the occasional taking of a life was just part of her profession.

Chapter V

A statesman is an easy man,

He tells his lies by rote;

A journalist makes up his lies

And takes you by the throat;

So stay at home and drink your beer

And let the neighbors vote.

Yeats

Mark Sarasohn settled back into the spacious first class seat of the jumbo jet. Just three years after his SB degree from the University of Chicago (every other college calls theirs a BS degree), he was not only a journalist for a large Chicago paper, but was assigned to cover a meeting of heads of state. It was hard enough to get a job in journalism when papers were merging and folding — a time when seasoned reporters found themselves at the unemployment office — but to be singled out for this assignment was a real plum.

He did consistently fine work in high school, so it was no surprise when he was offered scholarships at several excellent universities. Yet he was undecided about what field of study to pursue. A frustrated idealist and philosopher, he also loved the problem-solving challenge of mathematics and physics. One of Mark's greatest talents was the organization of ideas. Thus writing had always been his most natural and creative means of expression. How could a man with such diverse interests choose a curriculum? He found that the University of Chicago was a solution to his problem. Regardless of their field of interest, all students had to undertake the same core areas of study. The first two years were satisfyingly eclectic. He found that with careful scheduling he could delay the inevitable decision for another year. But as the end of his third year was nearing, he still was torn between the Arts and Sciences. It was then that two young men approached him. He was offered an introduction into a career that promised to utilize both his journalistic interests *and* his talent for basic sciences. The only requirement was that he gives up his summers for additional training in Colorado. At first he refused because he relied on his summer work. He needed the cash to carry him through the school year. But when he found that these advanced summer studies carried a very ample stipend, his objections vanished.

149

His new friends had tremendous influence. He was promised his choice of jobs upon graduation, but he thought they were like the Army's promises: full of light and hope and little substance. To his surprise, they not only obtained work for him on the paper of his choice, but he started as a reporter rather than at the bottom of the heap. The assignments he got were often of major significance, and took him out of the country. How he was chosen seemed a mystery to him. His work was of excellent quality, and he never disappointed his editors. He knew there were plenty of others with at least equal ability and greater seniority that were handed more mundane tasks.

The plane was beginning to lose altitude, and the "FASTEN SEAT BELTS" sign was lit. Unconsciously, he protectively cradled the camera case in his arms. He frequently did his own photography, and in the case was a fine Nikon with lenses of an adequate range of focal length. Carefully encased in a lead foil package, secure from airport x-ray monitors, were ten rolls of Kodacolor Professional. Below the layer of film was his .38 derringer.

It was not unusual for airport security to ask him to open his package. Because of his press pass, they never took the effort to dig below the layer of film. The first few times he passed through security, his heart was in his mouth, but now all he felt was a bit of a thrill as he beat the system.

The derringer was a poor excuse for a weapon except at extremely close range. Diligent practice gave Mark the skill to hit the chest area of his target at 20 feet.

Even this took careful sighting. Shooting from the hip, he couldn't hit the proverbial barn door. His first love was his .357 with the 3-inch barrel, but anybody lifting a package of film holding a .357 would know that there was more to the package than film. The derringer was a safe compromise.

Mark was promised a new weapon which was a collector's piece. Colt had run off a few revolvers made of solid brass. They were non-magnetic, and would pass through metal detectors at any airport. Needless to say, production had been abruptly halted.

Customs at Nassau gave Mark's baggage its usual cursory wave through, and he was on his way to the Royal Victoria Hotel. The hotel was an old, sprawling place still bearing the splendor of a regal past. It lacked the luxuries of the flashier new structures on Paradise Island, but it had its own compensations: a subdued grandeur, and a location just a block south of Bay Street, Nassau's main thoroughfare. This location was also convenient in that a small chemical company was a couple of blocks away.

After unpacking his bags, Mark spent much of the afternoon eating freshly caught dolphin washed down with Chablis Maison Blanc. He then decided it was time to make his visit to the local chemical company.

Lead acetate was widely available, and would be no problem. He must acquire the sodium azide first.

The chemical supply company was located in a large warehouse. A tall, black, muscular, clerk was leaning over a counter that separated a small reception area from the large supply depot as he took orders from customers. In a voice steadied by long experience with misdirection, Mark said, "Hi, I'm a new vet from the other side of the island. I need to get about 500 mg of sodium azide to make up solutions for my cell counter."

"Hey, Mon! You must have one of those ancient Coulter Counters. Don't you know the new counters don't use sodium azide anymore?"

"Yeah, I know. I don't want to spring for the cost of new equipment. Not when I just started practice down here."

"Well, you better spring for a new counter. You know why they stopped using sodium azide in those Coulters? I'll tell you why. Lab tech would pour the waste solution into the sink where the azide would combine with the lead plumbing. Then BOOM the whole lab would blow up way in the sky. That's why I don't carry sodium azide no more."

"Rats!" Mark thought as he left the supply house. He never carried explosives on the plane. Not only was there always the risk of the Plastique being detected by a bomb-sniffing dog, but he had too much sense of responsibility to put a plane-load of passengers at risk.

Now he had to do some hard thinking. Mercury fulminate was out of the question even though the ingredients were easy enough to get. All he needed was mercury, nitric acid, and some ethanol. The problem was you needed a large empty area with plenty of running room. The last thing he wanted was to attract attention.

Besides, the stuff gave him the willies. All you needed was to trip and fall after adding the alcohol, and you're doused with hot nitric acid. No thank you!

Mark turned the problem over and over in his mind. Silver acetylide was the answer. The only downside was the cost. What a waste of silver!

This time Mark went to the other side of the island. At a large photographic supply shop he purchased a quarter pound of a common photographic chemical— silver nitrate. He rented a small oxyacetylene outfit. It included an oxygen tank that he didn't need, but nobody uses acetylene without oxygen. The last purchase was the easiest of all. A large bottle of ammonia water from the local Seven-Eleven. He had a big argument with the clerk who was trying to sell him sudsy ammonia.

I just need plain ammonium hydroxide.

"Sudsy ammonia clean much better," the clerk said said.

There was no need to purchase laboratory equipment. The little coffee maker in his hotel room was all he needed. Using the coffee carafe to hold the solution, the silver nitrate easily dissolved in the ammonium hydroxide. Then he bubbled in the acetylene, and a heavy gray precipitate fell to the bottom of the carafe. Placing the coffee maker in the sink, he poured the slurry through the coffee filter. Then he poured fresh water over the filter to wash the ammonia from the filter, finally laying the paper with the precipitate aside to dry.

He washed the coffee maker thoroughly, starting out with plenty of soap. He knew that in spite of all his efforts, the next occupant might be doomed to taste ammonia in his first cup of coffee.

To test it, he took a small amount of powder on the tip of a teaspoon. Up on the roof, next to the noisy air conditioner equipment, he struck a match to the tiny pinch of powder. His ears rang with the noise of the explosion. It sounded like his .357. He hoped that nobody would be able to localize the sound. At a distance, they would think it was just a car backfiring. Gun laws are so strict in the Bahamas, that the last thing anybody would think was "gunshot."

The mechanism was simple enough. He bought a cheap clock at a drug store, and purchased some wire, a 6-volt lantern battery, and a soldering iron at Radio Shack. He could have bought a timer at Radio Shack, but that would have been easy to trace.

He removed the second and minute hands from the clock, and placed a wire through a tiny hole in the plastic clock face. Now he had a simple 12-hour timer. It was easy enough to make the hour hand close a circuit between the wire, battery, and ground. He knew from experience that the current flowing through the hair-like filament of wire he had teased from the braided cable would glow red-hot with the 6 volts passing through it.

At the shop, he was a bit concerned that a half-pound of silver nitrate would be more adequate for the job planned, but pulling that kind of dough out of his pocket would attract attention. Now, looking at the spoon, deformed from a tiny pinch of the acetylide, he felt confident that a quarter pound would be quite enough.

Carefully placing the "Do Not Disturb" sign on the doorknob, Mark left the hotel. He'd hate to have a cleaning woman throw his silver acetylide into the hotel incinerator. On the way out, he tossed the soldering iron, wrapped in a newspaper, into a hotel wastebasket.

A newspaperman on his first visit to Nassau would certainly play tourist, but Mark was uneasy. While leisurely roaming Bay Street, his eye had caught someone distantly familiar quickly stepping into a car. Plates and car were suitably memorized for later furrowing into local control. Again, at the airport, there had been another brisk impression of a known entity heading off toward Paradise Island.

Two glimpses of vaguely familiar people within just a few hours in a small place like Nassau disturbed Mark. His memory, trained to retain images of operatives from other organizations, couldn't catalogue these two. Just an obscure impression of having met these men on not unfriendly terrain. Were they with his special branch, also? Couldn't be. There was no reason for him to have a shield. Or, if his cover had been blown, he would simply find that his credentials as a reporter were insufficient to allow him entry to the conference. Well, he'd check their photos when he got back.

Still feeling uneasy, he took a taxi to the motorbike rental concession in the front of the Britannia Beach Hotel.

"Isn't Alfredo here?"

The muscular young man looked up from his magazine. With blond hair, tanned body, and an innocent face, he looked more like a California surfer. The strong, brilliant eyes gave him away.

"Nah! He's gone back to the States. Need anything?"

"That's funny. He always said he was going to get his instructor's certification and become a dive master in the Antilles." Mark shook his head convincingly. "Just can't see him back in the States."

"Yeah, well, a gorgeous, rich widow could change anyone's mind."

"He always gave me a special deal."

"I can give you the same deal."

"You're sure? I like a bike in perfect condition."

"You'll get everything you expect."

Mark handed the man a credit card, while getting on the bike that had been indicated. He felt a bit foolish. Anybody overhearing that conversation would have to know that it was a bunch of spy stuff. Shaking his head, he thought his people had lousy imaginations.

As the card was handed back to him, he was told, "be sure to turn left as you leave the driveway, and you'll find the best scenery in the Bahamas. Here's a map so you can't get lost."

The map proved to be more than a street map of the city. It was a minutely detailed census map with each address listed in its appropriate position; the more permanent structures like churches, government buildings, and cemeteries were carefully outlined. An address on Carmichael Road was circled in red.

Mark gaped at the incredible "safe house:" a huge, white monstrosity, with several different types of architecture, all bad, crazy-quilted together. The basic color was white, but the trim had gone mad: red green, and a few purple doors. He remembered seeing this kind of thing in Bonaire. He wasn't prepared for it now. Parking his bike against an old oak, he knocked at the front door.

"Who is it?"

"A tourist who's lost his way." Mark said loudly, but inwardly he was thinking, "I can't stand this spy crap."

"Can you use a map?"

"God, I hope the neighbors aren't listening," thought Mark. "I have a map, but it's not good."

"Here's a good map."

An exquisite white hand, with long magenta nails, and a multitude of silver rings, snaked out from behind the door, which had opened a mere six inches. He had just exchanged codes with a grating male voice. The sight of that feminine hand left Mark a bit slow to reach for the envelope held delicately between its graceful fingers, as he realized that the hand belonged to the voice.

Christ! Mark thought. "The neighbors probably think that this guy just handed me the plans for a Manhattan Project."

Wordlessly, Mark took the envelope, got back onto his motorbike and drove away.

Coming to a fork in the road, he opened the map, deciphering the message that held tomorrow's instructions. He chortled as he followed directions for the map's destruction. It was a good thing it was biodegradable. It really didn't taste so bad. Always such theatricality. Some day, he'd probably find out the Chief had plans to take over Hollywood.

The next morning, he met the other newsmen at the Prince George Wharf, where a small Bahamian naval vessel was waiting. The trip out was two hours of bucking four-foot seas. A squall came from nowhere and added its unpleasantness. They finally hove to about fifty feet from a one-hundred-foot yacht. Lines from the yacht were fixed to a Russian trawler. On the rough trip over the journalists had received their briefing. They were to wait in their crowded thirty-six footer until the meeting ended. Then they would be invited aboard the yacht and allowed an interview with both heads of state. The trawler was off limits. After their ration of information, the Russians would transfer to their trawler, and the newspeople would leave the yacht by returning to the launch

Mark had wisely applied a scopolamine patch behind his left ear before leaving port, and now, waiting in their tossing boat, his colleagues were retching at the rail while he was surprisingly comfortable. Three hours of tedium passed, and the rain finally let up, replaced by bright sunlight, oppressive heat, and sticky humidity.

Mark looked around for someone who was well enough to hold up one end of a conversation, and noticed a woman quietly sitting near the stern.

"Hi! Mark Sarasohn," he said, offering his hand. "You look like the only one around here who won't upchuck if she opens her mouth."

"Cathy Slade, *People Magazine*. Technically, I'm not sick, Mark, but I'm not too sure you're really there. You're more like a wavy blur," she grinned.

Mark took the seat next to her.

"You're supposed to focus on the horizon."

"What does that do?" Cathy asked.

"Makes you less seasick."

"How does that work?"

"I don't know," Mark said. "Now that I've been such a fabulous source of information, maybe you can help me out."

Cathy nodded, her eyes fixed straight ahead at some unseen point in the distance. "I think its working. I'm only partly queasy now." She thought to herself, what

159

a shame, he seems to be a nice guy. Boy! I've sure come a long way from Nurse Sibyl.

"I didn't get a chance to research this guy before I was thrown on a plane, and dropped over here;" she said, lying of course. "Can you fill me in on him?"

"Sure! Well, he's president of a little country the size of Virginia. It hasn't any industry or agriculture to speak of, and the median per capita income is $78.67 a year or something like that. Its only importance is its geographical location in South Africa. It's rather close to the Horn. Except for that fact, we wouldn't give a shit about that little pest hole."

The boat was roughly slapped by a wave.

"It's incredible, Mark! My stomach didn't even flinch. Too bad someone else discovered it. Otherwise you could publish."

Cathy daringly took her gaze away from the horizon for a few seconds as she looked at Mark. "Of course, it really hampers conversation when you can't make eye contact."

"On the other hand, if you're with a really grungy date, it wouldn't matter."

"Is that what you do, Mark? If your blind date is a dog, you take her on a boat ride when small craft warnings are out?"

Mark grinned at her. "I bet all your dates want to get you on some nice firm surface."

She returned her vision to a nausea-defeating point. The sides of her mouth flickered mischievously. "I didn't know you were here for a little raunchy flirting. All this time I thought you were like the rest of us. An overworked newsman, told thirty minutes before flight time to grab some clean underwear, and interview some guy he had no time to do background on."

"I am simply what you see. So keep talking, and I'll buy you a non-flirtatious, newsman-to newswoman dinner when we get off this delightful ride."

"I'll keep looking straight ahead so I can enjoy that meal. Anyway, President Magoto is an enigma. He came to power in Ubanga by what is loosely called an election. Why anyone would want to take responsibility for a place like that is beyond me. He's been playing East against West, like a spoiled kid manipulating divorced parents. For awhile he showed some signs of slipping into the Soviet camp. What screwed up his plans, though, is that there's no longer much of a Soviet camp. He's an out-and-out paranoid-schizophrenic with just enough reality to play with power, and get him where he is. On the other hand, he has enough delusions of grandeur fogging his brain to give him the idea that he can make Ubanga an atomic power."

"Another Idi Amin."

"Well, not quite. He hasn't had time to develop the technique yet. I suspect his people will suffer great hardships as he tries to raise them to the status of a so-called 'developed' nation."

"I guess that's one more port where our ships won't be welcomed. It's a good thing the USSR is folding. Otherwise, a few more Ubangas and we'd be another great sea power like Britain," he said sarcastically.

"You know, Cathy, I wish I had brought a book to read, or had something interesting to do like hang over the rail and throw up. I'm hot and sticky and bored — not that the present company isn't good— but I can't take this much longer. You'd think they'd invite us aboard, and stick us someplace unobtrusive and air-conditioned while they had their conference."

"Nothing to read? What are you carrying in that heavy attaché'?"

"Oh, I always carry my faithful laptop and modem. Maybe they'll have some nice hors d'oeuvres and wine. Oops, sorry I didn't mean to mention food in your condition."

"Listen, I'm fine," she giggled, "as long as I keep staring straight ahead."

"I'm afraid our friends over there," she pointed to the yacht without turning her gaze toward, "must share the popular view that reporters are like cockroaches—ubiquitous, but unavoidable, and not the sort of thing you invite into your home."

"Cathy, I see some activity on deck. I think the cockroaches are about to be invited aboard. By the way, that's some yacht. That's the first yacht I've seen that sports a deck gun."

The meeting contained no surprises. Magoto was the first to speak: "Gentleman of the press, my people and I are very fortunate to count among our friends the Union of the Soviet Socialist Republic. It has graciously offered to send its best minds to help lift our poor little country out of the past and into the modern technology of the present. We, in turn, will be leasing a few ports and inland areas for the Soviet's exclusive use. This day marks the historic beginning of a long, happy, and fruitful relationship between our two countries. I would now like to present Mr. Greganski."

"Gentlemen, I will not tire you with a long speech. My sentiments mirror those of my dear comrade, Mr. Magoto. There are refreshments on the deck. Please feel free to partake of them."

The reporters turned away disappointed, but not surprised at the paucity of information that was doled out to them.

"This is a big joke, Cathy," Mark said incredulously. "Don't these people read *Time,* or *Newsweek*? This Magoto is living in the last century, and what's worse Greganski doesn't even realize that his country no longer exists. Who's going to pay for those great minds to travel to that jungle? The USSR's ships are sitting gathering rust. They're going nowhere."

The food and drinks were lavish, and the remaining hours were spent with the newspeople wandering freely about the boat, drinks in hand. Some were invited aboard the president's gunboat, moored alongside. More refreshments were served on its deck.

Mark excused himself for a call of nature, and left for the head. With the door securely fastened, he opened his attaché, and removed a package. Space is always at a premium aboard a ship, and you can be sure that everywhere you go there are compartments in the bulkheads for storage. The package fit nicely in the one below the sink, and the sink was mounted on an external bulkhead below the water line.

As dusk approached, the media took their leave, and boarded their launch. When they cast off and began to pick up speed, Mark turned back toward the yacht to see four husky seamen struggling with a huge chest. It appeared to be made of steel and had rings bolted to the sides for line and hand grips. Progress was slow, but the heavy chest was finally slid down a gangplank from the trawler onto the deck of Magoto's boat. They were almost out of sight when trawler and the yacht went their separate ways and sailed over widely separated points of the horizon. The trawler traveled northeast, and the yacht, northwest. A moment later, as the sun had just set, and the sky was darkening, there was a bright flash of orange briefly illuminating the skyline to the northwest. Three seconds later the sound of an explosion shattered the inky air.

*   *   *

Mark's plane was on schedule. This time, it was a single engine Beechcraft, rather than a jumbo jet, and this time it was a grass strip in a little valley rather than the concrete runway of an international airport. Mark sat in the co-pilot's seat as the plane gained altitude and appeared finally as a speck in the Bahamian sky. A moment later the speck was replaced by a flash of light, and became a scattered mass of falling debris.

Chapter VI

Any fool can tell the truth,

but it requires a man of some sense to know how to lie well.

Samuel Butler

Happily nestled in blankets, and listening to the almost fetal throb of the rotors, Clara and Jack dozed fitfully in the back of the cabin.

As the helicopter made its ascent, there had been a quick conference, and the decision was made to say nothing of their find. Jack lost his new boat, which was underinsured, but they were alive. Jack elegantly summarized the situation, "Being a target is shit." Their episode was a complete mystery. Perhaps someone with the philosophy of Charley Chan might have pursued the mystery to its solution, but they, being of ordinary mettle, looked forward to their exodus from the Bahamas, and resuming their lives. Next year might find them diving in Fiji, or some place else on the other side of the world. The Bahamas would not be their first choice for many years.

"My name is Arthur Waldmann," the man in the co-pilot's seat said to them. Their response was inaudible as they half-dozed. Speech at normal volume is lost anyway in the noise from a helicopter's rotors. Their skins were wrinkled and parched. Second-degree burns with blisters clustered their lips and foreheads. After being pulled aboard the seaplane, they consumed an entire case of Heinekens before falling into a semi-comatose state.

After this rebuff, Waldmann, a man in his late fifties, turned to the plane's fourth occupant, who was a good decade his junior. Waldmann was clad as usual in a rumpled suit. Only this time, in deference to the tropics, the suit was white linen with huge oval stains under the armpits, and topped by a Panama hat. He was a corpulent man, and one would expect the fourth passenger to be Humphrey Bogart, or Peter Lorre. But, the younger man, Aaron, lacked Bogart's slightly dissipated appearance. He was lean and well muscled, in T-shirt, and jeans. His hair was close cropped, almost making him bald. The coiffeur screamed military — probably ex- Marine. A cigarette did not belong in this craggily handsome face.

Waldmann shifted his fatness in the small seat. "They look like they'll recover, but they'll be miserable for a few days with their burns, and exposure. I wonder if all that alcohol will exacerbate their dehydration. We really must carry something more than fuel and beer on the next flight."

Clara awoke, glassily trying to focus her eyes on the rotund speaker.

"Where are you from, Miss?"

"Miami."

"Well, I'm afraid we're headed in the opposite direction."

"How did you get in this fix?" Aaron asked.

"Fire in the engine compartment. Boat sank." Jack quickly chimed in. He'd already seen what damage resulted from truth. "Let's try lying for a change," he thought.

Aaron looked sympathetically at her. "What a contretemps. We have more than adequate accommodations at our club, and it will not inconvenience us to the least to see that you're made comfortable there. There's a doctor on duty, and he will see to it that your skin gets attention."

Fatigued by her effort, Clara had fallen asleep again.

"As soon as we get them situated, we'll have to change for dinner. You know, we have reservations at the Martinique this evening."

Aaron shook his head in amazement. "I can't understand how you got where you are with that belly."

"Life is so easily terminated that we must each savor our own delights. For some, it's adventure, love of country, sex. I am a sybarite, and receive my sensual satisfaction from a superb meal, served on fine napery, preferably in a room with suitable ambiance. Anyone's prime passion can lead to his obsequy. In this way, one can reach for death with open arms and a smile, instead of closed fists, and agonal defecation."

"I'm still surprised, Arthur, that with the way you eat your brain has not become a clump of fat."

"My dear Aaron, in apercus that's just what a brain is!"

Clara opened one eye and muttered, "Sphingomyelin."

*   *   *

Jack and Clara found themselves ensconced in a plush apartment of the Lyford Cay Club. The club was cloistered away on a private tip of New Providence Island. The wealthy atmosphere was evident as they passed the guard at the gate and viewed stately buildings of traditional Bahamian and Georgian colonial architecture. Their hosts ordered food to be sent to their room, while Aaron and Arthur went off to make their dinner appointment.

"Clara, this is a way of life I could easily become accustomed to."

"Look, we already owe our lives to these strangers. They seem to have an unlimited quantity of money, but I'd still prefer not to become more indebted."

"Well, let's enjoy the meal anyway. They've even sent wine. Then let's climb into bed and make love."

"You're kidding! How can you think of sex? We're both burned to a crisp, and I'm beginning to peel everywhere. If we 'do it,' it will have to be standing up. Let's think about it after we eat. I'm hungry, and believe it or not I'm thirsty again even after all that beer."

They proceeded to polish off the Caesar Salad, followed by Duck l'Orange on a bed of wild rice. The dinner was enhanced by a bottle of the finest wine. "Jack! This wine we just guzzled down is a 1971 Laffite Rothschild."

At the end, Jack gently removed Clara's clothing, being careful not to touch any areas that were blistered, reddened, or tender. Their lovemaking was gentle, and various positions were attempted to avoid additional trauma to these friable areas. The temptation was overpowering to fall asleep in each other's arms, but there was a strong suspicion that their friends would return after their dinner engagement. Reluctantly, they dressed and awaited their rescuers.

Arthur and Aaron sat on the verandah sipping cognac. "I don't see why we don't simply call in our own divers," Arthur said.

"Because I don't want any more new faces brought into the area. It'll cause too much suspicion. Stanger and his girl friend are already here."

"And it's obvious nobody is watching them."

"That's it, Arthur. They're just a couple of lovers in the Bahamas for fun. It's really perfect for us. I think we should take advantage of the situation when it's handed to us on a silver platter."

"Of course you don't intend to take advantage of the girl, do you?"

Aaron's look of annoyance did not stop Arthur from continuing. "I noticed you eyeing that half-drowned blonde's body. She has that fleshy look you so admire."

As the waiter was already hovering in their vicinity, Arthur waved him closer. "Would you please bring us some of those delightful chocolate mints?"

"But sir, I'll have to send all the way back to the dining-room for them. We don't keep them in the lounge."

"How jejune, you really should begin keeping them here, don't you think? I'm not the only member who feels so passionate about them."

"Yes, sir."

Both men watched the waiter's retreating figure. Aaron said, "I'm always glad to see that you haven't gotten careless."

"That was my first lesson from our mutual teacher."

"One of the first lessons that I like to teach is that the end-point must be reached by the simplest possible means. That translates to letting the girl and her boyfriend make the dive."

"Well," Arthur sighed, "I suppose the decision will be made for us as soon as you request permission to use them."

"I need no permission. The decision has been made."

Arthur's blood pressure rose a few points as he eyed his colleague with envious resentment. He watched the waiter place the sweets between them. As he delicately munched, he asked, "How will you get them to dive for us? We have to tell them something, you know."

"There's no problem. They're already in our debt, and we'll tell them only what they need to know. That's another one of those primary lessons I teach."

"Well, I hope you young people are refreshed and able to talk a bit."

"Let me apologize, Mr. Waldmann. If you hadn't come along we would have been fish food. I'm sorry to say that we were too exhausted to be sociable before, but we're well rested now and don't wish to impose further on your generous hospitality."

As Jack spoke, Clara wrapped the soft white terry robe closer to her body. The Lyford Cay Club Monogram disappeared into some folds.

"Tut tut, Mr. Stanger. You may call me Arthur, and I hope you will not mind me calling you Jack. You're not putting us out in the least. In fact, you were the major topic of our conversation. Our business associates and we agree that you may be very useful to us. For a small favor, you will more than repay our minor bit of inconvenience, and in addition, you will find our little task financially rewarding. It might be so financially rewarding that as a perquisite you will be able to purchase one of the properties at the club and afford to spend many vacations here."

"Arthur, let's get down to business," Aaron Forsythe broke in. "Our company designs and manufactures microelectronics. I'm sure you are aware of these little silicon chips that have replaced the whole roomfuls of vacuum tube circuits that were used in the Cretaceous age of electronics. Well, there is a cutthroat race to see who can build the smallest, the most complex, and the least expensive. The old RAM chips were measured in megabytes. Now if you want to run Windows efficiently, you need 75 megabytes. Believe it or not, we'll soon have the terabyte chip and none too soon. The companies that are leading the pack are keeping their heads above water, and perhaps even making a few dollars. The others don't last very long. At present, Intel is king of the mountain with their series 700. We have developed a new circuit, and an entirely new manufacturing process. Our machine can build a chip that has forty times the speed of the old Pentium, and has a bus four times as wide. In spite of its enormous power, it is no larger than the Pentium, and will fit in the same socket. The killer is that we'll be able to sell it for about one hundred bucks and still see an obscene profit.

"Gentlemen, the only micro circuitry I get involved with are what are in my camera, and I haven't the foggiest notion of how it works, but that price is certainly impressive."

"Our only working processor, together with a few of the chips, was on the way to our plant in Freeport. The boat met with an unfortunate accident. As great as our little process may seem, it won't be long before someone will do as well or even better. We have much invested in that little machine, and if we don't start using it soon to make some computers, our company will go belly up. What is worse, if our competitors salvage that machine, we might as well pack it all in.

"Now, we couldn't help notice that you were wearing buoyancy compensators rather than ordinary life vests when you were in the water. It doesn't take Sherlock Holmes to deduce that you are both trained in SCUBA."

"Hold it! Clara and I have basic certificates. That means we're skilled enough to play around in nice, safe waters. If you need to do a salvage operation, you'll need professional divers."

"Let me give you an exegesis. We'd love to use professionals, Jack. Unfortunately, the money involved in this process is considerable. Our competitors want to get their hands on it. You must appreciate the importance of secrecy in this operation. You, on the other hand, owe us a great deal, namely your lives. I know nothing of your sense of honor, but it's beyond my imagination how you could double-cross us. Moreover, the boat is lying on a reef at about seventy feet, and there is very little current. It should be duck soup for a sports diver."

Clara interrupted to reinforce their amateur standing. "You're right about us not being able to refuse, but what good does it do to have honest, willing, faithful, but dead divers?"

Aaron smiled at Clara. "The item is in shallow water, the currents are gentle, and we will pick a pleasant day so the visibility will be excellent. You'll also have lift equipment at your disposal, and the finest gear money can buy. In short, it will not be out of the capability of a sport diver with limited experience."

"The sea water must do wonders for your little machine," interjected Jack.

"The sea water would do the same damage as the sea air. For that reason, the machinery is sealed in a watertight case. It was never intended to be totally immersed in water, but the package is only at about three atmospheres of pressure, and I believe the seal will hold. Meanwhile, you'll have all of the facilities of the club at your disposal. You're free to leave of course, but for the sake of security I would rather you confined yourselves to the club grounds, and of course, you must consider our conversation auricular, and discuss this with no one else. Our only edge at this point is our exclusive knowledge that such a precious instrument has been lost at sea, and secondly, the approximate coordinates of its location."

At a brief nod from Aaron, Waldmann terminated the conversation. He rose from his chair, and benignly held out his hand to Jack.

"I'm afraid our business problems must seem boring to you when all you want to do is rest after your ordeal. Tomorrow, when you awaken, leave a message for room 503, and we'll make plans to meet for a magnificent meal."

As Aaron and Waldmann departed, calmness settled in. Jack, and Clara, in arm chairs, stared at each other, numb and anesthetized.

Wearily, Jack leaned forward, his hands barely supporting his chin.

She sighed, tenderly touching her reddened arm. "Wish we had some cortisone cream."

"Well, you just took care of question number one."

176

"Huh?"

"Is this really us? Yes, it must be. Who else would worry about what to treat your sunburn with. Shit! I think med school must have destroyed your sense of whimsy."

"Whimsy? No, no, Jack. This is insanity. Whimsy is light and frothy like chocolate mousse. This is heavy, sort of a burned soufflé loaded with gelatin."

"And the cheap kind, at that."

"Ain't nothing cheap about this place, old buddy." Clara turned her head surveying the living room of their suite, with its thick brown and white carpeting, plushly upholstered sofas, and huge glass doors through which the harbor lights created a scintillating pattern.

"What do you think, Jack?"

"Wrong question. You should have asked, 'Can you think, Jack?' How could you forget that my brain has been jolted, drenched, baked, and then assaulted with flights of ideas? This is right out of *The Arabian Nights*."

"I'm so tired I don't even know what I've heard. I've suddenly developed a totally unreasonable fear of the water."

"Can't understand that, baby. As soon as we get home, we'll set you up with one of your shrink friends. Maybe he can dig around in your psyche and find out why this fear suddenly occurred. He'll probably discover that when you were three months old and just starting to enjoy your baths, your mother almost threw you out with the bath water."

"It's always the parents, Jack. They get blamed for everything."

"You're trying to tell me those Bahamian cops had a screwed-up father and weirdo mother, and that's why my boat is now an interesting wreck for divers to explore."

Jack paused before continuing. "Clara, why didn't we tell Waldmann and his eight-by-ten glossy buddy, that the cops got funny with us?"

"What do you mean?"

"Well, they saved our lives, and somehow it didn't come out in the conversation. In fact, if you remember, we lied to them."

Clara got up and walked to the window. Jack joined her. He put his arm around her, supporting her head on his shoulder.

"Do you think we should have told them, Jack?"

"I don't know. I seem to have this insatiable desire to tell someone, but I don't know whom. My red, white, and blue upbringing says to run to the nearest cop screaming for help. If those guys dressed as fuzz were just Bahamian law enforcers, what then?"

"Then, that's even more sinister."

Jack tenderly took hold of her shoulders, and turned her toward him. "We have two choices. We can either leave immediately for home, or stay and do the bidding of our new pals."

"They saved our lives."

"I know, Clara, and they want to be sure we remember that, too."

Clara sighed as she put her arms around Jack, her nose burrowing into his chest. "I guess I've got so many left-over guilt trips on me that I'd feel like a turd if we left without helping them."

"But helping them means sticking around the Bahamas."

"Jack, do you think we ought to tell them about what really happened to the boat, and then go on home tomorrow?"

"Two things, Clara: One, once you fall off a horse, get back up damn quick. If you don't prove to yourself, right away, that you're the same person as before, fear sets in, and you never get back on a horse again. We have to make another dive soon. This will be a real soft dive. When we go after that expensive doodad, out friends will hover over us and give us plenty of support. Two, about our boat, well, according to all the adventure novels I've read, the less said the better."

Clara spent her first few waking moments staring at the clock embedded in the mirrored wall facing her. Another few seconds of blinking, and it came into focus. A little longer and she was oriented to place and person, but the time still escaped her. There were no numerals on its face. A great deal of concentration, and she realized those odd-shaped chrome things were probably hands. Although never at her best in the morning, she hated to admit defeat to a simple chronological device. With massive concentration, she was able to discern that it was a few minutes after twelve. From the sunlight flooding the room, she deduced it to be noon rather than midnight. Self-satisfied, she stretched. Jack's arm came around her. Cuddling against him she said, "If we just stay in bed we won't have to make any decisions, will we?"

"That's right. Stay in bed and you can put off the world. It'll always be *manana*."

"It's funny. It seemed like I had so many pressures last night. Now all I'm trying to decide is when to take my shower."

Jack reached for the Lucite phone. "Why don't you do that now, while I order breakfast?"

The terrace was cantilevered out over the water, and bedecked with flowers. The sun generously bathed them as they enjoyed an opulent breakfast.

Biting into a blueberry muffin, Clara watched a sailboat lazily tack its way out of the inlet. "Whoever said it'll be better in the morning was certainly right."

"On a clear day, nothing looks sinister, Honey."

Jack tenderly took her face in his hands and kissed her. As he came away with blueberry staining his lips, she laughed gently. Wiping his face with her napkin, she said, "You know, I guess we can stay and dive once more."

Jack nodded in agreement. "As soon as that dive is over, we head right home. I'll have to report what happened to the insurance people, and probably the sooner the better."

"That's it. They can take it from there. They've got their own maritime investigators."

The ringing phone interrupted their conversation. Looking frantically around him, Jack finally discovered it hiding in a rocky nook of their terrace. He did a lot of listening, a little mumbling, and hung up.

To Clara's raised eyebrows he answered, "That was Chubby. He took several thousand polysyllabic words to tell me that he knows we're awake since his spies tell him we ordered breakfast. He wants us to join them for cocktails in his room at seven, and also this place is at our disposal, tennis rackets, golf clubs and all."

"I'm still uncomfortable, Jack. When something disastrous happens, you report it. You don't just sit around on your ass, and allow an investigation to be delayed."

"Okay, but who's going to get your report? You can't run down to the Port of Miami and find the appropriate friendly American authority in charge of boats sunk by possibly ersatz Bahamian police. We've already decided we don't trust the fuzz here. Would you trust your freedom to, let's say, the Mexican police? We're foreigners in a foreign land, Honey." He took both of her hands as he continued. "Now, we could discuss this with our rescuers. They're the kind of rich, internationally connected men who should know who we can report to."

"I know." Clara stared at the now unappetizing remains of her breakfast.

"So, why don't we tell them?" Jack prodded.

Clara shook her head helplessly at Jack.

"Something bothers you," Jack went on. "I'll tell you something. Nobody expects to die in a miserable situation like that. Deep down, we always knew we'd be rescued. Simply because it couldn't happen to us. That's why those Westerns are so popular. The heroes always get rescued. It's the cavalry syndrome. They always arrive on time. It's some sort of confirmation of your own humanity. The good guys are always saved. So, when we saw that helicopter, it seemed natural."

Clara munched on a muffin, her eyes down, as Jack was speaking. He took her muffinless hand as he paused. "In the back of my mind, things do not quite seem right. I couldn't see it last night. Now that we're dry, fed, and safe, we can do a little analysis. What the hell is a helicopter doing cruising around in the Caribbean? A great little job for a search and rescue mission, but for a joy ride? It's not the usual type of craft down here, and they didn't seem to be just riding around. Guys like that don't simply cruise around a terrain they obviously know well. They didn't say they were going anywhere. I know that at least with the military helicopters, it takes about one hour of maintenance for each hour of flying time. Those aren't play-toys. And," Jack paused purposefully, while he sipped his coffee. Clara continued to stare, wide-eyed, and silent.

"And, we now come to a nerve-shattering conclusion, my love, that they may have been searching for us."

As Clara's eyes snapped to meet Jack's, the door commanded both of their attention. Jack wrapped a towel around him, while Clara raced for the bedroom.

When Jack opened the door, the threshold was filled with boxes. As he stepped back, a shopping spree entered the room, and he could see arms, legs, and bellmen. After the items were piled on the table, he was handed an envelope, and the messengers departed silently.

Clara's head appeared at the bedroom door.

"It's okay. You can come out without a towel."

Clara stopped in amazement at the table covered with boxes. "My God! Someone's been busy."

Attacking the parcels, they found golf outfits, tennis outfits, bathing suits, and an evening gown with accompanying men's suit and tie.

"Well, we don't have to keep wearing those ratty jeans they gave us in the chopper. I guess when you're a corporate giant, you think of everything," Clara sputtered.

Jack glanced up from the note he was reading. "Typewritten in gold italics, mind you, 'Dear Friends, These items should help fill the void until the lobby shops open later today. Please select your other necessities and have them put on our bill. You will find the golfing magnificent and the tennis courts superior. A.W.' There's a written P.S. From Aaron, I think. 'Been called away on business. Back in the morning. Will meet you, my room 503, for cocktails tomorrow. Enjoy the Club today.'"

Clara flopped on the couch. "Thank God, we have another *manana*."

Fingering a conservatively striped blue and white tie, Jack mumbled, "You know, I hate ties. I guess they're saying we dress for dinner here."

Clara exploded from the couch as she spewed tissue and boxes in several directions. "I can't stand it. I feel like a pig being fattened up for something. Well, I'll tell you, Jack, somehow the thought of playing tennis as if I had all the time in the world to vacation is absolutely unnerving."

"I know. Look Honey, if I had any of my credit cards we could rent a car and drive around Nassau, but my wallets at the bottom of the sea. Fortunately, for all the plastic people, it'll be pretty rough for a grouper to saunter into Macy's and go on a charging binge."

Clara stopped throwing boxes in the air. "Jack, I can call my office and have Casey wire us some money."

Clara had no trouble getting through to Miami.

"I know why you called, Doc," Casey said. "You're finally getting married, and you want Casey and me to come down there for the wedding."

"Wedding!" Anna breathed happily as she picked up the extension.

"Calm down, you two nuts. I called because we had a slight accident."

"You're pregnant!" Casey shouted.

"The accident is Jack's boat sank."

"That's slight? What would you call the sinking of the Titanic, a design flaw?"

"Casey, save your one-liners for the patients. Take a signed check out of the safe. Make it out for two thousand, cash it and wire it immediately. Also, send out that extra American Express card, air mail! Fast! Pronto!"

"Fine. Which reef do I send it to?"

"We're at the Lyford Cay Club on New Providence Island, The Bahamas."

"Okay, baby. We'll wire the money and send the card in a plain brown unmarked envelope, but what you two really need is some chicken soup and a rabbi."

"Remind Mr. Stapleton about his 4 p.m. blood sugar. He's such a brittle diabetic and always waits too long."

"Already done, **Sir**. Hey," Casey paused. "Hear that funny click, and that change in volume?"

"Casey, we are not calling from next door."

"No, no. Remember when your cousin Michael used to work for that detective agency? When you hear a drop in volume, that means you have another instrument drawing current from your line. In plain speak, that means you have a tapped phone. Ha! I told you not to kick out that pharmaceutical rep just because he wanted your body. The Sandoz or Merck reps have tapped your phone."

"Oh cut the paranoia. Were you hurt?" Anna broke in.

"No, we're both fine. We got picked up by a plane, and were given accommodations. I need about a thousand for the two weeks, and plane fare and underwear and stuff."

"A thousand dollars won't go far in a fancy resort." Casey said.

"Much of our expenses are being covered. Also, there's another reason I called. Since we'll be here a little longer, arrange coverage for me and rearrange all my routine office visits."

Casey answered, "That's no problem. Dr. Fishberg owes you some coverage, and things are quiet this time of year anyway. Have a good time. You really need it. Give our love to Jack. Let us know the exact date you're returning so we can start setting up office appointments."

The car rental desk was a magnificent alcove, surrounded on three sides by glass, overlooking a finely shrubbed lanai and pool. Huge wicker chairs with plump pillows surrounding coffee tables holding crystal decanters and glasses made it look like the Florida room in one of the more reekingly expensive Miami waterfront homes.

The Eurasian beauty smiled as Jack sat across from her. She managed to illuminate her whole face without crinkling those huge almond eyes. "Let's see, with an ASA of about 400 and that dark skin...about f2.8 at 1/125 in this light, or maybe...."

"You desire some mode of transportation, sir?"

Her suitably modulated voice jolted him. Yet, her accent escaped him.

"Transportation? How about a rickshaw? Though a camel would do better in this heat."

"Oh sir," she laughed, with the right amount of giggle in it, "we can arrange plane trips to some of the other islands, or perhaps you'd prefer a boat, with captain, cook...?"

"What about a helicopter?"

"I'm so sorry, sir."

Jack was definitely, emphatically convinced that she was unhappy. God! She was good; a whole portfolio, or just her face. To bad he couldn't get that voice on film.

"All we have," she continued, "are single-engine Cessnas."

"That's all right, honey." She made him want to show her that he was not disappointed. "I really want a car."

At that strategic moment, an obtrusive buzz caught her attention. Suitably pardoning herself, she lifted a wicker apparatus, listened charmingly, said "of course," and smiled again at Jack.

She informed him, very sorry of course, that there were no cars available.

Somewhat jolted, Jack said, "anything," and remembering Clara, "as long as it's air-conditioned."

Leaning forward, the silken fabric of her blouse parting to reveal lovely dark breasts, perfume numbing him, she persuaded him of how truly sorry she was.

"A moped?" he managed to croak.

She shook her head.

"I know. You're sorry you have none available."

"Oh no, sir," she brightened. "We never carry them here."

"Not even a bicycle?" he wheezed.

Her head shook. A volcanic dark mass of hair moved every tendril unhappy that no transportation was available.

"Isn't there anywhere else?"

"No, sir. We're the only place around. I'm so sorry."

Dejectedly, Jack returned to the room. Now, he felt like he was in a trap. This pink paradise was not the dungeons of the Bastille, but it was a prison nevertheless.

"What do you mean there's nothing available?" Clara whined, while slipping into a tennis outfit. "We've really got to get out of this place for a while. Didn't you ask if there was anywhere else we could get a car?"

"Of course I did."

Her frenzy suddenly dissipated, she collapsed in one of the chairs. Reaching for a tennis shoe, she said more calmly, "I've really got to try to find some kind of transportation to get us to Nassau. I just can't seem to handle the isolation here."

"I know, honey." Jack gently removed the shoe from her hand and laced it up on her foot.

Brightening up, as she reached the door, she said, "Maybe some place in town can send a car out for us. I'm going downstairs and see what I can dig up."

Jack did not care to share his thoughts with Clara. He wouldn't know how to handle her hysteria. Maybe he was wrong, but some how it would be fixed so that no transportation would be available to them, anywhere. They were in an unbelievably luxurious prison.

An hour later, Clara entered the room quietly and looked at Jack. She walked to the railing of the balcony. "I really felt angry when I left our room. By the time that glass elevator had deposited me in the lobby; I began to feel more sneaky than mad. So, when I saw a man going over to the transportation desk, I pretended I was looking at some magazines on the other side, and peeped through the foliage. She rented a car to that man."

"Clara, he could have had it reserved a while ago."

"No! I distinctly heard him ask her if she had any cars available. She even gave him a choice. He could have a white Mustang, or a Camaro, or…."

"Shit!"

Downstairs, in her lush corner of the lobby, the Eurasian beauty sat at her desk, her well-manicured hands turning the pages of a European travel brochure. As the phone rang, she tore herself away from "The Best Paris Shops", and gracefully identified herself.

"Yes, I'm alone," she murmured. "Of course, I'll place the call immediately. Always so happy to serve you, sir."

Upstairs, another phone began to ring. Jack answered. He recognized her voice and swore to himself that some of her perfume wafted over the wires.

"Fantastic! We'll be down in a couple of minutes."

"I was wrong after all. Clara," he grinned, "We have a car."

"You weren't wrong Jack; they just wanted to demonstrate their power over us."

*   *   *

Draco always enjoyed the boat ride to the island. Especially on this assignment, the solitude was refreshing. He never worked well when he was with the fat man. Whether he called himself Jonathan Smith or Arthur Waldmann, he would always be the Fat Man to Draco. No one really had names any more in the Special Branch, except a base name for identification. After your fiftieth passport, a name was like a meal: necessary, but quickly over and on to the next one for survival. Draco thought over his many names, each associated with a totally different character. There is Draco the spy, Cliff the soldier and most recently, Aaron the business executive. Was he all of these people? What was his real personality? Did he have any identity, or did it somehow evaporate away in this business?

"That big ass!" Draco thought, as he yanked the steering wheel more viciously than he needed to stay on course. "He would always be fat. Even three years ago,

191

in Istanbul, he was seventy-five pounds thinner, and he was still fat. His goddamn *personality* was fat."

On the island, he found the old stone Chinese lantern half buried in the sand. This was his starting point. The other signs were much subtler. A notched palm here, a subtly arranged group of stones there, and he followed the almost invisible path to a small shed. The shed was on low ground, and surrounded by mangroves. It could not be seen until you were right on top of it. Nobody got that close unless they were willing to wade through thirty yards of knee deep brackish water.

He must have been the first one there. There was no sign of Mr. D. Opening the door, the blast of hot moist air was stifling. He quickly walked to the rear and raised a large window for ventilation.

"You're early, Draco."

Stunned, he whirled to face the Director.

"I'm impressed. I didn't see any of your cover. How in hell can you sit here with the window closed?"

"Excellent, aren't they? Or, maybe I'm alone this time. But it doesn't matter, does it?"

The Director moved his chair to the small table and indicated a chair to Draco. "Sit down, please. We'll only be here a few minutes, but I do want you to be comfortable. As you can see, I have long ago trained myself to forego comfort."

"Another Lawrence of Arabia, huh?"

"Very funny, but remember, Lawrence owed much of his success to his ability to withstand environments that were challenging even to the Bedouin. He beat them at their own game. He could ride a camel greater distances and go without water longer than any of his Bedouin soldiers. And what was most amazing, he could do what no other Britisher could do; he could eat Bedouin food — including the eyeballs"

Draco sat, annoyed by the heat in the shack, by the fly that buzzed only around him, and by the partner he despised down at Lyford Cay.

"Now, Draco, since the boat sank two days ago, what are your plans for retrieval of the object?"

"Completely consolidated," Draco said, with noticeable smugness.

"Really?"

"Yes." He paused before continuing. "I'm just surprised to see you here personally for a mere plan finalization."

"I have other reasons for being here. You do not have the need to know."

The Director leaned closer to Draco and spoke in slow, chilled words. "Waldmann has not been told of this meeting."

Draco nodded. He pulled his sweaty shirt away from his body for a few seconds. "I decided that professional divers would only call attention to us. I was planning to go down as a sport diver, and let word out that I was waiting for a friend who was into spear fishing. My original plans were to call in Theo. But then, I was informed of a couple out fun-diving that found the boat and might still be alive."

The Director leaned back in his chair. He could picture the scenario.

"So Waldmann and I rescued them, and fed them a story about a piece of scientific equipment in bad need of a rescue."

"My, aren't you the Good Samaritans."

"We are indeed, sir."

"All right."

A fly lit on Draco's hand. As he slapped it away the Director repeated, "All right, you can go, Draco."

Clara could tolerate many discomforts, but heat made her insane. Sitting in a small black car with a broken air-conditioner converted a sweet, easygoing woman into an irascible grump. Jack was about to turn back to the hotel's cool, garden pool when he saw a moped shop.

Caribbean breezes soon fanned Clara out of her cantankerous mood as she tried out a moped, by making vertiginous circles around the little street. Finally, Jack, struggling to pay for the bike rental without credit cards or money, talked the owner into calling the Lyford Cay Club for verification of their credit.

He drove back to the Club. Ahead of him, Clara's rump happily bounced on the moped.

A long swim in the pool and Clara was ready to be fed. Nothing seemed ominous. Blue skies can chase away a hell of a lot of bogeymen, even when they are real.

As Clara towel-dried her hair, Jack ordered wine from room service. Before he could hang up Clara yelled, "And some potato chips, either Pringle's or Munchos."

That doesn't go with a '72 Schloss Eltz."

"Well, what does go with potato chips?" she shrieked.

"Nothing!"

He uncovered the phone's mouthpiece and said, "Also some fresh strawberries with no sugar. Thank you."

"I thought you didn't care what I looked like."

"I don't care what you look like, as long as you're not fat."

"Jack!"

"Hmmm?"

"I love you even though you keep me junk food deprived."

On the terrace, with their wine, Clara said, "I've had my fill of the fucking Bahamas."

"Now what, the heat?"

"I don't know," she sighed. "Maybe just pre-dinner depression, or wine on an empty stomach, or something much more realistic, like fear."

Jack drained his glass. "Look, I'll feel a lot better when we're back in Miami too, but that dive is a debt."

"God, I'm tired." Clara rose from her chair somehow managing to upset the wine on herself. As she crawled under the table to retrieve the errant bottle, Jack met her at the other end. He began to kiss away the wine that had spilled down her cheeks, neck, and breasts.

"Why don't we get into bed?" she whispered.

His hands began to tug at the zipper of her jeans. "Don't you like the floor?"

"For a Parquet floor, it's beautiful, but I meant get into bed because I was sleepy to begin with and this alcohol is putting me out."

"OK, honey. I'd carry you into bed if I had the strength."

"Jack, I'd never ask that of you. You might need your back some day."

Jack helped her up and put their wine glasses back on the table. "Wait until you see what I have planned for tomorrow. We'll leave an eight a.m. wake-up call."

"Eight!" Clara groaned. "Didn't I ever tell you that my one ambition in life was to sleep until noon? Now, I have the chance, and you're spoiling it. You may have to cook for the next year."

"How about ten? Is that more humane?"

"Noon is elegant."

"I'll agree to noon, if you promise not to scatter your midnight snack crumbs in our bed."

"You drive a hard bargain," she sighed.

The phone awoke Clara from her usual sound sleep. After mumbling an automatic thank-you at the operator, she managed to replace the receiver with some difficulty. Not finding Jack next to her, she planned to burrow deeply into the covers for a few more minutes of sleep.

Jack's voice destroyed her plans. "Come on, it's another great day in the Bahamas. Get your eyes on, kid," he panted. Crawling to the end of the bed, she saw Jack at his morning exercises. She preferred to get her exercise by watching him work out, but in Miami, he dragged her to a gym several times a week. It cut into her science fiction and trashy novel reading time greatly.

"You don't have to exercise this morning. Just get dressed. I have sybaritic plans."

197

Clara staggered into the bathroom, picking up the trail of scattered clothing she had left on her way to bed. As usual, she thought she looked awful. Jack loved her. So it didn't matter.

"Tell me again how Marina Sand looks worse than me without make-up"

"Get dressed!"

"I need to hear it."

"You've got great skin."

"Thanks a lot," she growled as she tried to attach a recalcitrant eyelash.

"Jack poked his head into the bathroom, watching her fight with the lash. "Well, you're a big morning crab until you get your face on. Where did you find false eyelashes anyway?"

"From a sympathetic maid."

"Well, don't forget your bathing suit."

"But if we go swimming, my lashes will float away."

"I'll hold your head above water."

She came close, wrapping her arms around him and nestled against his chest. "You know, I have a confession to make."

"Oh, here it comes," he said. "Two years of bliss and now she's going to tell me all she's really interested in is my body."

"It's worse, "Clara whispered. "Most of the time I really dread diving and swimming because I can't wear eye make-up. It's out. Oh God, I feel so much better."

"You sure it's not because of all those near death experiences you have when you're diving? Anyway, when you're in a bikini only idiots look at your face."

A loud knock brought Jack out of the bathroom. "Get yourself together. I'll see who's at the door."

"Mr. Stanger?"

"Yes."

"Room service with your order."

As Jack handed over the tip, he was relieved that he had taken that handful of cash from Waldmann. In return he received a huge straw basket with garish ivory inlaid handles.

"Who was that?"

"You mean your nose isn't working? That was food, but to be eaten later."

Clara poked her head out of the bathroom as far as the cord on her blow dryer would allow. "A picnic! That's beautiful. Let's find a big tree with green grass. That's one of my sexual fantasies."

Clara was prowling around the room, throwing towels and jeans in various directions. "Where's my bra?"

"I swear I'm not wearing it."

"How could it disappear? It's my yellow and green print bathing suit top. That makes it very hard to be lost in the protective coloration of this hotel room."

"Here it is, honey. I'm afraid I was sitting on it."

"Are you going to give me your lecture on putting my things away, and then I'll always know where they are?"

"No, I'm about to whisk you off on a romantic picnic."

Clara presented her back so Jack could hook her straps. "You know, it was thoughtful of our friends to send us those Cardin Jeans and tops, but a girl needs underwear and nightgowns."

"What do you need nightgowns for? I'll only take them right off."

"But what if we have breakfast in bed, or sit on the terrace sipping wine, or there's a fire?"

"If there's a fire, I'll wrap you in a sheet. If you really want some clothes, I'll take you shopping early in the morning so we don't waste the whole day."

Clara found herself stepping into a rowboat. She stared in disbelief at the foam rubber contoured seats, and the oars with their padded handles. Usually there is a standard inch of water in most rowboats. This one was immaculate. "What a place. They can't even have a plain, slightly battered wooden rowboat."

As she began to search around the boat, Jack asked, "What are you looking for? The food is right here in this basket."

"I'm looking for the power steering. How are we going to get anywhere?"

Jack lifted one of the extravagant oars. "With these."

"You mean you're actually going to row?"

"Listen, if I can lift a few weights, I can row a boat."

"I didn't doubt your physical prowess. I just can't believe that people like Aaron and Arthur would actually row a boat, even one as ludicrous as this."

"You should have seen the other rowboat we could have had. It came with twelve matched oarsmen from Princeton's sculling team."

Clara snapped her finger. "That's it. When Aaron and Arthur go rowing, they just buy someone to row for them."

Jack found that rowing was a bit more than muscling the oars. They made a couple of complete circles before he learned to get an equal pull on port and starboard. Finally they made it to the middle of a beautiful lagoon. "I should be in some frivolous organdy dress, with bare shoulders, and a matching parasol."

Jack located a secluded clump of trees, gentle, green, and cool. He opened the basket, and removed the blanket from the top. Spreading this below the shade of a tree, he then removed a lace tablecloth. This covered the central area of the blanket.

"If you bring out paper plates it'll ruin everything," Clara said.

She didn't have to worry. The top of the basket came fitted with racks of Spode China, and appropriate silver.

Jack took off his T-shirt and carefully draped it over his forearm as he displayed the wine label. "For madam, a nice Matras, so madam would not have to schlep ice."

"Those glasses look like lead crystal. What a spread!"

"It's really nice here. I don't care if we never get back to Miami. I escaped down to Florida because I thought it was so much calmer than New York. Then came the crowds, the traffic, and the crime. This really beats both places by a mile."

"Jack, you'd go balmy spending more than two months like this."

"Possibly."

"Possibly?" Repeated Clara as she began her excavation into the picnic basket. "You're too bright to just eat, and screw, and do push-ups all day."

"I have my camera, too."

Clara stopped her digging for a moment. "Camera? That's odd. I never think of it in the singular. It's several different bodies with an infinite number of lenses, viewfinders, motor drives etc, which somehow multiply as fast as unicellular organisms. Soon we'll have to buy a huge home with a large guest house next door to keep all your attachments."

Jack sat up, pulling Clara's busy hands out of the basket. Then he leaned back against the tree with his arms encircling her. "I love you more than my camera."

"Even more than your ancient Nikon FTN?"

"That camera does not bring chaos into my life, nor does it scatter potato chips over my bed."

Clara bit Jack's shoulder as he pretended to ignore her.

They ate their lunch, drank their wine, and dozed in each other's arms beneath a motherly Bahamian tree.

"You really don't mind staying a while, do you?" asked Jack.

203

"Well, I don't feel as hysterical as I did, but I'd rather be dallying in Hawaii than here. Those hours in the water were like one of my worst nightmares in living color. I'm afraid to sleep; afraid I'll play it over in my dreams."

She was quiet for several minutes as Jack held her. When she spoke again, it was in a hushed voice since she really didn't want to he heard. "I'm a coward."

"How can you say that after all you've been through?"

"Because I was petrified."

"Fear is not tantamount to cowardice."

"Oh, stop it Jack." Clara tried to pull away from him, but he held her more tightly. "You've proved you're brave. You've got all those goddamn medals, and you don't cry."

"That's what it is, what's really bothering you. Not the shipwreck. Clara was scared shitless, and it screwed up her self-image. You thought you were such an independent chick, and independent chicks don't get scared. Well, let me tell you something. That whole time in Vietnam, I was frightened out of my gourd. I never slept. I dozed, always listening for that metallic click of an AK47, that footstep. Every time I took a step without blowing off my legs or my gonads, I took a sigh of relief. All I cared about was surviving, and all I could see was that many of my buddies were not surviving. The only intellectual or philosophical exertion I had was to count how many more days I had until I could go home."

Clara looked up at him in amazement. "I don't believe it."

"It's true. Cowards and heroes are both equally scared. It's just that the heroes do the best they can even while they're terrified, and the cowards do nothing. You're OK. When I was unconscious after I ran into that Man-O-War, you took care of me. You were frightened, but you did everything you could. That's all bravery is."

"I love you, Jack Stanger."

Jack kissed her eyes closed. "You're exhausted, and you don't even know it. Until I lived with you, I had no idea what a doctor's life was like. Seven days a week, dragging around, and all those interrupted nights' sleep."

"But I'm crazy about medicine."

"It's a good thing. You have to be crazy. There's got to be an easier way. It's inhumane."

"Ben Fishberg was talking about an arrangement where we alternate weekends, covering for each other."

"Well, every other weekend off is a start in the right direction."

Clara put her head in Jack's lap and looked up at him for a long time before speaking. "It's good to be alone again."

"Again? What do you mean?"

"Well, ever since we met Aaron and Arthur, I've had this feeling that they were taking us over — manipulating us."

"I have the same feeling. We're entangled in the world of the high-powered corporation masterminds." Jack stuffed a strawberry into Clara's mouth as he continued. "They have to be able to manipulate others in order to survive. Come on. Let's walk off some of our lunch."

As Clara reluctantly arose, he added, "You know, without me, you'd probably turn into a great big hunk of chicken liver."

"But think of how content I'd be, sitting there, oozing schmaltz."

"Nah. You'd hate yourself in the morning."

Wordlessly, they walked. They only stopped when Jack found frogs, toads, or small insects to fascinate. Clara pretended to be frightened. She didn't tell him that she once raised cockroaches for a grade school show-and-tell.

They stopped at a waterfall and Jack began to undress.

"But I left my bathing suit with the picnic basket."

"Since when did we ever need bathing suits?"

They played in the cascading water, forgetting everything unpleasant. When they finally dressed and returned to the club, they kept their repose.

Back on their terrace, Clara said, "I just want to stay like this forever. Today was better than Xanax."

"I bet this island could use a good doctor. Maybe I could work out a deal with the Bahamian government as some sort of photojournalist in the Office of Propaganda."

"Well, if you plan to work for any government, you should know that it's a news story when you do the story, but it becomes propaganda if it's the other side's story."

*   *   *

Clara rose and walked to the terrace railing. After gazing at the view for a few seconds, she said, "I guess I'd better get some sleep. After all, we want to start shopping by ten."

"That gives you only fourteen hours sleep. How will you ever function, my love?"

The persistent knocking annoyed them both. As Clara went toward the door, she said, "It's got to be Aaron or Arthur, because I wasn't expecting Tom Hanks this evening."

"Then don't answer it."

"They must know we're here."

Aaron stepped in, wearing a perfectly tailored navy blue suit with a pale blue Quiana shirt. Jack couldn't help estimating the value of his outfit at about $800.

"You both look marvelous." His eyes were fixed on Clara. It was doubtful that he had any idea if Jack was wearing anything at all.

"Just a little rest, food, and incredible surroundings," Jack answered.

"Won't you sit down," Clara invited.

"Actually, I was on my way to dinner, and I thought you might join me."

"Thank you, but we're really not hungry now. We had a huge, late lunch."

"You may not be hungry, Jack, but Clara has such a healthy appetite, that I'm sure she'll accompany me."

Clara shrieked in mock horror. "My God! How did you find out my secret?"

"Ah Ha!" Jack grinned. "Somewhere a little gnome is keeping a dossier on you. No skeletons in your closet shall remain undiscovered. Can't you just see it? Clara Weiss feed her and she's your slave."

Aaron laughed courteously. He was disappointed. Prying Clara loose from Jack for a few hours would have made a pleasant interlude. Hiding his regret, he said,

"Well, I'm sorry I can't interest anyone in joining me for dinner."

They took the usual amount of time with polite good-byes, and as Aaron went through the door, he turned and said, "If the weather holds, we'll probably make our dive in about five days. I've got some business to take care of, so I won't be around for a while. You can always call on Arthur Waldmann if you have any problems."

Clara held out her hand. "I really can't conceive of anything we could need. You've been more than generous."

Aaron kept her hand a shade too long as his eyes lingered on her. Jack didn't notice, but Clara knew she was being stalked.

Sitting on the bed, she began to remove her shoes. As Jack sat beside her, she said, "You don't like him, do you?"

"No."

"Why?"

As Jack pulled her down and began kissing her neck, he said, "Because his T-shirts are pressed."

Much later he whispered, "Clara, he doesn't really know how to enjoy anything. All he knows how to do is exploit. For him, people are objects to be maneuvered for his own purposes."

"I feel that way, too. Like he really calculates. Nothing on impulse," she yawned.

As Jack drifted to sleep, he automatically slipped his arm around Clara protectively.

"I think he really likes me."

"Mmmm?"

"Jack, I think he has designs on me."

"That's nice."

She extricated herself, sat up and turned on the light.

Jack groaned, rubbing his eyes as light assaulted his stunned pupils.

"Clara, I'm in no shape for philosophical disputations." Jack covered his eyes with his hands.

"If I turn off the light, will you talk to me?"

He nodded as he tentatively lifted an eyelid.

Nestled once more in his arms, Clara continued, "You know, he's really on the make for me."

Jack patted her shoulder.

"He's a very attractive man," she whispered to Jack's left axilla.

"Doesn't turn me on."

"Don't you think he's got incredible confidence? I mean, ogling me when he knows I'm with you."

Jack's answer was smothered with a yawn.

"I'm boring you."

"No, no, I love talking about men you find sexy when I'm exhausted."

After a few minutes of silence, Jack said, "Listen, Clara when we get back home, we'll get married. You've never really been comfortable just living with me, have you?"

"That's a lousy way to propose." There was another two seconds of silence. "But I accept."

The next morning, after a breakfast that was a massive assault to their intestinal tracts, they used their motorbike to go shopping.

"I'm pretty cagey. If my chariot has restricted baggage space, that means there's a limit to how much crap you can buy to stuff into our closets at home."

"Remind me to get rid of the junk I don't wear," said Clara as she critically eyed her reflection in a new long gown.

"That's at least three-quarters of our closet space. Every time you put on something, you scream that it makes you look too fat, and throw it right back into the closet."

"Well, what do you think?"

"It looks great."

"OK, I'll take it."

"Clara, can you wear it to the office?"

"Of course not."

"Can you possibly scan back two weeks when you said you had nothing decent with which to make your daily entrance to the hospital and stun all the patients?"

"Yes, but I need another gown."

The bar was dimly lighted and cool. The paneling was darkened by centuries of oxidation, and old brass fittings, green with age. After dragging themselves all over Bay Street, this was the only hospitality they needed. Ordering the house concoction of rum, fruit juices, and lots of ice, they found that only its frigid temperature made the hideously sweet brew tolerable.

A comfortable silence was broken when Clara said, "I think Casey's right."

"Well, when she's not right, she's at least funny."

"She says her goal is to be kept by a rich man. Think of the life, Jack! Spend the day shopping, and then off to the 'in' bar of the month."

"Oh, come on Clara, You'd really miss those three a.m. phone calls."

"Especially when it's some lunatic who's had a post-nasal drip for four days."

Jack moved his chair closer and put his arm around Clara. Her head dropped comfortably to his shoulder. "I've never seen you so tired."

"I don't really feel like I'm on a vacation." Her head rose abruptly.

"What's wrong?"

"Look," she whispered, nodding her chin toward Jack's right shoulder, "but don't let him notice you." She pulled her newly purchased straw hat down, partially obscuring her face.

Jack tried to turn his head casually in the direction Clara indicated. There was no way he could do this without making himself obvious. The large mirror behind the bar was his next gambit. "Clara, I don't know what you mean."

"In the corner, you see the man with his back to us, in a striped shirt? Well, the one facing him is the boat captain."

"Which boat captain?" Jack was still trying to correlate her directions with the reversed reflection.

"The one who tried to kill us."

Jack lowered his eyes to his drink, and then slowly shifted the position of his head.

Turning back to Clara, he grinned with relief. "He doesn't even look familiar to me."

"Nobody looks familiar to you. You didn't remember half your classmates at that reunion you schlepped me to."

"Clara, that can't be him."

"It is. I'm sure."

"Oh, my God!" Clara grabbed Jack's arm.

"What is it?"

"The man in the striped shirt talking to him — it's Aaron."

*　　　*　　　*

It was quiet on the terrace.

Jack toyed pensively with the five-hundred-millimeter mirror lens, part of the photographic equipment Aaron lent him.

"We should have gone over and talked to Aaron. Now your mind will never be at rest. You'll see Aaron talking to gunmen behind every corner."

"It looked like that captain."

He laid the lens down gently on a towel. "Clara, how close were we to the captain? Several boat lengths, right? You didn't have your contacts on, did you? How many inches can you see without them? I think you're spooked, and so you're over-reacting."

"It's because of my myopia and astigmatism that I've developed a feel for shapes and mannerisms. I really thought he was the captain," she added haltingly.

"Thought? And now?"

Clara stared at her hands. "Now? Now I don't know."

"I think by tomorrow you'll realize you've had a hysterical reaction."

Jack was disturbed to see Clara so dejected. He now understood the extent of her exhaustion. He reached over and gently took both of her hands. Tenderly tracing the vein pattern, he said, "I think as soon as we get things straightened out at home, we'll take off again. Remember that cabin we rented in North Carolina? It was near Hendersonville, and the entrance to that great national park."

"With the two fireplaces, one in the living-room, and one in the bedroom."

"Yeah!"

"That lake by the cabin was so beautiful."

"Maybe the same farmer will catch us skinny-dipping again."

Jack smiled as Clara laughed in remembrance.

She shook her head as she said, "But this was supposed to be a vacation."

"Oh, Clara, you work so fucking hard, and then come out here to find all kinds of trauma and pressure." He made a gesture of helplessness. "Lay off guilt-tripping yourself. You deserve another vacation."

Jack grabbed Clara. Hugging her, he said, "I suppose that's part of why I love you. My motivating principle is pleasure. You put a whole raft of other people's problems before your own enjoyment." He kissed her gently. "Let's get some sleep."

*   *   *

Five days after the mishap at sea, their skins almost healed from the onslaught of the sun and the Man-O-War, they found themselves at sea again. This time it was in style. The ship was fifty-four feet from bow to stern, beamy, and with a deep "V" hull. This was a ship built to weather rough seas, and not for those in the least concerned with fuel economy. The bridge would have been roomy, but almost all-available space was taken with electronic gear, and a large chart table. This was a gadgeteer's dream.

They were taken below decks and introduced to their quarters. Their diving gear occupied one cabin, and as promised, the equipment was more than adequate. There were four sets of twin eighty-cubic-foot aluminum cylinders. Each set would give them about an hour and a half at sixty feet depth. While diving with one set, the empties could be filled with the Joy Compressor and its thirty-five-hundred PSI bank of tanks above on deck. This kind of diving was going to take some careful decompression stops. There was a locker filled with lift bags which, when filled with air, could lift well over 1000 pounds, but if that was inadequate, there was a heavy duty hoist carefully concealed under canvas.

The map coordinates were not precise, and in spite of all the high-tech equipment, days were spent in a search pattern. All passengers and crew took their watch at the instruments. Jack and Clara usually found themselves paired. While Jack watched the moving chart paper on the depth sound, Clara would watch the gauge on the metal detector, earphones tightly clasped to her head. Together, they hoped to separate coral reef from steel hull. In mid-afternoon, Jack and Clara would take a break, and lie on the fantail cultivating a tan. Today, the sky was becoming overcast, and with their sunlight going, Clara was fastening her bra in preparation for going below. "Jack that boat looks like it's following us."

"It's more than following, babe. A while ago it was on the horizon. Now it appears to be closing. Let's let the rest of the team in on this."

It was Arthur and Aaron's turn on the bridge. Arthur was at the depth sounder, while Aaron had to split his attention between the magnetometer and the helm. Arthur turned away from the sounder to scan the oncoming vessel through his seven by fifties.

"You have sharp eyes. Yes, I believe these are competitors. The captain's below checking out a noise from one of the engines. I'll ask him to come to the bridge, and we'll try some evasive maneuvers to lose them."

Both engines were jammed into full throttle; the bow lifted a few degrees, and the boat cut through the water at maximum speed. Jack had to wonder at the power rumbling under his feet. The boat was seriously over-powered. The engines were more suitable for a drug runner than for a pleasure craft. In spite of this, it soon became evident that the competitor had the faster craft as the distance between them steadily decreased.

As Waldmann lowered the binoculars he said, "Aaron, unless providence is with us, and they hit a reef, or run out of fuel, I'm afraid we are faced with a confrontation. If we're forced into a fire-fight, our young friends will get a bad opinion of us and our industry."

"There's another possibility. I'm going to head us toward that hovering black cumulus to port."

The sky darkened and the sea piled into high breaking waves. All hatches were battened as wave after wave broke across the bow. The sea churned to white foam everywhere. Clara and Jack were below decks, their stomachs queasy and their tanned complexions turned to a sallow white.

"Oh Christ," Clara moaned. "I wish I hadn't stuffed myself during lunch."

"What difference would that make? I lost my lunch ten minutes ago, and now I'm working on last night's supper."

"Jack, that Dramamine didn't help a bit. I couldn't keep it down."

"What about the Scopolamine patches?"

"I'm wearing one behind each ear."

"Well at least we're alone together."

"You're incredible. My mouth tastes awful, my stomach's about to heave again, my legs are shaking, and you have a hard on. Where did this storm come from? The forecast was for good weather."

"Why do you think this place is called The Devil's Triangle? Only the Devil can predict the weather here."

On deck, Aaron and Waldmann struggled with the helm to keep the bow headed into the waves. Then, suddenly the sea became quiet, and the heavy black clouds were whisked away as if some giant unseen hand had snapped a massive blanket at them.

"Do you see the other boat?" Waldmann asked, peering along the horizon.

"No ship in sight."

"Then let's proceed with our search."

In the middle of the fourth day the wreck was located. Nylon line was carefully laid out on deck, and

the divers were assisted into their gear. Waldmann helped
Jack on with his tanks and attached spools of line, a knife,
and a supply of lift bags. Aaron worked with Clara. Both
needed assistance in standing and maneuvering to the
ship's ladder. The double tanks and the plethora of
additional equipment more than doubled the weight that
they were accustomed to carry on a dive.

Using the anchor line to control descent, they
slowly worked their way toward the bottom, pausing
every couple of feet to equalize the pressure in their ears
and sinuses. At fifty feet they could clearly make out the
form of the wreck below them, and in another few feet
they were both shocked to recognize the deck gun,
machine gun mounting, and the gaping hole of the wreck
that *they* first discovered two weeks earlier. They were
relieved that they had not revealed their earlier discovery
to Aaron and Arthur. Yet, they were frightened to again
confront the wreck under these circumstances. Their first
task was to secure two lines; one to the bow Samson post,
and one to a hatchway cover near the large, ragged hole to
port. Approximately one hundred feet of line was laid out
at each site. The ends were secured to a lift bag. Jack
used a blast of air from his octopus regulator to float the
lift back to the surface. In short order, the lines became
taut, indicating that the ends of the lines had been secured
to the vessel above them. A third line was rigged around
the hatch cover. This was to be their safety line so that
even in the darkness of the sunken hull they could find
their way out by pulling themselves along this line. Jack
slowly fed out the line as he entered the darkness of the
ship. Clara, using the same line as a guide to keep close
to Jack, aimed the narrow beam of her light in the

direction of travel. The cabin they were in proved to be a dead end. Its watertight doors were frozen to the warped and corroded bulkhead. Their combined efforts couldn't budge it.

They returned to the outside through the hole, and this time approached a large cargo hatch on the forward deck. The weightlessness of water is like the weightlessness of space. Astronauts cannot accomplish work without anchor, and similarly there was no way to turn the balky handle without body stability. Clara wrapped her legs around a nearby stanchion while Jack wedged his body between the hatch and a deck pipe. Working together, they slowly turned the balky handle. The cover proved heavy in spite of its counterweights. Being careful not to lose their safety line, they made their way down the companionway into a dark cabin. The beam from their lamps cut a small tube of vision through the inky black darkness. On one wall they could make out a couple of bunk beds. Then sweeping their lights in a slow arc, they saw a chest stowed in a corner. It was metallic and large. It looked at least three feet by four feet, and three feet deep. Along its side were several sturdy ring bolts. Chains through two of the ring bolts fastened the chest to a ring bolt in the bulkhead.

Jack had been hesitant about bringing those long bolt cutters along for the dive. Before the dive he and Arthur had an altercation over the risk of being encumbered with excessive equipment. He finally conceded when Arthur informed Jack that he knew what kind of problems he would meet, and the cutter was a critical tool.

The corroded chain snapped easily as Clara busied herself attaching a lift bag to each ring on the chest.

When their tasks were done, Jack checked his watch. Thirty-seven minutes had passed since they had started their descent, and they were at a depth of seventy-five feet. Jack signaled to Clara to leave the ship and begin ascent immediately. A few minutes more, and decompression stages would be necessary—something they would try to avoid.

At the surface, Aaron was standing on the last rung of the ladder. He helped the divers off with their tanks, and passed them to Waldmann. Once on board, Clara gave the progress report.

"Great! We have two pair of fresh tanks all ready while the first are being refilled," Aaron said. "When will you be ready to go down again?"

"I'm afraid Clara and I will have to rest up a bit. We have quite a bit of nitrogen dissolved in our tissues, and our blood is probably fizzing like Pepsi-Cola. If we're to get, say, another forty minutes down below without decompression, we'll have to wait eight and a half hours before we can dive again."

"But then it will be dark," Aaron responded. "How soon can you dive by just taking a short decompression stop at ten feet? What do the tables say, Clara?"

"If we rest for three hours, we can spend another forty minutes at depth, but then we have to float around at ten feet for seventeen minutes."

Jack made the decision. "It will still be light then, so let's give it a try."

When they were alone, Clara frantically whispered to Jack, 'why couldn't you postpone the dive until tomorrow? That gunboat," she whispered, "that was the wreck we saw when we got blown out of the water."

"Clara, listen. I just want to get the fucking dive over with. We've got to get away from these characters."

He cradled her head on his chest. Then her voice spoke the thoughts he was desperately trying to bury. "How safe are we?"

Jesus! All kinds of primitive floodgates opened up in his mind. He loved Clara. He wanted to protect her, physically and mentally. He wanted to be able to say, "Everything's fine," but it wouldn't wash. Not with Clara. She had always been on intimate terms with truth.

He chose his words carefully, his voice calm and low as he answered her. "I think that being dumb will give us a good safety factor. If they don't know that we discovered the wreck when our boat was sunk, that increases our survival odds." She shuddered in his arms. Oh God, if I only had a rosier picture to show her.

Jack went on. "But, even if they knew, honey, they're probably feeling secure because, remember we were barely conscious; our senses obviously pretty well addled when they picked us up. They could easily expect us to be confused over what happened and what we saw. Look," he paused, "whatever purposes they have, or whoever they really are, it's plain that we're dealing with rational people. I don't think they'd do anything to us unless they really thought it was necessary for their own well being. We just won't make it necessary."

Clara shivered. "I just can't believe we're talking like this. We're coolly discussing our prognosis, and I just don't feel sick, Jack. It's insane!"

"It's gonna be okay, Honey."

Clara looked up at Jack. Tall and strong, with the sun highlighting him. A girl could really feel safe around him. Protected from natural disasters, monsters, ruin, and every day run-of-the-mill cataclysms, but not whole sets of happenings beyond control, and manipulative people with implausible power and unplumbed intentions. Clara felt stunned by the unknown. If a terror had some shape, at least you could get a handhold.

Jack smiled at her reassuringly, and Clara had one of those flashes instinctive to almost every woman. The kind of thought she had spent years trying to repress, but its time had come.

"He likes me."

Jack didn't have to be told who. "So what?"

"Maybe we could use that." Jack tried to interrupt, but she wouldn't let him. "I just mean that I could very tactfully pump him and act very stupid and innocent."

"I think you'd be safer with a Great White. You can't play that kind of game. You don't even know how to flirt without tripping over both feet and your stethoscope. Believe me, I know."

Clara smiled and looked out over the water. When she turned back to him she felt calmer, because at least this was a plan.

"Really, Jack, I'd be careful. I'd simply talk and be nice and girl-like. I've read the books; I could talk to an attractive man and not let him know I'm too bright."

"And if you're too stupid, that's a dead give-away."

"I'll be careful."

There was nothing else they could do. They didn't know the lay of the land. Reluctantly, Jack said, "Just let him do most of the talking."

She grabbed his shoulders and gently kissed him. "Go downstairs and take a nap. I'll wake you up in about thirty minutes."

Shortly after Jack had gone below, the heavy-set captain, known only to Clara as "Match," appeared on deck. He motioned Aaron over to the railing for some discussion.

When Aaron returned he announced that they would have to postpone the dive until tomorrow.

"Why?" Clara looked surprised.

"Match says he's seen a couple of tigers in the area."

"But that's ridiculous!" Clara said. "Propaganda to the contrary, sharks are not known to bother divers. We've met some friendly sharks over at Pennekamp."

"Nevertheless, Clara," Aaron smiled, staring at her, "Tigers are different, and I'd be mighty uncomfortable knowing you were down there with that breed. Match is an experienced captain, and he knows his sharks. If he feels the dive is dangerous, let's humor him."

Aaron sat down next to Clara and said, "now that we have this perfect afternoon, shall we go up to the sun deck and work on our tans?"

Suddenly apprehensive, she moved away from him. "I think I'll get down to Jack. He may want some food before he really sacks out."

Aaron seized her hand before she could move. "Don't be long, Clara. I'll wait here."

After Clara had gone below, Waldmann questioned Aaron. "Why did you postpone the dive?"

"We have some eyes on us. Match spotted them. I doubt if they're more than mildly suspicious right now. A few hours of loafing in obviously perfect diving weather should make us look more like a party yacht." Aaron looked out at the calm water. "A nice, loud, carousing party tonight should help. Tell the chef to break out the case of Taittinger."

Clara sat on Jack's bunk. The slight pressure of her body awakened him.

226

"I'm glad to see you, honey."

She shook her head in annoyance. "I'm so disgusted. You know, I took one look at that bronze Sun God up there, and I just couldn't play the prom queen."

Jack captured her face in his hands. "You don't have to. I told you it wasn't a game you could play."

"It wasn't that," she broke in. "He was just so damn arrogantly perfect. It's like he knows he oozes sex appeal, and every girl will just naturally grovel at his feet. I just didn't want to give him the satisfaction of 'Ha! She may have a boyfriend but she can't resist me.'"

Jack laughed. "I can understand. You are a very independent woman. In fact," he whispered softly as he nuzzled her ear, "I first realized you loved me when you began to depend on me."

Jack brushed her lips with his. Sighing, she snuggled against him. "They canceled the dive."

"Why?"

"They believe all that idiocy about the terror in the depths. Our Neanderthal captain thought he saw a shark."

"I don't believe it, "Jack chortled. "Too bad all those friendly monsters we meet can't hire some public relations men for themselves."

They sat a while, comfortably quiet. Then Jack frowned, "you know, the weather is perfect right now for a salvage operation. I just hope it holds out tomorrow."

227

"I think it will. Aaron says the forecast is for several days like this."

Jack stretched out on his belly and Clara began rubbing his back. "Should I get you something to eat before you go to sleep? I know you were hungry before the dive."

"No, I'd rather get some rest now."

She kissed his cheek lightly and went back on deck. What did the Greeks call it? "Hubris?" She was too proud to pretend she liked Aaron? As Aaron came into her mind, a torrent of painful memories welled up. Clara, as a chunky little Jewish princess, a brain, left out at parties, watching slender girls with perfect hair, and perfect bodies, tantalize football players. Trying to comfort herself with the belief that it didn't matter, because in a few years, her mind would put her far ahead of all the beauties. Now, respected and successful, none of that mattered. Thinking back to those days, she still could feel the pain of a teen-aged Clara. It had mattered then.

As she walked up the stairs, a realization held her. It was not a chunky adolescent, but an accomplished woman who was emerging into the Caribbean sunlight.

Aaron was sitting alone, examining the wineglass in his hand. As Clara came up the ladder, he rose and helped her. "I've already brought some blankets and some refreshments to the sun deck. We have the whole afternoon to get tan."

"The sun goddess should not always be worshipped, especially by women. We don't look good all wrinkled and craggy. I use sunscreen even before I go for a dive."

She walked over to the railing. As Aaron joined her, he said, "Let's go upstairs. There's an umbrella you can hide under, and the view is so impressive that you feel suspended in a daydream."

Taking her hand, he led her to the ladder-way. Aaron spread a blanket under the huge yellow umbrella. Then, like some fastidious housewife, he carefully smoothed the creases.

As Clara lowered herself to the floor, she forlornly hoped her awkward movements might somehow conceal her discomfort. She felt like an idiot. She had no confidence at all in her ability to play clever games with Aaron. What was she going to say? "Listen, Aaron, baby, whoever you are. Please don't kill us, because we really don't know anything, and if we did, we wouldn't say anything, anyway." Shit! She felt like the school's best trigonometry student suddenly pitted against Einstein in a new mathematical system. She wanted out of this match. With no game plan, how could she find the opening gambit? Now, all she could think about was retreating down those stairs.

Clara was on her stomach, trying to hide her lack of aplomb. By now, Aaron could probably smell her anguish. It must be radiating from her and floating toward him in fat, black clouds.

Oh, shit! His hand was caressing her back. She sat up, poured herself a glass of wine, and smiled at Aaron. When in doubt, smile. Now, what dimwit in the depths of absurdity had said *that*? She shivered to realize that it was a fifteen-year-old Clara sitting painfully in a corner at her first high school dance. She had panicked when a boy came near her chair. What if he asked her to dance? What if he didn't? She cringed at the memory.

Retreating from her adolescent nightmare, she realized Aaron was talking.

"You are very courageous, diving again so soon after a bad experience."

Good Lord! He was making the first move. Now, if she had even a couple of brain cells still connected, she should be able to take the ball. Diffidently lowering her eyes, she swirled the port in her glass. As she watched the legs recede down her glass, she spoke hesitantly. "It's just like a dream, Aaron. I can't believe that it really happened. Besides, if I didn't dive soon, I was afraid that I'd never be able to dive again."

Looking at Aaron with just the right touch of the bewildered, somewhat simple blonde, she continued. "So, you see, I'm not so brave. Maybe if I remembered more, I'd be scared out of my wits."

"Well, it was an awful experience for you and your friend."

He squeezed her hand to comfort the poor little thing, and she realized she was doing all right. She didn't know if blondes really had more fun, but it did make it a little easier to be deceptive. She understood what his last little tactic meant. She was getting adept at this. Pausing before he said, "friend." Fishing to find out how permanent she and Jack were. Instinct made her start to protectively blurt out "fiance," but a wilier Clara decided that, although it would be easier for her to ward off his advance, she might get a lot more out of Aaron by dumbly ignoring his last maneuver.

She repossessed her hand. Couldn't let him think his attentions were welcome. First of all, they weren't. Secondly, she just wanted information, not attention. Putting the hand to good use, she snatched at a cracker. Food was always a fine mechanism for a strategic pause. Time to marshal defenses, or plot an offense. As she crunched the cracker into oblivion, Clara quickly found some Gouda to sandwich between two thin slices of rye bread.

Aaron watched her, amused. Her dossier was imbedded neatly in the data storage banks of his mind, ready to be retrieved all or in part at his discretion. He allowed his mind to dwell on her personality profile. *Emotional pubescence counterpoised against maturity and a firmly directed sense of responsibility.* How much did she know? Did the guns on the wreck register suspiciously? Being unfamiliar with pleasure boats, could she think this was normal armament? Most of the boats now were well fortified against yacht-napping. Watching her slowly grind away at a cracker, it was hard to think there was anything more important on her mind than a suppressed desire to be the next Playmate of the Year, but he knew better. She was a Phi Beta Kappa, Alpha Omega Alpha in medical school. Fellow of both the American

231

College of Cardiology and the American College of Physicians—he knew one hell of a lot better.

"Don't you want to be cadaverously slim like every other girl in the world?"

"No, I think I'm just far too seductive already," she grinned.

Aaron laughed with her as he poured some more wine. *Extreme sensitivity to wine, bordering on a pathological intoxication.* "Here, gargle with this."

Slowly sipping the Chablis, she murmured, "Pretty good gargling." Thank God there's some food in my stomach to slow down this booze. If I eat enough I can probably spend an hour sipping half a glass safely, she thought.

"Drink up. I have a few more bottles stashed for dinner tonight."

Holding her hand over her glass, she said, "Maybe we shouldn't celebrate until we've found your hardware. It might anger the gods, or something."

"The gods get thirsty, never angry."

She lay down on her stomach again, apparently contemplating the waves. She didn't know the techniques. How could she get any information from him?

Aaron leaned back, indulging himself. Romantic liaisons, although frequent, were always brief. Now, over the past few years, he had become aware of a faint, but bitter angst. No one really cared whether he won or lost. Seeing Clara and Jack, who placed each other's comfort above their own, made his bitterness more pronounced. He didn't know if he wanted a permanent relationship, a woman that he could fuck one minute, and be his best friend the next. Maybe it wasn't his style. Clara certainly wasn't demonstrating any of her vigorous mental powers. He stopped cold. Suspicious! Why? Then he laughed at himself. He had always felt that one of his greatest talents lay in his manipulation, and understanding of how each individual functioned. Having had any sense of humanity, he would have been a brilliant psychoanalyst. She wasn't playing dumb to soften him. It must be one of her essential defense mechanisms. A beautiful and brilliant woman. Probably found it hard to get dates in school if the boy knew she was smarter than he was. This role she slips into with any man if she's not his doctor or colleague: The pretty blonde. Like a battered old shoe for her. Except with Jack, he mused. They probably honed their wits on each other.

They sat on the upper deck, mesmerized by the tranquil water. Then some rougher swells made Clara aware that she was alone with Aaron, and her hand automatically sought refuge in the tidbits of food laid near the wine. Maybe if she could get him talking about himself, she could eventually steer the conversation to more critical areas.

"How did you get into the computer business?"

"What do you mean?"

"Well, I mean it would take a lot of foresight to get in on the ground floor of a new industry. It also takes a lot of money."

Watching the endless cavalcade of food disappearing down Clara's throat, he realized she was nervous. However, he concluded that the nervousness was standard when she was with an attractive man, and forced to take a role purely as a woman. He relaxed.

"Not so difficult. I was getting a degree in Business Administration, and my roommate was an engineering genius, passionately in love with mathematics. His uncle, Waldmann, was a bored wealthy man, who financed us for the pleasure of getting back into the corporate wars."

Another half-hour drifted by uncomfortably for Clara, but pleasantly for Aaron. She wasn't getting anywhere. Frustration set in as she cursed herself for her ineptitude as a spy. Although it often took great skill at interviewing, and psychology, to ferret out a patient's real complaint, no amateur could garner intelligence from a craftsman.

Judging that any further probing might make him suspicious, Clara stood up, brushing cracker crumbs from her suit onto the blanket. "I'm going to shower before dinner."

"I'll help you down. If I didn't, you might trip on those treacherous stairs, and I'd feel guilty."

"Ha," she beamed, "but then you could appease your guilt by bringing me chocolates while I was in the hospital in traction."

On the next day, the last fifteen minutes before the dive was spent nervously watching the clock. An extra tank with octopus rig was lowered to the ten-foot level just in case they ran out of air before finishing decompression.

With backpacks on, Jack turned to Clara for a last briefing. "We have forty minutes. That's plenty of time to do it slowly and carefully, but not enough time to screw up and make a second attempt. What we have to do is add just enough air to the bags to make the box light enough for me to slide it over the hatch. Too much air and it will slam into the overhead, dump its air, and come crashing down on us. Once we have it exactly under the hatchway, we'll add air to each bag so that it has negative buoyancy of just a few pounds. We will rely on a line to the hoist to do the actual lifting, and thereby have a controlled ascent. The most important thing is to have a balanced amount of air in the bags so the thing doesn't turn over. Air expansion should decrease buoyancy as it gets to the surface. If we figure it wrong, and have added a bit too much air, it may start flying to the surface at the last ten feet."

Jack did a back roll entry from the port side, and after making certain he was clear, Clara followed. There was no time wasted in searching, and they were adding air to the lift bags ten minutes after entering the water. Jack found that by bracing his feet against an adjacent bulkhead he was able to inch the heavy chest under the hatchway. More air was added, and after a signal tug on the line, the box began its way to the surface. Clara and Jack worked opposite sides of the crate to make sure it floated clear of the hatchway. The remainder of the salvage operation went smoothly, and the chest was hoisted aboard without incident. The divers had finished their job well under the forty minutes allotted to them, but because of the physical exertion involved, they took their seventeen minutes at ten feet to avoid the bends. Their air reserve was adequate, and there was no need to use the extra tank hanging on the line.

With the chest on board, faint whiffs of tension began to escape from the boat's inhabitants, like bits of steam from a simmering teakettle. Each had his own release. Waldmann continued to gorge himself following a more than ample meal. Aaron studied some cryptic charts in his cabin. Jack and Clara collapsed in their bunks, deeply asleep on the ultimate waterbed.

Unaccustomed to such an early bedtime, Clara woke in the dim hours of the morning. With the sun not yet raised, and the ocean unruffled, she found a comfortable seat from which to ponder all this tranquillity.

"Good morning."

Startled, she turned to the adjacent deck chair and found Aaron settling in. "I didn't think you were an early riser."

"I'm not," Clara said. "In fact, for the first twelve years of my life, my only ambition was to sleep until noon."

"A noble goal."

"My parents didn't think so."

"Wanted you out of the house and working, huh?"

"No, just out of the bed so they could make it."

Aaron laughed. The peacefulness of the dawn was further disturbed as he pulled his chair toward Clara.

"I can't believe I'm not asleep. Usually, four raucous, nasty alarm clocks have to drag me out of bed in the morning. Here I am, at five a.m. staring at nothing. This can't be me."

"The ocean does that sometimes. It lures you awake and you rush on deck so you don't miss anything, and then there's really nothing to miss. Somehow, you stay anyway. Must be the stillness. Like the placidity on a ski lift. Even your thought processes seem quieter."

"You can't think red," Clara murmured.

"Pardon me?"

"Well, on a hot miserable Miami day, if you're idiotic enough to stagger around in the heat, it's easy to think red and orange. Out here it's hard to have red-tinged reflections. All your thoughts are suffused with blue."

"Ah Ha! You must paint in real life." Aaron lifted Clara's hands, inspecting them as he said, "I smell linseed oil. One hundred hours in seawater wouldn't erase that odor. I have discovered your secret. You paint with oils."

Clara laughed, pulling her hands away.

He leaned closer to her and said as gently as he could, "You know, you are quite lovely."

"You won't say that in another hour. Because then the sun will be up and I don't have my eye make-up on."

Aaron could add a page or two to her dossier. *Banters her way around the serious spots. Basic insecurity. Very precarious in male-female relationships.*

He gently reached over and took her hand. Direct approach. Cuts through all the crap.

"Look, I find you very attractive."

Clara retracted her hand. As she did so, Aaron took her face and turned it toward him. "I like you very much," he said slowly.

Clara pulled back her head, wishing for a carapace into which she could further retreat.

"I'd like to take you out when we get back to Nassau." He had now imprisoned both her hands. *Sweaty palms* noted Aaron. Brushing her cheek with his lips he murmured, "And there are some inviting hideaways in Miami I want to share with you."

Clara was transfixed. Aaron had magnetism and elegance. He was obviously used to having his own way. The rebelliousness that had lured a beautiful woman into medicine began to assert itself. Clara's nettlesome traits rushed all kinds of brilliant and cutting ripostes to her mouth. As she was about to let loose with a few feisty words, sanity intervened. *Don't alienate him. Just a nice, friendly no.*

"Aaron, you know I'm flattered that you'd want to see me, but I don't think you understand my situation."

In the gathering light she thought she detected a quizzical expression in Aaron's eyes.

"Jack and I are engaged."

"Is your relationship so tenuous that you can't see another man? If you have to grab on to something so tightly, maybe it's not worth holding."

"You don't understand, do you? It's not a clutching, grabbing kind of thing. It's a matter of choice. Jack is so many things to me that I don't want another man. In fact, as long as I have him, I don't feel as if I need anyone else at all."

"You're really shackling yourself up."

Clara smiled, as she watched the sun begin to rise. "Maybe that's what it would be for you, Aaron, but for me

I've never had so much freedom. Intellectually, and sexually Jack's given me the confidence I've never had."

She looked at Aaron as she found herself voicing things she had not quite thought about before. "I have the freedom to be myself. I am so confident with Jack that when I feel miserable and bitchy, I don't have to hide it. I know he'll indulge me. I can tell him whatever is on my mind, and if he doesn't understand, he'll try to."

She couldn't read what was in Aaron's eyes. Probably sounded foolish and gushy to him, but shit! That's the way it is.

Standing, she stretched as the sun rose. What a lovely scene for Aaron. Impulsively, she kissed his forehead. "Good morning. See you at breakfast."

Watching her go down the stairs, Aaron felt a few bizarre twinges. She had something he'd never have. For some seconds, he remained switched into a new emotional level. Focusing quickly back to an intellectual plane, he smiled to himself. He did get something out of this. She obviously knew nothing of what was really going on. Probably swallowed their whole story. Otherwise, she would have played along with him, thinking a sexual liaison would force some protection for them.

With a great sense of security, Aaron strode back to his cabin.

"You may have noticed, Jack, that we are not headed back to New Providence, but to the Exuma Cays.

Our company has a refueling station there with some capacity for storage. It would not be feasible to transport our cargo all the way to the West Coast in this glorified pleasure craft." Waldmann then turned back to the chart table. A course to a minor cay was already marked on the overlay. The cay was unnamed, but Jack could see that he was using *Harry Klines's Yachtsman's Guide to the Bahamas*. A few hours later they were approaching a small island, which appeared to consist entirely of a mass of mangroves. It was only on close approach that they could differentiate a simple crude dock from the surrounding wilds.

As they made fast their lines, four unshaven, burly men came to assist them. Each man appeared to be a distant cousin of the gorilla, and each wore a .45 sidearm.

Poles were inserted through the ring bolts of the metal box, and then the four men hefted the poles to their shoulders. Jack and Clara followed behind Aaron and Waldmann as they trod up a narrow sandy path. The path then turned downward, below the water table, and they found themselves walking through sucking mud, and at times, ankle deep water. After the short stretch at the beach, the path was never dry again. They walked less than fifty yards; for certainly the island could not have been longer than seventy-five, and arrived at a windowless building on stilts. It looked like a freight car, somehow derailed from tracks at least 500 miles away. Now ripped off its wheels by some errant teenagers, it stood on blocks in the middle of nowhere. Its only port of entry appeared to be a large sliding freight door. One of the great apes removed the padlock and slid the door open. The crate was lifted into the door way, pushed well to the side, and the door bolted again.

A couple of hours later, Jack and Clara helped tie up at the marina of the Lyford Cay Club.

"Well, we should all congratulate ourselves on a job well done, but congratulations are not all you get, my friends."

With these words, Waldmann handed each diver a fat envelope. "Aaron and I made reservations for you at the Britannia Beach Hotel. You're now well-supplied with cash, so I trust that the remainder of your holiday will be a delight."

*   *   *

"Success is wonderful," belched Waldmann as he fondled the moist cork from the '*70 Fixin Clos de la Perriere*'. "I'm sure you will find that this wine will bring your palate to life. It's a Premier Crus from a small village in the Cote de Nuits district. I was surprised to find a bottle here as it is produced in too small a quantity to be exported in any volume. May I say that I hope we always feel as satiated and wealthy as we are at this moment."

"Wealthy, yes," Jack grinned, "but I think Clara should pass up the satiated. She has always had this problem with her fat cells."

"Mr. Stanger feels an obligation to remind me that I used to be plump," Clara muttered, as she put a pat of butter on a roll.

"I think Clara's one of the loveliest women I've ever known," Aaron said quietly. Jack deftly placed his hand on her elbow, halting the roll's journey.

For an instant, Waldmann's face appeared angry, but if anyone at the table had blinked, the anger would have been missed. Waldmann was adept at many things, and one of those abilities had been most important at insuring success in his profession. He allowed only those emotions to become evident that he felt were advantageous to his game plan.

"A waltz!" Waldmann's eyes lit up gaily. "There are a few things more serene that the sight of a waltzing couple. Mr. Stanger, would you bring pleasure to one too corpulent to be a graceful participant, and dance with Miss Weiss?"

After Clara and Jack were no longer near their table, Waldmann turned irritably on Aaron.

"What are you trying to do?"

"What do you mean?"

"Must your glands always be massaged?" Waldmann's eyes narrowed.

"A little flirtation won't jeopardize anything."

"Please," Waldmann gently used his napkin to sponge wine residue from his lips, "we must keep things as uncomplicated as possible. This whole expedition has been rather cumbersome. It would better serve our purpose for our friends to be, uh, blissful and unsuspecting. If you get mixed up with this girl, Stanger will get jealous. A jealous, angry man is more likely to become inquisitive. We have enough on our hands now."

There was silence at the table. Aaron said nothing. He looked at Waldmann. If it's really possible for a face to be expressionless, then Aaron's was. Waldmann began to pick at the crumbs on the tablecloth. This gave him an opportunity to look away from his partner; down at his busy fingers. There were only two people who had the facility to make Waldmann feel vulnerable, and Aaron was one of them. Waldmann could only whisper, "I'm sorry, I've overstepped," but Aaron had already left the table, and was cutting in on Jack.

Jack sat down as Waldmann angrily speared leftover steak from Aaron's plate. Suddenly, Waldman began clutching at his chest, while making panic-stricken hand motions at Jack.

"Clara! Quick! Waldmann's having some difficulty," Jack shouted.

She was at the table in three long steps, then stood back to survey the situation. Waldmann was cyanotic, and there were deep retractions of his suprasternal fossa.

Clara stepped behind his chair, reached around him, and rammed her clenched fists beneath his sternum.

The first thrust was non-productive, but then Waldmann relaxed in unconsciousness. On the next thrust a huge chunk of meat flew from his mouth.

"My god," he wheezed, "I thought I was a goner." Waldmann collapsed in his chair, even more rumpled, sweaty, and unappealing than usual. He continued to pant, but his color returned to normal. The maitre d', now that the crisis had been expertly handled, could safely hover around his wealthy guest. He skillfully moved Clara out of the spotlight, taking center stage. This was accomplished with an adroitness polished through years of maneuvering, always in the best restaurants, the best hotels, the best clubs—the best, the very best. There were infinite Arthur's to sop up his elegant attentions.

"Monsieur, please, shall we call the hotel physician?"

"No, no, I'm fine now."

"As you wish, Monsieur, but I shall personally help you to your room. Armand! Be sure there is a bottle of Amaretto at Monsieur Waldman's bedside. Have the maid turn down his bed." Turning to Arthur, he dabbed the sweat away from his brow with masterly skill, and guided him out of the room. Another triumph of the true artist.

The three remaining celebrants stood awkwardly around the table.

Aaron held Clara's chair as she seated herself. "I'm impressed, Clara."

With noticeable discomfort, Clara smiled briefly.

"It was fantastic," Aaron pushed. "You knew precisely what to do."

Jack too, felt disquiet if Aaron were to learn that Clara was a physician. Would it shatter the image of naiveté they were trying to project?

Jack forced a laugh. "Look, it's no big deal to unstuff someone's windpipe."

"But she was so cool about the whole thing."

Clara stared dejectedly at the crumbs on the table. Then she lifted her head to Aaron, seeming to search for something in his eyes, as she said, "I'm a doctor."

Aaron feigned a stunned expression. "You're kidding!"

"Well, along about 4 a.m., when some dodo calls with an earache he's had for six months, I might wish I were kidding."

Aaron, shaking his head, continued to portray astonishment. "How come you never told me?"

"You never asked," Jack said.

"I'm so exhausted; all I want to do is sleep for the next week."

"Of course, Clara," Aaron signaled for the waiter. "Call me whenever you awake tomorrow, and I'll take you over to the Britannia Beach. Though Arthur and I both wish you'd spend the rest of your vacation as our guests."

"Thank you, Aaron, but Jack and I really want to be on our own."

The Britannia Beach Hotel was located on Paradise Island. The Island was joined to New Providence by a short bridge for which the ridiculous sum of two dollars was the toll. This princely amount even applied to pedestrians. Only the wealthy have any interest in passing over this bridge anyway. On the side of Paradise are a few luxury hotels, a beautiful beach, and lushly decorated casinos. There are also strange ruins. Partly buried in the sandy beach, long stone stairways that climb to nowhere. The effect is that of being lost in one of Dali's landscapes.

Early in the morning Jack left the hotel looking for a phone. The note he left for Clara merely described his sudden yearning for ocean air.

Once, Jack had spent two months accompanying Carl Felton on a photojournalism tour of the Ivory Coast. Discovering a similarity of political and professional views, they went on to establish a great camaraderie. Through the years, they had remained in close contact. When Felton was chosen to head up *Time*'s Washington bureau, Jack gave him a party that's still a legend among many eastern journalists. On occasion, a hushed rumor would drift over to Jack regarding his friend's tenuous CIA associations.

"Hey, Jack, how you doin', old pal?"

Relieved to find Felton in, Jack said, "listen, Carl, I really need help." He paused then, as a new worry jarred him. "Carl, you may think I'm crazy, but could your phone be tapped?"

Obviously not surprised by the question, Felton answered, "No! This is a private number. Anyway, we've got a service that checks it pretty frequently. Where are you calling from?"

"A pay phone in Nassau."

"What is it? The story of the century or you just need a few hot phone numbers?"

"I'm in trouble."

Jack completed his narration of everything he and Clara had been through. There was silence on Felton's end.

"Carl?"

"Just a second, Jack. I'm trying to figure out who'd be best for you to talk to."

"You believe me?"

"Listen, if you say the Bahamian cops took pot shots at you, I believe you. Don't you think we go back far enough that if you told me you took a ride in a flying saucer, I'd believe that too?"

"I really think there's something fishy going on."

"Look, give me the number on that booth. I'll call you back in exactly one hour. If for some reason I don't get back to you in an hour, you call me."

It gets real dull standing at a phone booth for an hour. It's also hard to look inconspicuous. Jack spent the next fifty minutes looking into store windows, trying to find anything to make the time pass. He couldn't help it. Ten minutes to the designated time, Jack found himself standing in front of the phone booth. He got the phone on the first ring. Listening carefully to Carl's instructions, he memorized the number he was to call, and then dialed.

After going through the identifying mumbo jumbo, the voice on the other end of the phone continued. "OK, I'm Bruce Rand, an old college pal. Get to Maxie's bar tonight at seven—alone. Try to get a seat at one of the stools not far from the stage."

"That's just terrific. What do I do, carry a purple umbrella, or just pin on a red rose?"

"Look, Stanger, you're the one asking for help."

"Sorry, but my fiancée' is not gonna understand my running off in the evening without her. What about early tomorrow morning or very late tonight; about midnight. She's usually zonked out about then and she won't flip when I leave."

"Seven, tonight."

The click of the broken connection annoyed Jack. Sanctimonious schmuck! Clara would be off the wall when he bugged out on her tonight. Couldn't blame her.

249

What a detestable quandary. If he told Clara he was meeting some CIA-type dude, she would worry that things were not as light as he was trying to paint them. If he didn't tell her, she'd think he was a shit for leaving her alone instead of spending their waking hours together. Once he fueled her worry, it would be hard to calm that down. Better to be a shit. That would only last for the few hours he'd be gone tonight.

*   *   *

Clara was not understanding.

"Honey, listen. This is an old buddy from school. I bumped into him when I was shooting this morning with that lousy rented camera."

"Then why can't I go too?"

"He has this thing about women."

"What thing?"

"Well, he feels they're a distraction."

"I certainly hope so."

Clara folded her arms, and if she were ten again, she would have stamped her feet before using her final weapon, tears. Now, she just glared, lasering her annoyance at Jack, out of eyes that were both frightened, and furious.

Stomping off to the shower, she angrily ruminated over the scene with Jack. How could he do this! With the hot water kneading her strained muscles, she began to cry. It wasn't like Jack. He always put her first. Something was wrong. Her melting anger was replaced by fear. Quickly toweling herself, she grabbed a robe and padded into the living room.

Aaron stood near the terrace doors, a piece of paper in his hand.

"How did you get in here?"

He turned to her, charming, with a smile that could send the top billing ad agency rushing for a contract.

"I just wanted to see how you and Jack were getting along."

Shit! How could he be so ingenuous? It was tough to stay incensed at him.

"Your door was open. So, when nobody answered my knock, I'm afraid I took the liberty of just walking in. I really didn't think either of you would mind."

Handing her the paper, he continued: "Since it looks as if you're going to be alone for dinner, please join me. I promise I'll get you back by ten."

She looked at the note. "Sweet thing…since I wasn't sure I could find Maxie's, I left a few minutes early. Promise to be back by ten. Love you."

Such waves of annoyance engulfed her that she wished Jack was here just so she could throw something at him. She didn't want him to be hurt, just miserably uncomfortable. Great mounds of spaghetti, sticky with tomatoes and cheese, clingy custard pie, faintly rancid, and just a tad undercooked. A nice, trashy, but colorful mess.

Aaron, redolent with confidence and sophistication, was describing some paradigm of culinary adventure. Obviously, her life would be incomplete if she didn't sample its pleasures tonight. Exasperated with herself, and angry with Jack, she agreed to have dinner. Pavlov's dog must have felt that way. Irritated at salivating whenever that goddamn bell rang, but nothing else to do.

Furiously dressing, it wasn't until she ripped her third pair of panty hose that she realized why she was so annoyed. Damn Aaron! He was the first to know that Jack had really gone on without her. She felt exposed, her store of privacy vastly depleted. Oh, hell! So she'd waste an evening with Adonis. It was still a better alternative than hysterically pacing the floor until Jack's return.

From sparkling Bahamian sunlight, Jack plunged into the murky obscurity of Maxies's. The bar scene had never been one of his recreations. At best, he found the most elegant ones depressing. Maxie's was certainly not the best. The miasma from a million carcinogenic cigarettes soon attacked Jack's nostrils. Something is wrong with the ventilation. "Fuck!" thought Jack, as he coughed his way to the bar. There *is* no ventilation. No windows. Must be some law that says bars can't have them. No air-conditioning. As he desperately tried to expand his lungs against the heavy effluvium, he searched for the stage. His burning eyes accommodated to the darkness, and he began to thread his way through closely packed tables.

"Jack! You old bastard."

Had to be that CIA asshole. The voice was a bit raspy. Most likely the result of hanging around smoke-filled bars. Must be the only people around who thought it was macho to refer to friends as bastards. Jack grinned as he reflected that maybe that was the only noun that really described agency people.

He turned toward the sound of the voice, vainly trying to orient himself in the vaguely lit bistro.

"Over here."

He thought he saw a flash of light as a shape, probably a hand, waved near a candle. He veered in that direction. Approaching what he assumed to be the appropriate table, he cursed when his shin banged into a chair.

As he tenderly massaged his injury, that galling voice continued. "Goddamn it, same old Jack. Just as clumsy as you were in college."

The laughter that followed was so irritating that Jack thought his entire spinal column was being abraded with coarse sandpaper.

"Why don't you shut up, you putz."

253

"Huh?"

"'Putz', it's a complimentary Yiddish term."

"Listen Stanger, just talk quietly, fast, and smile a lot."

"Smile? What the hell for?"

The agent leaned across the rickety table and gripped Jack's arm. "You idiot, so they'll think we're happy to see each other—old college pals. Remember the scenario?"

"Who can see in this cesspool?"

"That's part of the cover." As the agent said that, Jack sensed the self-satisfied smirk on his face.

"Stanger, you can unload now. This place is perfectly safe. It's checked out constantly."

"Oh, great, and all the locals can sell tickets while you CIA nuts run around looking for hidden microphones in the ashtrays."

"You asked for help, shithead. I wasn't just waiting around here hoping a Boy Scout like you would turn up. I have a few other things to do, you know. Now wipe your ass and start talking."

Controlling his rancor, Jack chronicled the events.

"Terrific! A real bunch of crap. It was boring, Stanger. You can't even tell a good story."

Jack could never remember feeling more furious. He wanted to punch this creep's face out. If only he could find him in this lousy sewer. He had nothing to say to this lout, calling himself Bruce Rand. No words, no logic, no remonstrances. Just a kick in the balls would be relevant right now.

Stumbling out into the moonlit night, Jack's lungs gratefully sucked in air uncontaminated by cigarettes. As he started back to the hotel be began to feel better. He had a plan.

The voice was pleasant, and as Rand reported on the meeting to his superior, his phrases were concise. There was none of the raspingness he'd affected in Maxie's. "The subject was so provoked that he will not be likely to investigate on his own. We can run him with a loose tail, and pick up on whatever he finds. That way, we won't have to risk an operative."

Clara was exhausted. Such an expenditure of energy being charming and yet distant. Subtly, she let innuendoes establish that she was friendly, but not amorous toward Aaron. Why was it so hard for her to tell Aaron she'd rather wait at the hotel for Jack? People were always asking her to do things she didn't want to do. Maybe she ought to head for the nearest shrink when she got home.

She fumbled with her key in the lock. The door was suddenly pulled open, and she found herself in Jack's arms.

"Clara, I'm sorry. I met this guy from school, and I couldn't say 'no' to him. He was all alone."

"Seems like neither of us can say no. I had dinner with Aaron."

"Well?"

"What do you mean, 'well'? Well, did I have a good time while you were gallivanting around bars being macho man? Or, well, did I find out just who or what Aaron is? Or, well did he sweep me off my feet, and I went to bed with him?"

She flopped on the couch.

As Jack approached, she pulled her feet up, wrapping her arms around her knees.

"You're glowering."

Jack sat down. He searched through the mass of blond hair, and when he located her ear, whispered, "I can tell you're glowering because of the steam escaping through your ears."

"I'm not mad at you."

"I would never have guessed."

"I mean, I'm not mad at you anymore."

"Ah ha! So, you *were* mad at me."

"I know you had to go out with that guy. I was just pissed at the timing. It's okay back in Miami, but not here. I needed you."

"I know, honey."

He tried to put his arm around her, but she was a compact ball, enveloped in white satin, without handles. He wanted to have sex with her, right there on the couch, but she was hard to approach without feeling clumsy.

"Do you unfold?"

Jack was heartened by the giggle he heard.

"I'll tell you, I can unfold, if I know we're going home soon—like tomorrow."

Uncoiling her legs, she turned to Jack and took his hand. "This was not one of your better ideas. Staying here to finish out our vacation. Yeech! Let's get back to Miami. "We can spend the rest of the time playing tourist there. Even check into one of those garish edifices they've cluttered up Collins Avenue with. We can stay in bed and have room service. When you are satiated, we can wander through the Parrot Jungle. Okay?"

"Okay, hon. I'll call the airlines first thing in the morning, but don't get your hopes up. We probably won't be able to get out right away. This is prime time down here. Should be able to get something in the next couple of days, though." That would give him enough time to do what he needed to, Jack thought. I'll show that CIA boob.

Come up with something concrete, but get it right to Carl, and let him decide what to do with it.

Jack gave her a long, warm, wet kiss. She met his tongue with hers, and she knew what was planned for the next couple of hours. She didn't feel romantic. Sure, she forgave Jack, but she was still uptight over the stress of his leaving her in Aaron's hands. She thought, I'm not going to be aroused, and if I get aroused, I know I won't come. Clara's sense of honor would never let her fake an orgasm and she knew that when it was over, he would take it as a personal failure, and she would feel the same about herself.

"Maybe we ought to hold off for a while, Jack. I'm still a bit tense."

"I'll give you a rubdown. That always calms you down."

Jack started with her feet, slowly massaging away the tension in her muscles. He then kneaded her calves until she was so relaxed she was falling asleep. When he reached her thighs, she woke up again. Her inner thighs were her most sensitive erogenous zone, and soon her juices were flowing. When Jack finally entered her she was well lubricated, and she surprised herself with orgasm after orgasm.

Jack spent much of his time at poolside perfecting his tan. Clara loved the outdoors, but her fair skin didn't tolerate the sun. The thought of those penetrating ultra-violet rays cross-linking the collagen molecules in her dermis with the resultant aging appalled her. When she couldn't avoid the sun, she covered herself with a sunscreen lotion. So, Jack left Clara dozing in their air-conditioned room. He had been lying motionless for about fifteen minutes and was just considering baking the other side when he heard a clatter next to him. Raising one eyelid, he made out the shape of a trim blonde stretching herself on the adjoining chaise. Beginning at her toes, the young woman methodically applied a heavy coat of grease.

When she saw his eyes flutter open, she swooped. "Hey, I'm sorry. Was this taken?" She indicated the lounge that she occupied.

"No."

Jack turned his face to the other side, settling in to let the sun bake away his anxieties.

The girl frowned, while the Barbie-doll look in her eyes briefly lifted to reveal sagacity.

A seasoned angler, she carefully threw her next line. "Listen, I didn't pick this particular lounge chair by accident, you know."

Shaking off his torpor, Jack turned back to face the blonde.

Now that she had some of his attention, she continued. "Just look around. You are the only single-looking man in this whole goddamn beach. All you see are couples."

Jack sat up, smiling at her. "You really know how to snow a guy, don't you?"

"Well, three days here, and I'm getting desperate."

Resuming her grease application, she lifted the string of her bikini bottom and languidly applied the oil to her groin— clearly conscious of Jack's eyes.

"That won't help."

"Pardon?" she said, one eyebrow disappearing beneath the shock of hair waving over her forehead.

"It's not going to protect your skin from burning, and it's not going to make your tan any tanner."

"Are you a suntan expert?"

"I'm a close friend of a physician who is, and I have been lectured on the matter incessantly."

"Well then, Mr. Close-friend-of-an-expert, what do you recommend?"

Jack reached beneath his chair and brought up a small bottle of lotion with a large 25 SPF. "It'll take a hell of a long time to tan with this stuff, but you won't burn."

She flopped over and deftly undid her top." Would you mind lending a hand?"

"A pleasure! I, by the way, am Jack Stanger."

"Hi, Jack Stanger, I'm Cathy Slade," she mumbled, her chin resting in the crook of her elbow.

As Jack obligingly applied the lotion to her back, he observed that although both Cathy and Clara shared blond hair, Cathy had a lithe body, which was almost the antithesis of Clara's.

"Do you come down here often?"

She nodded her head. "No, as a matter of fact, this is my first time in the Bahamas, and I'm not exactly thrilled with it."

"How come? There's this great beach, nice hotels, it's always sunny, never rains, and there are magnificent reefs if you're into diving. There's also a plethora of good food."

"Well, maybe it's because I'm really working now."

Jack stopped oiling to ask, "Who's your employer, and does he need another hired hand?"

"*People Magazine* owns me, but right now I'm scratching up some local color copy."

"That's hardly reason to get turned off on the Bahamas."

After a pause, she leaned closer to Jack, and said huskily, "I think Nassau's looking a little better."

Lying on her side, she positioned herself so that her nipples were now barely covered by her top. With so little time, she had to be obvious, and a sunlit Bahamian beach was a good setting for a little blatancy. It was apparent that coyness was not going to entice him.

Brushing an ant off his leg, she queried, "What are you doing down here, Jack? Pleasure?"

"Yeah! I'm here for the diving and some rest."

"And what do you do when you're not diving or resting?"

"Hmmm?"

"I mean, what do you do in civilian life? You know, back in Chicago, or Poughkeepsie, or wherever you come from."

"Just a country boy from Miami. I'm a free-lance photographer."

Sitting up, she clapped her hands. "Ahah! I knew we had a lot in common. I'm a writer, and you're a photographer. Let's go share a drink or something. You are alone, aren't you?" Cathy added as an afterthought.

Jack shook his head. "I'm here with my fiancée."

"Do you realize that you've just spoiled a fantastic relationship?"

"I know, I know," he laughed. "But, listen, you're such a sharp gal that I can't let you get out of my life without a drink." He signaled to one of the beach boys. "What would you like?"

"Well, since it's our first and last drink together, I'll just have whatever you is having."

"Two Pina Coladas."

As they sipped the thick, sweet beverage, Jack asked, "Why do you have to get a lot of atmospheric stuff on Nassau? That doesn't sound like something *People Magazine* would be willing to let a reporter pad an expense account for? I'm sure the travel editor has done and redone it to death."

"You're right. The local color is for a background on a feature piece. I scrounged a commission from *Harper's* to do an article on the President of Ubanga, and while I was here, I thought I'd plug in some human-interest stuff on the luxurious life of Paradise Island. Kind of tie it in for contrast with the carnage in my story."

"Carnage? What carnage?"

Cathy stared incredulously, while Jack grew defensive.

"I haven't seen the newspapers lately, but I thought I saw some headlines mentioning President Salazar being down here."

"You're kidding," Cathy's eyes widened. "He was just assassinated. It was incredible. I couldn't believe it. I managed to sneak on board with my *People's* ID. For some obscure reason, none of the magazine people were allowed on board. There was this little tin creep puffing himself up. Talking about alliance with our friends, the Iraqis, for the good of our country and all that old shit."

Cathy took a breath before plunging on. "Some crackpot had put a bomb on Ubanga's only naval vessel, and blew him and his crew to pieces."

"That's wild. Did you see the blast?"

"We were returning to shore in a launch, and just far away enough so that all we saw was a flash on the horizon." Cathy began to munch on the orange slice that had decorated her drink. "Later, the whole group of us journalists were rounded up and questioned for hours. I guess the Bahamians thought one of us could have planted the bomb."

Cathy had become very quiet. What a lousy experience. His gentle nature wanted desperately to cheer her up. Again summoning the beach boy, Jack ordered a couple of hamburgers and French-fries. Maybe food would lift her spirits. It always worked with Clara.

Chewing away at her sandwich, Cathy brightened again. She acted as if she were entranced with Jack. Subtly questioning him, she never seemed to tire of hearing details about his work and personal life.

Finally, Jack said, "listen Cathy, I'm really sorry, but I have to get on up to my room."

"I know, you're an engaged man."

"You're a lovely lady, and if I wasn't almost married, I'd show you around this place."

"I guess that's better than nothing," she sighed.

As he walked toward the hotel, she yelled, "If you see any single men, send them on down, but under fifty and no paunches, please."

Turning, he waved at her. Continuing up the beach, he mused that she had learned more about him than he knew about her.

The "DO NOT DISTURB" sign was still on their door. Clara was probably sleeping. She was so used to her sleep being broken that when she had a chance to get away from the phone, she seemed to sack out for a couple of eternities. He entered the room quietly. As he approached the bed he saw a large, stagnant lump under the covers. As he came even nearer, the lump stirred, and one long, slender white arm reached out and hugged the pillow.

"Clara," he whispered.

"Hmmm?"

"You still asleep?"

"Tired," came her muffled reply.

"Listen, go ahead and get some more shuteye. I'll go down to the bar and fatten up on Pina Coladas."

A few fingers waved as she settled back into her previous level of coma.

The dark, cool bar was almost empty. Most of the vacationers had forsaken its rich mahogany for the sun. He was glad to be alone.

Even before his drink arrived, he found himself making mental flow sheets. That CIA dude thought there was nothing unusual in his narrative. Shit! He had enough of the reporter in him to know something bizarre was going on. There was a hell of a lot of questions. Why was their processor on an armed vessel? Only under very unusual circumstance would a private American corporation own fully automatic weapons. There were other irritating things that kept cropping up in his mind. Did he really believe their story about why they couldn't use commercial divers? Surely there were plenty of reputable diving outfits around. A big fancy corporation would logically use one of them rather than waste a chance on amateurs bungling a salvage operation. There were two other things that really made him sweat. That minuscule cay was a damn funny place to put a warehouse. No boat with a decent draft could reach that small dock, and a little rain, much less a class I hurricane, would put that entire island under water. Stirring the heavy mixture, he agonized over why they were paid in greenbacks, no less. No check and no receipt asked for. How the hell were they going to declare it as a business expense? As he drained his drink, he pondered over the fact that he had never heard of Electronics Investments Incorporated. He had a few connections among the select coterie of investment analysts. He could spend the next half-hour or so on the horn, and try to find out about this company. That could, at least, tell him something concrete. If there was a real story here, it could be worth a mint to some news syndicate. Jack was not a greedy man, and normally the fat fee he had collected would be more than adequate compensation for his time and energy, but his curiosity was piqued. He hated being lied to, and he was both angered, and frustrated, by his encounter with the CIA.

He had never been in a position where he had laid his life on the line. There was that incident with the police out on the water, but that couldn't be called a voluntary commitment. He had spent his year in Vietnam, but that was 1970, in an engineering battalion. The only danger he faced then was boredom. Somehow, they never saw real action. Most of the time he was stationed in Cam Rahn Bay, a rear echelon, if any place could be called that in that war.

Whatever was in that box they raised was worth much effort and money. All these things compelled him to investigate further.

Clara didn't awaken until the afternoon. As she staggered into the bathroom, her half-opened eyes found a note taped to the mirror. "Clara. Can't find any such stock as Electronics Investments Incorporated. Seems strange to me that a company can have enough R & D to beat out the big boys, like IBM, and yet be too small to be even listed on the NASDAQ. Gone for a look into the contents of that box. Don't wait for me for dinner. Gorge without me and I'll grab a sandwich when I get home, though it may be a couple of days."

*   *   *

The midday sun blazed as Jack climbed the long, arching bridge between Paradise Island and New Providence. There was no shade. There was the bone white bridge, the bright reflecting water, and the pastel buildings in the distance. All this contributed to the sensation of walking into Dante's Inferno.

Commercial fishermen mostly used the Nassau Wharf. Here and there the commercial boats were separated by a lone pleasure craft. His eyes scanned each craft in turn, on the lookout for a "FOR SALE" sign.

When he returned to the states, he would leisurely shop for a nice cruiser. Maybe a Bertram, or a Hatteras, big enough to take him and his diving gear wherever he wanted to go comfortably, but small enough so that it would be handled easily with a one or two-man crew. Right now he had different requirements. The deal would be a hurried one. It would have to be made today. That shed was certainly not the final resting-place for that chest, and he had to get there before it was moved. The waters in this area were treacherous. This part of the world had the deepest point in the Atlantic Ocean; the tongue of the ocean, seven and one-half miles deep. A nice big "V" hulled cruiser would be a great comfort in a rough sea, but he was not an old hand in these waters, and would find much of the area blocked by shallow reefs. There was little doubt that he would have to settle for a small, shallow draft boat, and sacrifice stability if he was to do any exploring and be freed of the anxiety of running around on the reef. Besides, there were the financial restraints.

The tide was out, and lying at the shallows, half on its side, was a sixteen-foot Fibercraft Open Fisherman. The hull seemed sound, but sorely needed paint. The fifty-five-horse power Evinrude at the stern seemed well cared for on the outside, but the inside was the only thing that mattered. Shallow draft it was, but it was a bit smaller than he bargained for.

Twenty minutes after calling the number on the For Sale sign, he was talking to Mr. George Stern at the dockside. At first he couldn't make out whether he was talking to a Bahamian or a weather-beaten Yankee whose skin had never seen shade. His speech was that of a man who had spent most, but not all, of his life in the Bahamas.

"Oh, I know it don't look too glamorous lying on its rub rail like that. The tide is at its low, and in a few hours she float free. They don't charge me nothin' for tyin' her up here. She needs paint, mon, and her bottom's not cleaned, but she's seaworthy."

Jack knew his limitations. He felt like an idiot, buying a second-hand boat without using a marine surveyor, but the fewer people who knew about his purchase the better. He tried to look savvy as he went over the hull with his pocketknife, looking for soft spots. Next he examined the transom and stem for dry rot. The wiring was a bit brittle, but appeared to have some life in her yet. A layer of oil puddled around the engine mounts, but at least there was no visible leak. The fittings were secured with stainless steel bolts rather than screws, a reassuring sign that there was some care in her construction.

269

"Mr. Stern, it looks like it will float, but I'm not sure it will do much else."

"The only way your go'n to know is to come back in an hour. She'll be afloat then, and I'll take you on a sea trial."

Jack spent the next hour nervously wandering through the stores on Bay Street. The hour crept past and finally Jack was at the helm, cautiously guiding the boat around the bay.

"She handles OK, but can I rely on that engine? It looks like she leaks oil. I don't care to be out in the middle of the Caribbean without power."

"Now don't you worry nothin' about that, mon. I just got clumsy and spilled some oil. Here's a receipt showin' that I just had that motor overhauled just six months ago. The boat, she has no leaks, and you got a real reliable engine. What more can a mon want out of life."

Then followed the usual dickering, a skill that Jack felt he had never developed, and they finally compromised at fifteen hundred dollars. This just about maxed out his American Express.

The ease and low price for which Jack acquired the boat caused him a bit of concern. This was a single engine craft. Gone was the security of his old twin engine boat. Jack was a poor mechanic, especially around marine engines, so it was not uncommon for him to limp into harbor on one engine. Now that insurance was gone. One factor was working for him. The weather for the next few days was favorable for small craft.

The next step was to visit a marine supply shop. The boat was already equipped with an oversized fuel tank, but he was going to add a couple more. There would be little room for him, and certainly no comfort except for the shade from a Bimini top. Just in case he didn't find his destination the first day out, he also bought camping supplies, a sleeping bag and some canned goods. Jack also acquired a chart of the area.

At 5 a.m. the bleach-white streets were deserted. The coal-black African with her Gauguin-colored costume was still home. Her corner of the City Square was still awaiting her stacks of intricately woven dolls, hats, and baskets. The horse-drawn carriages would find no tourists at this hour, and automobiles were few in number at any time. Only the wharf was teeming with people. Fishermen casting off for the day's run, and last among them, Jack loading provisions. The engine started without a cough and the small boat planed smoothly through the light chop of the inland water. Confidence quickly turned to concern as the low waves were replaced by the long, high swells of the open sea.

He pointed the bow straight into the swells, and gritted his teeth. Just one swell catching him broadside was all that was needed to swamp his boat.

The Exuma Cays were only a few miles southeast of Nassau, but there were hundreds of these small islands, and every one looked alike. He spent the day searching for signs of habitation, while at night he was moored to mangrove, fighting mosquitoes. Late on the third day, as he cut close to one of many identical little islands, he spotted the familiar dock. The light was getting poor, but this was actually to his advantage as he remembered those goons with the big .45s.

He moored his boat to a tree one hundred feet south of the dock, and carefully waded in knee -deep water until he reached the dock and the path leading inland. Except for his training in the army, he was a stranger to firearms, but this time he felt naked without anything except his machete. It had not taken him long to discover that Bahamians have extremely strict gun licensing regulations. He had found it impossible to buy even a rifle, at any price, at short notice.

There was no sign of any guards, and Jack reached the storage shed without difficulty. The padlock was sturdy, but the sea had taken its toll on the doorframe. A few minutes later, he'd pried the hasp away from the door with the machete and slid the door open. The crate looked formidable. It appeared to be heavy steel. Jack was quite surprised that it took only a few exploratory jabs with his machete under the lock to reach metal that proved to be very soft. But then it took more than an hour to pry the lock away from the lead in which it was imbedded. The cover was extremely heavy, and it took several attempts before he could muster enough strength to swing the lid back. Inside he found another metal container. The light was dim, but he could just make out a large label with no words, consisting of three orange rays arranged symmetrically around an orange disc —the universal warning that the contents were radioactive.

CHAPTER VII

Death: A black camel which kneels

at the gates of all.

Abd-El Kader

Annoyed with her penchant for sleeping, Clara crumpled Jack's note. If only she'd been awake when he'd come back, maybe she could have stopped him, or at least gone with him. Damn! She was almost Olympic quality, a real laureate in snoozing. Irritable and groggy, she squirted toothpaste in the vicinity of her toothbrush.

Brutally stabbing at her gums, she continued to harangue herself for not being clairvoyant enough to stop Jack. She'd never felt such anguish for him, not even when he was hanging by a ladder from a helicopter, taking the background shots on some idiotic fashion layout.

She quickly dressed and ran down to the lobby. Once there, her purpose dissipated. Who could she ask? Where could she look? Dispirited, she sat down on the nearest chair, a massive, overstuffed creation with orange and pink flowers. Its flowery exuberance did nothing to lift her mood.

She thought of going back to her room, but five minutes alone with her fears, and she'd probably tear the furniture to shreds.

Walking! Maybe that would help. As she rose from her chair, she saw Aaron come striding through the lobby. If only she could vanish. Before she could figure out which direction to flee, Aaron's effusive hello was hammering at her ears. She really hated him. Her helplessness turned into a frenzy of hatred. At least it was a more constructive emotion. There he was, Herculean in his golden tan, blue eyes sparkling, dashing in his cream-colored slacks and expensive sport shirt. Perfectly tailored. She despised him. Other women stared as he strode through the lobby and envied her as he took her arm. She just wanted to shriek and pummel him furiously. If not for this flawlessly handsome bastard, Jack would he at her side.

"The Bahamas are really agreeing with you. You look even more beautiful than when we pulled you out of the sea."

Dutifully chuckling, she plastered a smile on her face. It won't help to call him names. She could hear her mother back in Miami chiding that honey catches more flies than vinegar, so she bantered with him. "What are you doing here?"

"Had to meet a business associate nearby, so I thought I'd stop over and see how you two were doing."

"We're fine, Aaron."

"Good. You know, I'd like to take you both out for an evening before you leave."

"That's really not necessary, Aaron." Oh God, she was sounding cold. There was no motivation for her being aloof to Aaron. After all, he had saved her life, and just bestowed a nice hunk of money on her. Think, she railed at herself. Be a typical blond twit. Be Grateful and friendly. Hide the hysterical worry about Jack.

"I mean," she smiled glowingly at Aaron, "it's not necessary for you to take time away from your business to entertain Jack and I."

"Oh, but I insist. You've helped us out and now I'd like to spend a little time with you."

"That's so kind of you," she gushed.

From the periphery of her vision, she could see a trio of post-adolescent knock-outs eyeing Aaron with the intensity of sharks, teeth fully bared.

"But we have to get back to work. So, we're trying to leave tomorrow."

"What about tonight?"

Think, Clara. Make excuses.

"Well, the only problem is that Jack met an old college buddy. So, they're off somewhere. They mumbled something about getting a boat and maybe going night fishing, or night diving, or something."

"Well then, that's perfect," he beamed. "We can spend the evening together."

Oh shit! What an idiot. Really walked into that one. But, she had to find a way to explain Jack's absence.

Numbly, she smiled and nodded her head.

"I'll call you later and we'll set a time."

He took her arm, pulling her close. "Wear something beautiful just for me, Clara."

The rest of the day was spent in her room awaiting word from Jack, and dreading the call from Aaron.

Her concern for Jack coupled with the distrust and loathing she felt about Aaron made her anxious to avoid this encounter. Being totally unskilled in the art of the devious, she couldn't find a comfortable way of evading

276

him. She had to answer the phone. What if Jack was calling? Damn, she missed her answering machine. When she heard Aaron's voice, she pleaded a flu-like illness. His rejoinder was, "Great!" They could have dinner *a deux* in her room. "How marvelous!" she choked. She managed to dissemble that getting dressed, and having dinner downstairs might be more therapeutic.

Aaron took her to a predictably fabulous place for dinner, after first stopping at a romantic, plant-stuffed bar for drinks.

Over dinner, while he told her droll anecdotes of his world travels, she acted impressed. When Jack's name came up, she prayed that she was a good enough actor. Did he note the concern in her voice? No. She could always cover it up with a giggle, and he'd think it was normal female nervousness caused by a date with Aaron the Urbane.

He held her hands, gazed longingly into her eyes, and whispered, "I'd really like to see you in Miami." As she started to sputter, he smiled tenderly and continued, "I know. You're engaged, but we could certainly be friends."

Almost deranged with worry, she composed herself enough to beam at Aaron.

Midway through the entrée, she insinuated a few flu symptoms, such as headache, and muscle discomfort. She was able to end the evening early, but with promises to get together in Miami.

Once in her bed, she lay awake thinking of all the combinations and permutations of possible fates that Jack met. What was her next move? There was no trusted friend from whom she might get assistance. Gone was the confidence that was her cloak as a physician. Now, she was a lone woman in a strange land. Someone's life may depend on her next move, and all of her training as a physician was not worth a hill of beans here. She was not about to buy a boat for herself. She did not have the nautical skills to maneuver a boat through narrow, shallow channels. Whenever she went boating, it was always as a passenger. On occasion she would be asked to hold a line, or tie a line to something, or untie a line from something else.

That morning she took a taxi to Coral Harbor. There was less chance of her being seen than in the more public Nassau Harbor. Charter boats were plentiful, and she slowly walked along the pier, looking for one that was tailored to her needs. The boat had to be large enough to carry adequate food and fuel for several days at sea, but small enough to be both inconspicuous, and have a shallow draft.

CHAPTER VIII

The sea drowns out humanity and time;

it has no sympathy with either,

for it belongs to eternity,

*and of that it sings its monotonous sound for ever
and ever.*

Oliver Wendell Holmes

A youngish blonde, slender and long-legged, strolled to the rear of the lobby of the Royal Hotel. Walking past the passenger elevator, Cathy entered the large grimy freight elevator. The walls were covered with protective padding, and the floor was scuffed and dirty. She removed a small key from her purse and inserted it into the fireman's access lock in the button panel. She next pressed two keys simultaneously, "EMERGENCY STOP" and "OPEN DOOR." Every time she went through this hokey maneuver, she would almost laugh out loud. She could not get out of her mind that old TV spy spoof, *Get Smart*. The doors closed and the elevator descended.

The room was small, measuring perhaps six by eight feet. Cathy's walk-in closet was a bit larger than this office space. The office was crowded with a couple of folding chairs, an old rusty steel desk, and a rather beaten up, corroded file cabinet. Furniture did not last long in rooms below the water table. An old, gray-skinned man with matching gray hair and gray beard sat behind the desk. It seemed doubtful that he ever left the desk. His skin never saw sunlight. Perhaps he left his position for the usual calls of nature or to get a bite to eat. More likely he didn't have those kinds of needs.

"Hello, Cathy. What have you found out about this Jack Stanger?"

"Freelance photographer, just like he claims. I suspect it's a cover. I've asked him repeatedly what he's doing in the Bahamas, and he either evades my questions or he lies. Why would he do that if he were an innocent?"

"The next question is, is he an ally or theirs?"

"I don't know who he belongs to yet. I probably would have gone to bed with him. Not because of duty, mind you. He was just a nice guy, and I liked him. I doubt that making the relationship more intimate was going to make him suddenly open up and confess his mission. He was probably a professional, but it's a moot question now.

"What happened to Mr. Magoto?"

"Magoto got what he deserved, but it got me into hot water. They grilled me for two hours, and checked, and double-checked my connections with *People Magazine*. Sarasohn didn't make it home. As per your orders, I put him away. He died in an explosion in a small private plane. I'm really very sad over this. I never got to bed him."

"Next subject: Let's talk about Clara Weiss, MD?"

"She's a physician, and a member of the Dade County Medical Association. I can't believe she's anything else."

"Well, good hunting. Report back when you have more."

*   *   *

"Hey Harv, there's a dame outside with money looking at your boat. She's talking weekly charter."

Harvey was sitting at the bar with his glass of ice and a bottle of bourbon. A crisis was at hand, now averted by the promise of money. The bourbon was down to the last inch. Harvey Jackson didn't look like the typical charter captain. He lacked the weather-beaten face with its deeply grooved skin. His color wasn't right either. He was pallid, rather than tan. His friends told him that he looked like a Pookah, whatever that meant. It was easy to see that Harvey had not been a seaman for long.

A few years back he had been a lawyer. He was not a big, flashy, trial lawyer, but one of those quiet, competent people who dealt in contracts. Big corporations used him to formulate reams of typewritten paper to protect their interests. Boring it was, but somebody had to do it.

It was not uncommon for him to hold vast sums of money in escrow. His income was well above average, and normally more than adequate for a comfortable standard of living. He suffered, however, from problems that are common to many professionals. Expenses seem to rise with income. Taxes, as we all know, rise faster than income.

Harvey had many friends. There were other lawyers, a few judges, many businessmen, and one or two others in the commodity market. "Listen Harv, I owe you a favor. You really got me out of the soup with the Securities and Exchange Commission. Let me give you a tip that will put you on easy street. The schmucks think that the price of wheat is going to hit rock bottom. All they can see is that gigantic crop coming in, and a limited American market. I've got it straight from friends in Washington that Russia is hurting and they are about to swing a tremendous wheat deal with the good old USA. Buy all you can on margin now. The price is going to climb sky high."

Harvey Jackson wasn't going to let a golden opportunity like this pass. He scrounged up his small savings, borrowed what he could, and bought wheat on margin. The only trouble was that Russia didn't swing that deal until two years later, and it was a bumper crop, and the price of wheat did fall, and his friend kept asking for margin money almost every day. The Russian wheat deal was always just around the corner if he could just hold on. Harvey found himself dipping into his escrow accounts.

The final outcome — disbarment and prison — was unavoidable. When you're released from prison, you start over from scratch. In fact, you start out a little below scratch, because now you have a prison record. So, it's best to plan ahead before going to jail. If you're going to steal, at least keep a cushion for yourself, and with this in mind, a few thousand, remaining in escrow, was hidden away for the future.

It was a first offense, but it was a public trust. The years of confinement passed slowly. Freedom came at last. What remained was the usual claustrophobia of the ex-con. How can one find less confinement than on the open sea?

The money purchased the boat, but not the self-respect or the license to practice law, lost years ago. The bottle brought amnesia, if not esteem.

"Hi, lady. I'm Captain Jackson. I understand you're looking for a boat. I know these waters like my own apartment. You go out with me, and you'll come back with the biggest sailfish you ever saw."

"My name's Clara Weiss. I'm looking for something besides fish. If we make a deal, I'll tell you where I want to go."

"I don't run dope, guns or anything else that can get me into trouble—and that's at any price."

"All I'll tell you is that we're not doing anything illegal. I'll pay for all this mystery by giving you double your regular fee. Just think of this as sailing under sealed orders."

"Let's have an understanding. Those orders become unsealed as soon as we're clear of the harbor, and if I don't like the deal, we turn right around, and you get your money back. The only promise I'll make is that your business is your business, and even if I turn you down, it'll stay that way."

"Fair enough."

"There are a few additional details. We'll have to go to ports for fuel. I don't carry oars on my boat. Thirty feet of boat doesn't row too easy."

Once at sea, she told the captain of their destination.

"You mean you want me to explore the Exuma Cays? There are over a hundred islands out there, and they all look alike."

"This one has a little primitive dock. Part of it has collapsed into the water. I promise you, you pass it and I'll recognize it."

"What's on that island that's so important to you?"

"That's not part of the deal. Let's just say I'm looking for a friend."

They rationed the limited stores of food and water. Plans were to catch fish to supplement their meager supplies.

Charters are extremely competitive in the islands. Stories like Shangri-La, and Bali Hai are in everyone's dreams. Many of us long for the day when we can retire to some island paradise, and use a boat to earn a few dollars for necessities. If you can do it right, you enjoy a life for which normally you would pay dearly. Being the smart guy, this time you are selling. As a result of the market being flooded with amateurs, you can't expect to have a charter every day even during the height of the season. No, the captain had a charter that might last for a week if he had any luck, and he was not about to question her motives too closely.

Three days had passed. They were now into the fourth day. As Clara had hoped, food was not a problem. There were plenty of fish in the sea, but they repeatedly had to make runs into Great Exuma for fuel and water. Each time they made port, Clara would call the hotel desk to find that Jack had neither picked up his messages nor checked out.

She spotted the island on that fourth day. The dock was there with its port side collapsing into the sea over rotted pilings. If she had approached from the opposite direction, she would not have seen the dock, and she would never have recognized the island.

It would be impossible to explain the need for secrecy to the captain. So, she had him set anchor well off shore, and each retired to their separate space to rest. Clara was frightened. Couldn't sleep. Huddled in a corner, her knees drawn up to her chest, she berated herself. What could she find alone? If she found some trace of Jack, could she follow it? Thank God that boat captain looked tough. Must have had his share of barroom brawls. If she found anything, she'd have to tell him at least a little to enlist his aid. Terror shared, can at least be abated. But she realized that telling him was a futile thought born of fear. She should have found some remote phone and called Casey's husband. He knew a lot of influential people and could probably help her find someone down here for some counsel. She rocked with the motion of the boat, a small tight figure, with forlorn strands of blond hair tangling freely in the wind. She had no protection. What a fool. Even if she had thought of a gun while she was looking at boats, she hadn't the slightest idea of how to buy one. She dozed and awakened again as nightfall began to approach.

Uncoiling herself, she walked stiffly to the other end of the boat in search of Harvey Jackson. Shit! As soon as she saw him, she knew his was not the posture of a sleeping man. Sprawled on his back, his legs and arms were so relaxed he could have been a rag doll. One emptied Bourbon bottle lay near him, and another that was rolling near his hand was closer to empty than to full.

Bending over to shake some life back into him, she recoiled as his breath spun out at her. She managed to get him to some state resembling consciousness, and they half-tumbled into the little dinghy. Approaching the dock, Clara shuddered with the realization that she would have to explore that inland path alone.

Dusk is when biting insects swarm, and in the tropics they become particularly annoying. Strangely, it was not mosquitoes that bothered her, but large flies. They were big, what are commonly called horseflies. Their eyes were large, multifaceted green gems, and their bodies were a metallic blue. The farther she went, the denser the fly population and the more numerous were the painful bites. Damp air was heavy with the odor of putrefaction, and perhaps this was what was driving the insects into a swarming, biting frenzy. They probably thought she was another scavenger, a lover of carrion, and they did not want to share their meal.

Being a physician, the sight and odor of blood and tissue never bothered her, but insects were another matter. The flies that buzzed around her disgusted her, and the odor was overpowering.

Parts of the path lay under water; the border delineated by impassable vines and mangrove. There was no choice except to march through ankle-deep water covered with a green scum. Periodically, she would spot some long, living thing snake its way beneath the surface. Every few steps she stopped to retch. An unremitting force urged her to turn back to the boat, away from this miasma. She drew on her last reserves of will to move forward. If there was any chance of helping Jack, she would have to see this to the end.

One last bend in the path and the storehouse came into view. The door was open, and now the origin of the flies was obvious. A partially decayed body lay across the entrance. Extending from his buttocks to his head was a neat row of bullet holes. The last bullet had passed through the back of his head, blowing away the entire face.

Someone was screaming. Someone's agony tore through the trees, vibrating the heavy, humid air. Animals scattered through the underbrush, running from the throat-ripping cries they thought pursued them. Mercifully, the vocal cords were soon too inflamed to sustain such wretched sounds. Now, many minutes later, there was only hoarse sobbing.

Clara lay on a bed of leaves and twigs, gasping at the damp air. It was a long time before she became aware of the pain in her throat, and a longer time until she realized those screams had been hers.

Shivering, although her body was saturated with sweat, she still visualized the storehouse. Even with an unrecognizable face, she knew his clothes; she knew it was Jack's body. She didn't have to search for the scar on his left calf, or the stellate mole on his right wrist. It was some more primitive sense that told her it was Jack. She knew it in the same way that she knew so much of her was now dead. Ants swarmed over her hands, their mandibles vigorously injecting formic acid into her flesh. But those hands must have belonged to someone else, because she felt nothing. She had no thought beyond this moment. Moving from this spot was inconceivable. Was this shock, or simple numbness? Just a few superficial layers of her brain were awake. Emotions, reason, insight; all narcotized.

I will be one with this island and Jack, she thought. I'll stay here. I won't feel hunger or thirst because all the feeling parts of me are gone. I will never move from here.

A frog hopped toward her, his erratic motion like Captain Jackson's drunken attempts to navigate round the boat. My God! The Captain was waiting for her, helpless in his drunken apathy. A deeply imprinted concern for others tried to propel her body. Not a muscle responded. Insistently, the Captain reverberated in her mind like shards of glass being dropped down a circular stairwell. Instincts, training, or whatever had motivated her throughout her medical training made her sit up. Her legs now stretched uncomfortably in front of her. Head hanging limply like some forgotten doll, she watched blood drain slowly from cuts on her ankles. Making no attempt to staunch it, the slender red streams sliced through the dirt on her skin. Somehow muscles played against each other, raising her body, and turning her first faltering steps into purposeful movement.

Lumbering along the path, she plunged through mud puddles; the normal responses that would have guided her around them were absent. Stopping at the fork she had mentally marked on her way into the island, her brain began to focus. The horror of her discovery hit her anew. She froze. Her hands clawed futilely against a giant Mangrove when the emotional part of her brain began to function. As the anesthetizing effect of the numbness began to unwrap itself from her mind, fear quivered through her consciousness. It poured into her arms, coursing into her gut, and down through her legs. It was a psychic sledgehammer to action, a steamroller trying to move her along. At the same time it weakened each muscle until she sank slowly down the trunk of the tree to its roots that held the trunk out of water like a giant hydrophobic spider.

She would not return to Miami. There was no reason to go back. Could she still minister to the sick? Mechanically, she could go through the motions; examine a body, input the data, and out of her brain would flow a logical diagnosis and treatment. What of the art of medicine? The loving mind and hands of the healer come from a balanced, caring physician. She was only a shell who no longer cared. She willed her body to merge with the dead leaves beneath her. She wanted to be with Jack. Yet, the fear insistently throbbing in her head demanded that she move; fear that blended into a concern for herself and a concern for the captain.

Her progression was slow until she plunged into the cool water. Now awakened, she began to swim with maximum effort. Along with washing away the sweat, the

water cleared some of her frenzy, allowing her to seize
fragments of calmness.

Several yards distant, Clara near-sightedly
squinted at an object. It floated so serenely that she felt
no fear in approaching it, only curiosity. A few more feet
and she realized it was a man. With horror she continued
her slow crawl; knowing even though it was face down in
the water that it had to be the captain. Beyond terror, she
moved slowly toward his body. She was now a clinician,
closing in to ascertain the cause of death. It was not
difficult. She rolled him over to find an entrance wound
clearly visible a few centimeters to the left of the sternum,
and another small hole through the right eye.

The cruiser had been anchored at least one
hundred yards from the island, a difficult distance even
for a good swimmer who was husbanding her strength.
This time, the fates favored her, and a following current
allowed her to reach the boat.

Her knuckles whitened as she grasped the ladder,
preparing to climb aboard. Then she stiffened. Perhaps
the boat wasn't empty. Where was the killer? Was he on
the island, or was he on board? She waited silently,
listening for any footsteps or conversation. All that could
be heard was the lapping of the water against the hull, and
her own tortured breathing. If he was on the boat, he most
certainly could hear her noisy approach, but then her only
move could be to swim, against the current, back to that
terrible island. Slowly she climbed the ladder. As her
head became level with the top of the gunwale, she
expected some heavy, blunt object to come crashing down
on her, or some hideous monster to reach over and sink its

talons in her throat. She was finally able to see into the boat. An expanse of deck lay before her. An empty deck with a deserted helm slowly rocked in the gentle sea.

The right side of the windscreen was shattered. Flecks of blood covered the windscreen. Here and there, there were particles of pink jelly that she was certain were brain.

The keys had been left in the ignition and soon the twin diesels roared into life. The first few minutes were occupied in just increasing the distance between her and the island. When she had regained some semblance of calm, she throttled back and put the engines in neutral. She couldn't just plow ahead until she rammed into a reef.

A decision would have to be made regarding destination. The easiest island to reach would be Great Exuma. Once there, where could she go? Perhaps there was no air service. Nassau was close, but the boat was known. There was nobody there she could trust. How could she explain the fate of the captain and Jack to the police who sank their boat?

Miami was home, and she knew that if she just kept a compass bearing of northwest, she would have to hit the southern tip of Florida. Between her and home was the Great Bahama Bank. She was facing thousands of square miles of shallow water. In many areas the depth was less than a foot. It would be madness for an amateur to navigate that in the dark.

Clara switched on the "fish finder." Its little green marker showed her depth to be only six feet. Slowly she moved the throttles forward, and then steered due east, away from the United States, away from home. She watched the indicator intently. With no land in sight, the little green dot would float down to three feet. Clara would slow the engines, and as they crept ahead, the dot would change direction and move back up to six feet. After an hour of inching along, backing away from vast shallow areas to try new directions, the little green dot rose off the scale. Now she knew she was in depths greater than twenty-five hundred feet. This was the deepest part of the Atlantic Ocean.

The little boat climbed the wall of one swell to rush down the deep valley behind it. She turned in the general direction of northwest, trying to keep that little green dot on the scale, and the boat away from the open sea. The trick now was to keep out of the real deep water, and yet not let the boat creep back in the shallows. As daylight approached, she directed the boat due West. The shallows were at port, and the deeps at starboard. This had to be the Northwest Providence channel. Westward had to be South Florida's Delray Beach.

Eight hours later, with fuel gauges nearing the empty marks, Clara passed under a double leaf drawbridge to enter the inland waterway. A few hours south, and many bridges later, brought into sight the familiar skyline of Miami Beach.

CHAPTER IX

It is waste —

and worse than a waste—

of effort to ignore the element of brutality

because of the repugnance it excites.

Von Clausewitz

The room in which the three men talked was spacious. Aaron estimated the dimensions at more than thirty by fifty feet. This was a totally obscene amount of space for an office. It reminded him of Hitler's massive room; designed to intimidate the visitor who was dwarfed by its elephantine dimensions.

The boss's desk was on a low dais in one corner. Even though you stood on the hard white marble floor, and he was sitting, you were forced to look up at him. There was no carpet, and no other furniture. Within ten minutes the floor's cold hardness traveled up your feet until your knees hurt. This ploy worked only the first time. Aaron was careful to keep a pair of Nikes in his desk drawer. He would don them before each meeting. The red and white shoes were a sore point with the Director, but Aaron didn't give a flying fuck.

The stark white marble floor contrasted with a wall of dark cherry wood bookcases that went from floor to sixteen-foot ceiling. There was no ladder, so the upper shelved books were just for show. Perusal of the lower shelves gave one an insight into the owner's basic character. There was Karl von Clausewitz's *On War,* TE Lawrence's' *Seven Pillars of Wisdom,* Chun's *Tae Kwon Do.* Every book was on war, or martial arts, or weaponry. This man was focused.

The other walls were covered with weapons. This was a museum quality collection under sheets of glass. The North wall began with flint head arrows and war clubs, and ended with pikes, broad swords, and maces. Gun powder was discovered on the east wall beginning with matchlocks, moving on to flintlocks, and ending with the old western six shot repeater and the Winchester lever action. The final part of the collection was on the south wall. It began with the First World War rifles, featuring the Springfield, and ended with the epitome of man's barbarity. The final wall was covered with weapons such as the rotary magazine fed shotgun called the "Street Sweeper," the M16 fully automatic carbine, and the shoulder fired ground to air missile, the Stinger. Only the west wall was reserved for books on the science of killing.

The Director always spoke first. "This operation is not what one could call watertight. We have spun a web, which has required patch upon patch—a far cry from your usual performance. I suspect that part of the fault must be laid to you, Draco. If you could keep from becoming romantically involved with the pawns of our little game, I believe we would get into less trouble. Wouldn't you agree?"

The question was rhetorical.

Years of training forced Aaron's silence. Excuses, even if justified, were never acceptable.

"It now remains to clean up the operation," the Director continued.

"Sir, with Stanger out of the picture, there's no other laundering to be done. Sybil is still bitter. She suspects that Mark Sarasohn was one of ours, and that she killed a friendly to obscure the trail. In short, she feels used. A couple of days ago she told me she is planning to resign."

"Draco, her job is to be *used*. She's a big girl now. . Let's see how many years has she been out of nursing? I can just imagine what her résumé will say about these last few years. She'll get over it. Tell her she needs to get back to work. And, oh yes, it is still necessary to caulk the remaining seams."

The Director than turned to the third, rather obese man. Obesity always makes standing a chore. The floor made that chore torture. He shifted from one leg to the other. This only shifted the pain, and leaning against one of the far walls, covered with glass, was unthinkable.

"Arthur, you will of course, continue to assist Draco in this. I do not consider this assignment completed until that doctor has been totally accounted for. She is no longer in the Bahamas. However, she should not be difficult to pinpoint."

"Yes sir. By the way, I suppose the documents that we obtained from Nyuzu have gone through the shredder."

"Ah, yes." Responded the Director. "Those grandiose plans would be an embarrassment to President Magoto. They certainly have *not* seen the shredder. They are safely in my private file cabinet. I wasn't a student of J Edgar's for nothing."

At this point in the conversation, a beautiful brunette entered the room, teetering on three-inch heels. She tried to find partial support against the fragile glass panels of the north wall. Cathy (or was that Sibyl), wore a pained expression as she said, "Excuse me! Is all this violence really sanctioned by the executive branch?"

The Director turned to her with disdain painted across his face. "Miss Rosenthal. I am in the oval office on a weekly basis. The President has the utmost confidence in me, and is well cognizant of the steps we are taking to insure the security of this country."

There was silence in the room, as the Director rested his chin on his hand in an attitude of deep contemplation. If they only knew. His last visit to the Oval Office was with his chief, Casey. That was eight years ago. The Chief is dead, and oh yes, we have a different President. They had formed the Special Branch of the NSA at that time. They made his department independent, living off covert funds from the National Institute of Health. Let's see — I believe that's the last time I ever conferred with a President, or anyone else.

*   *   *

Clara found herself in a small, spartanly furnished office of Customs at the Port of Miami. She had narrowly avoided being cut in two by the bow of the cruise ship *Mardi gras,* and then rammed the dock as she made fast in front of the Bahama Star. Getting ashore proved to be difficult, as the dock was intended as birthing for cruise ships, and stood a good five feet above the deck of her little boat. It took two Customs officers to pull her up to the walkway.

Sitting at the desk, Clara dictated her story to a stenographer. In spite of her agitation, her training enabled her to give a clear, chronological history using an economy of words. She was then given a cup of coffee and asked to wait in an inner office. Hours passed and finally a Customs officer entered.

"Doctor, I don't quite know what to make of your story. We checked you out. OK, you're a doctor. But the rest of your story has holes like Swiss cheese. The Bahamian police say no boat has been reported stolen, and no boat captain is missing. No boat's registered to them that fit the description of that boat you claim to have found on your dive. At our request they flew a chopper over the Exuma Cays, and although there's a small building here and there, there's nothing that fits your story — and certainly no bodies. There is no contraband on your boat, and it seems about all you've arrived with is your crazy tale. I suspect you've been smoking too much Bahamian hash, Doctor. We have no real reason to hold you so please leave before we have to charge you with filing a false report.

During this entire conversation, Clara sat mute. There was nothing she could think to say or to do except to rise wordlessly and leave the building.

*   *   *

It was strange to be alone again. The townhouse wasn't large, but nevertheless had become too huge for her; too empty, too filled with space. If she left a dish in the sink, it stayed. A couple of bras had been strewn on the bathroom floor for two days now.

Without Jack's penchant for keeping things in their places, nothing seemed to get done outside of her practice. For once, Clara hoped her beeper would sound, forcing her to some emergency that would demand her consciousness.

It was all so damn incredible. Just one month ago her constant lament was never having time enough to do what she wanted to. Now time was all she had. Just one month ago she was constantly trying to get out of her office as soon as possible. When the last patient was seen, and the last call made, she'd race out the door, leaving her desk in chaos, and speed home to Jack. Now she didn't know what to do with herself. She felt abandoned, alienated, as if she didn't quite belong in this room or this society. She should have been ended forever in that shed with Jack's body, or maybe by bullets in the water. Oh, shit! She was getting maudlin.

She was losing control, and drifting down a vortex of depression.

She went into the kitchen and slammed the refrigerator door a few times. Kicking her shoes off, she sat at the table, hearing again her own screams when she found Jack. Her eye caught the canister of Jack's granola, and the bottles of Vitamin E that he was sure kept his penis operating at stellar capacity. Upstairs, she sprawled on her bed and hoped to escape into a senseless sleep.

She was on a dive in a huge fish bowl replete with artificial rocks, and a bubbling filter within a little plastic castle. She pressed her face against the glass to look out. All she could see were sharks' jaws circling around. Then she was in the ocean near a remarkably beautiful coral reef. She saw an octopus, and wanting to show off her find, turned to look for her partner. Swimming away from the reef, she searched with a growing sense of anxiety. Her arms and legs became heavy. Suddenly, she felt a crushing pain and turned back to see the jaws of a shark clamped on her left leg. The shark had Aaron's face. The next breath brought not air from her regulator, but a sticky, salted fluid. She spat out the regulator, and blood poured from the mouthpiece. Clara awoke gasping, her clothing drenched, and her mind in fragments.

She wanted to shower, but as she undressed in the bathroom, she felt panic. She was alone.

With her hair washed, in a clean nightgown, a modicum of peace came to her. She went downstairs and poured a large glass of Chablis. Back in bed, she decided to attack the pile of *New England Journals* on her night table. That and the wine should be a great soporific.

It didn't work. She could not recall a word of the last article she read. She put down the journal and began dialing Ben Fishberg's private line. As she heard him answer, she hung up. What was she thinking of? Ben was a fine gentleman. He was a superb physician who often covered for her. She needed advice. Unfortunately, getting that advice would only involve some innocent. No, better to keep Ben, or any other friends out of it. All they could tell her to do would be to go to the police. She ought to be bright enough to get that answer for herself.

Maybe she should go to the police, or the CIA. How do you contact the CIA? Are they in the phone book? Is it under "S" for spies in the Yellow Pages?

"Clara, you are cracking up," she said to her wineglass. "There's no way you can bring him back. There's nothing you can really do except keep you mouth shut from now on."

She must have fallen asleep because that obnoxious digital alarm was pinging away. She turned it off and started her day.

Summer in Miami has often been described as living in a humid oven. When Clara stepped outside to her car, she was greeted by soggy hot air. She settled into the seat of Jack's vintage 240-Z, leaning back cautiously as she met the blazing hot black vinyl of the seats. The clean response of the engine to the tight four-speed gearbox was healing to her haggard mind. Open up the choke, turn the key, and then shift into first.

She needed to drive his car because the automatic transmission in her Jeep made life too simple. Such robotic driving left room for too many painful thoughts. A stop sign. Remember to clutch and brake. Now clutch, and shift into first. As she wove her way to the hospital, Clara fought the desire to feel sorry for herself. Thank God she was a doctor. Being immersed in other people's problems didn't leave a lot of time to think about herself. Just the nights would be bad. With all the lights on, the world contained enough books and journals to hold her together until morning. Catnaps at lunch and between patients would provide all the sleep she needed.

After hospital rounds, she drove to the office. The routine of issuing orders, handling crises, visiting patients, and dealing with their families had stabilized her. She was back on comfortable ground.

Casey regarded Clara with a cool eye. "Well Doc, that was quite a vacation. You have no idea how I had to call everyone on the staff to get the coverage. You owe Dr. Fishberg...." On her way to setting up a brilliant quip, Casey stopped, sensing Clara's wretchedness, her loss of spirit.

Anticipating a joyful account of two lovers in the Caribbean, Anne rapidly approached from the lab, but the aura of depression that emanated from Clara was a palpable barrier. Casey's arms managed to work their way through that unseen bulwark. The next few seconds found them as one huddling mass in the corridor, sharing Clara's tears.

"I'm sorry; I just can't tell you the whole story. Maybe later I can talk."

The waiting room was full and stayed that way through most of the day. The last patient was finally seen. Then Clara whisked away to evening rounds.

While she waited impatiently for an emergency chest x-ray to be developed, a new thought occurred to her; she was stonewalled. Customs had investigated her story, and believed it to be a bizarre fabrication. There were no avenues open to her. If she persisted, all she could accomplish would be an admission to the psychiatric service.

That first week was back-breaking. Everyone's routine physical had been put off until she returned. Many of her ill patients resisted going to her covering physician, preferring to wait for the doctor they knew well. Her day in the office began at 9 a.m., and by skipping lunch, she was able to see her last patient at 7 p.m. Soon, she had a full hospital load and was making 7 a.m. rounds.

Strangely, the world appeared to go on as if Jack never existed. She had never met his family, and their friends always seemed to be her friends. Until now, it hadn't seemed strange that she never met any of his friends. Being free-lance, he had no boss calling to ask when he was going to show up to work. Nobody ever called to give him an assignment. Maybe the police were right: Jack existed only in her deranged mind.

The second week passed. Exhausted and tense, she hoped a quiet dive trip with Dr. Fishberg would give her some peace. Late Saturday morning she met him at the hospital after rounds.

Ben Fishberg was a pleasant, elderly physician, who kept himself in good physical shape. He had started diving many years before Clara, and held several badges for advanced training. As a test, perhaps to convince himself that he was still a young man, he earned certification for cave diving. He proved his point, but he was smart enough to know that cave diving was not his hobby.

His specialty was renal medicine. It would have been more ideal if she cross covered with another cardiologist, but their personalities meshed, and they worked around these little difficulties to continue their loose coverage association.

She had been too busy to get air earlier in the week, so they made a stop at the local dive shop to fill her cylinders.

Ben was surprised when she pointed out her boat docked at the Marina Bay Club. "Clara, I didn't realize your practice was going so well. I thought you still had all those debts from training."

"Well, I sort of got a deal. It's hard to explain. Let's get our gear on board. How about Molasses Reef today?"

The sea thumped out a light chop, and the broad blue sky was clear as they passed boats clustered over various popular dive sites. They stopped over a particular coral reef, being careful to lower the anchor in a patch of sand. The sun was bright, and the depth only thirty-five feet. The fish and coral were a collage of saturated colors. A school of Queen Parrotfish, with electric blue stripes about their beaks, nibbled at large brain coral. As both divers swam over a forest of fire coral, hundreds of silvery spadefish swam unafraid above, below, and around them.

Molasses Reef probably has the highest density of life of any known reef in the world. The fish flocked round Clara, hoping that she was one of the many divers that gave handouts of free food. There were brightly colored Triggerfish, Angelfish, Damselfish, and even a couple of friendly curious barracuda. On both sides of them, towering walls of coral extended almost to the surface.

Now and then they would swim into a tunnel passing through the walls of coral. Every few feet, chimneys would extend from the tunnel to the surface so that they were never in darkness. They swam with their arms close to their sides so as not to get an elbow full of Sea Urchin spines.

The riot of colors and sea life normally captivated her. She was now annoyed by a nagging headache. Clara prided herself on being a fairly experienced diver, and yet here she was becoming fatigued by mild exertion. She paused, hanging onto an outcropping of dead coral.

In spite of the rest, she found that she was hyperventilating. Above, a pair of disinterested barracuda swam past as her headache reached a new level of intensity. Her head separated into two halves as the fish took on bizarre and impossible forms. The colors swirled about her, twisting and merging, and forming new colors and new creatures of the sea. Then the colors went to purple hues before becoming muddy and finally deep brown as darkness closed in.

CHAPTER X

Murder may be done by legal means,

by plausible and profitable war, by calumny,

as well as by dose or dagger.

Lord Acton

     The headache was still pounding, pressing, boring in with splitting intensity, but the colors were gone. Instead, there was gray everywhere. Her eyes drifted over steel walls inches from her face. When she focused, she saw rows of closely spaced rivets, and a pipe coming from the gray somewhere near her feet, and going through the gray elsewhere, somewhere past her head.

She became aware of a thin, firm rubber mattress. It took several minutes for Clara to realize it was her body on the mattress. By turning her head slightly, a move that sent the pain to new heights of ferocity, she could see a row of small portholes.

As Clara scanned the expanse of gray steel, she thought, "Is any 'fun' worth killing yourself over?"

She was sixteen. No longer an adolescent, but still a bit of a tomboy. Tim was two years ahead of her in high school, and quite an athlete. Clara still tried to be one of the boys. After school she played some baseball and basketball, and was as good as any of the guys at sinking baskets on the courts.

She felt honored when Tim invited her to go boating with the rest of his friends. She was so elated that she did not notice the strange gear they hauled aboard the boat. At the reef she hungrily watched as one by one they back rolled into the water, leaving a trail of bubbles as they disappeared into the depths. It was not until thirty minutes later that they began to pull themselves back on board.

"Hey! That looks like great fun, Tim. Let me grab a tank and go back down with you."

A sneer wrote its thoughts across Tim's face. "You're kidding! You're not certified. We didn't bring you here to drown you. We needed you to watch the boat while we went down, and help the first guy back to get aboard."

The reality of how she had been used swept over Clara in waves. She silently turned away. Any response would be a tearful and angry one, and she wanted to appear cool at any cost. She'd show that bastard, somehow.

She had passed the little store every day on her way to school. They didn't sell fish, but somehow you felt that the store should smell of fish. In front of the store was a pole carrying a red flag with a white diagonal stripe. The flag didn't seem to represent any country that she was familiar with. The window display held artifacts that had obviously been exposed to water for a long time. A small anchor, a corroded brass porthole, and various other items she could not identify were neatly arranged.

She waited until the store was empty of customers, and gingerly stuck her head through the half-opened door.

"Hi! Come on in. Can I help you?" The boy behind the counter appeared to be in his late teens, and not dangerous at all.

"Well, yes. That is, maybe you can help. Is there any place that I can take lessons and learn to SCUBA?"

"There sure is. Right here. We're starting a basic class in one week. The course is eight weeks long with three hours at the pool twice a week."

"I'd like to join the class, if I may. How much will it cost?"

"Here's a flyer with the details. The fee is $80 for the course. If you can't qualify to enter the course we will refund all but $10. After all, we can't stop to teach people how to swim. To get your certification, you need two open water dives. We'll take an additional $50 from you when that time comes. Look over the sheet I gave you, and if you're still interested bring your money or plastic. You'll need to get the equipment we listed for the first class. You can buy it or rent it from us. I advise you to rent it…just in case."

The costs sounded astronomical, but they were not beyond reach. She had been saving for a mountain bike, and had over $200. The idea of turning back hardly entered her mind. She was thoroughly pissed at Tim. She was quite shaken, however, when $50 went for the bare essentials listed on the sheet. She purchased fins, mask, snorkel, and weights that were the cheapest she could buy, and yet be assured that they would be useful and safe in the future.

The class met beside a city pool with Olympic dimensions. The first order of the day was to make sure you were a strong enough swimmer for the class. Then came the Herculean task of swimming 300 meters without mask, snorkel or fins. Clara's previous experience was splashing around the beach, or a friendly small pool. Even though this pool seemed to be three miles long, the first of the six laps was not too difficult. She was careful to swim as slowly as possible. Time was not a factor here. By the second lap, she found herself exhausted, but was able to keep afloat by changing to a backstroke. On the third lap she was ready to put her feet down and give up, but then she thought of the consequences. She would either have to try again, beginning at yard one at the next class meeting, or take her money and give up. One saving grace was that Tim didn't know she was taking this class.

"That asshole," she thought. "He must have gotten through this somehow. If he could do it, and all of his idiot friends could do it, I can do it."

She spent the last fifty meters on her back, slowly sculling her way to the finish line. Clara was the last one in, but not once did a foot touch the floor of the pool, and she saw that almost half of the class had given up before finishing the 300 meters.

She enjoyed the total freedom of cruising along under water with no shortage of air, and unlike many of her classmates, she was totally enthralled with the physics and physiology of diving. In spite of this, each date at the pool was viewed with much trepidation.

Each class began with a 400-meter swim encumbered by mask and flippers. In the later classes the distance was extended to 800, and finally 1200 meters. Of the students that remained in the class, she was always the last to finish, and at the end of the swim her classmates would be sitting on the side of the pool, patiently waiting for her so that class could resume. She managed to pass all of the skills. The final pool session was called harassment day, and was a training session in a 50-foot deep diving pool called the "well." SCUBA is not that difficult if you know certain skills. In most sports, a problem with equipment may lead to injury. In SCUBA a defect in equipment often means death. You must be trained to react to a failed regulator if you are to survive.

311

Clara was not the least bit surprised that she ran out of air at a depth of twenty feet. Calmly she reached back and turned the air back on. She thought how lucky she was that her instructor had merely turned the valve rather than remove the entire yoke from the tank.

The last skill to be tested was the open water dive. She found herself in water that was forty feet deep, and in open ocean. They had swum 50 meters from the boat and in no direction could they see land. Large ocean swells periodically obscured the boat from sight. The dive itself was a joy. Beautifully colored fish of more than a dozen varieties came over to curiously examine her. She appreciated the beauty in this alien world, but ever present in her consciousness was the knowledge that she could not breathe the fluid that surrounded her. When her air ran low, and it was time to surface, it was with mixed feelings. She wanted to stay longer, and yet was relieved to get back to the surface where she belonged.

A couple of weeks later, after using all of her feminine charm, she wrangled another boat trip with Tim. She was careful to observe and savor the expression on his face when she almost effortlessly pulled the 80-cubic ft. tank from her father's car and slung it over one shoulder. She may have been a weak swimmer in class, but she was strong otherwise, and she handled the tanks with ease. Some of the others had to be assisted to a standing position after putting on a tank.

Thereafter, Tim looked upon Clara with great respect. These were the early days of sport diving, and few women had invaded this macho world. Clara's parents did not view her relationship with Tim with pleasure. Good Jewish girls did not go out with "goys," and after every date they would be waiting up to argue the point with her.

At first Clara found Tim interesting, and went with him for a good time, but slowly Tim's immaturity showed and she began to lose interest. However, inevitably she would go out with him again. Generation after generation of parents, plodding through the same parenting problems, doomed to make the same mistakes. Was it ingrained in mankind's DNA? Was some heavy curtain of stupidity destined to obliterate the recollection of their own youthful feelings? Sure, just tell her over and over, "He's not good enough for you. Find another boy etc."

Of course the normal response by any self-respecting adolescent is to keep going out with the schmuck. You would think that after the first ten centuries, parents would learn.

They had parked in the last and darkest corner of the drive-in. A few weeks earlier she would have pushed away any hand that had advanced beyond the knees. The hand was on the inside of her thigh, and her hand was lying gently on his. Her underpants were soaked from her excitement, and she was half embarrassed. Tim sensed that change in her also as he boldly placed his hand over her panties, and gently began to massage. Clara felt herself burning up and couldn't bring herself to offer the least resistance as he slid her panties off.

Clara had been using tampons for two years, so when it became time to enter her, she was tight, but felt no pain. Thereafter, the drive-in was on a regular weekly schedule.

Her parents finally realized that they were accomplishing nothing, and stopped their nagging. Without her parents' nagging to focus her defenses, Clara gradually lost interest in Tim, and they drifted apart.

*   *   *

"Clara, it's Ben! Nod your head if you can hear me. Keep calm. You're in the recompression chamber at Key Biscayne. We've got you back down to sixty feet and have been giving you short blasts of one hundred percent oxygen."

"Oh, that's what happened," she thought. "How do you get in trouble at thirty-five feet? She couldn't have gotten the bends, and how could she have gotten an air embolism without going toward the surface?"

Hours felt like days. The gray steel walls were monotonous company, but at last her headache eased, dimmed, and then cleared. Finally, ambient atmospheric pressure was reached and the door was opened. Amid protestations of good health and heavy schedules, and just plain crying and pleading, Clara was pushed into an ambulance, and transferred to the Miami Heart Institute for observation.

"OK Ben, what happened down there?"

"You began to act strangely, so I came over for a close look. At first, you just hung on to that rock, then, right before my eyes, your skin turned a bright cherry red. Jesus! There was no question as to what was going on, so I dropped your weight belt and got us up. As soon as we surfaced I got the second stage out of your mouth and you were still breathing. I wished we had some oxygen on the boat. I called the Coast Guard and got you to the chamber as soon as possible. The lab says the air in your tank contained twelve hundred parts per million of carbon monoxide. We checked with the dive shop. After we left the shop, someone noticed that the inlet pipe to the compressor had been knocked from its manifold and kicked near the exhaust of the engine. A real stupid accident. They tried to get hold of us, but didn't know our names, our boat, or where the hell we were diving."

"Ben, I'm feeling OK. I want to get out of here."

"There's been a role change. You, my dear doctor, are now a patient, and will follow orders, not give them. Considering the fact that you came within a few hairs' breath of dying, it is not being overly conservative to watch you in ICU for another, say, twenty-four hours. If all goes well, I will then transfer you out of this fish bowl and into the privacy of a telemetry bed. People who have been poisoned with carbon monoxide have the sneaky habit of looking robust one minute, and going sour the next."

"All right, I'll try to cooperate, but now that I'm awake, please have them take out that fucking Foley catheter. I believe, my good and faithful physician that I can pee without the help of a tube."

The Intensive Care Unit was not at all pleasant for someone who did not consider herself seriously ill. An intravenous line was running in the antecubital fossa of her right arm, which meant limited mobility. Two wires were glued high on her chest, and two were glued low on her chest. They were plugged into the wall monitor. She could use her left hand to scratch her nose and feed herself, but she couldn't turn in bed without jiggling the wires and setting off all sorts of alarms. She spent the long hours watching television, a pastime she despised. At last the hour grew late, the lights were dimmed, and the nurses in the unit at least made an attempt to be quiet. In spite of this, meaningful sleep was impossible. At 0500 hours, the lab tech came in to draw blood. One hour later, an LPN took blood pressure and pulse. In the ICU, vital signs were checked every four hours. This and other nursing chores assured the patient that she would not waste any time sleeping.

In spite of her discomfort, she managed to doze off, but was quickly awakened by loud alarm bells. Across from her bed, in the cubicle opposite and through her open door, she could see the nurses of the unit and respiratory therapy furiously working. It was late, and it was unlikely that there would be another cardiologist in the hospital to answer the "Code Blue." Clara removed the IV, and telemetry wires. Blood dripping from her antecubital vein, she ran to the opposite bed.

"OK, what do we have here?"

"He's a fifty-six year old male who was admitted to the unit today with an acute anteroseptal myocardial infarction. His blood pressure has been about 90/60. Just a couple of minutes ago, he started to run premature ventricular contractions, but before we could bolus him with lidocaine, he went into ventricular tachycardia, and now he's fibrillating."

"Charge the defibrillator to two hundred watt-seconds. OK, everybody away from the bed. Fire! OK, what have we got now?"

"Still fibrillating."

"Let's take it to three hundred watt-seconds. All clear? Fire!"

"V-fib," responded the nurse.

"Crank it all the way to three sixty, and let's try again. Stand clear. Fire!"

"No change."

"OK, let's continue CPR, and get him intubated. Let's push a milligram of epinephrine."

"Epi is in."

"Let's give him another three sixty. Stand clear."

"No change."

"Lets bolus with 100mg of lidocaine, and try again."

"Lidocaine in."

"Stand clear!"

317

"Sinus tachycardia with rate of 120, and BP in 90/60."

"Great! Let's hang a drip and run the lido at 2 milligrams per minute. I think we'd better call this guy's doctor, and maybe I ought to climb back into my own bed."

"Well, just what the doctor ordered." Ben Fishberg glared at her like a teacher annoyed at his best pupil. "Intravenous fluids at a keep open rate, monitor, frequent vital signs, complete bed rest, and what do we find? You run the codes in the ICU. Obviously, you don't need the Intensive Care Unit."

"Which is precisely what I've been trying to tell you."

"I'll see you in your new room tomorrow, and I'll probably discharge you in a couple of days."

It was the first time Clara had ever seen a hospital from the patient's side of things. It was difficult enough to face the necessity of having some stranger insert a catheter in your urethra; what was worse for her was that these were all acquaintances of hers. Nurses that she dealt with professionally on a daily basis. Chained to an intravenous line, they had to help her on and off a bedside commode. Earlier, when she was acutely ill from the carbon monoxide, she had soiled herself. Again, these people went about their business of cleaning her up as it she was any other patient.

The bed in telemetry was a step in the right direction. She was not surrounded by glass so she was no longer under continuous visual observation. She was monitored, but the wires did not plug into the wall. They were hooked to a transmitter belted to her waist. She was free to walk about the room, and even into the hallway, and still have a continuous cardiac rhythm monitored on the scope at the nurses' station.

One thing certainly was silly. She didn't need an IV, but the rules on the telemetry service were that all patients had to have a ready access to a vein — just in case. She had a heparin lock, a needle in a vein attached to a short piece of tubing that was capped off. Every now and then a nurse would come in to inject some heparin. This was to keep the line from clotting up.

Funny, she had never seen this nurse before. She was about to complain that the heparin was burning her arm, but then a profound sense of weakness passed over her, and in spite of the severe pain she could not gather the strength to cry out. Her only alternative was to rip out the line, but now her arm fell across her body, completely flaccid. Only a groan passed her lips. Blackness clouded over her eyes as the ringing of alarm bells echoed from an infinite distance.

"We almost lost you, Clara. You went into ventricular fibrillation. It took quite a few shocks to get you converted to a stable rhythm. We got a blood screen. Your potassium was sky high. I can't see how that could happen. I can't find a relationship between hyperpotassemia and carbon monoxide poisoning."

"Ben, I hope you're not going to be too angry with me. I can't tell you right now why I'm doing this except

319

to say I have a sound reason. I am leaving the hospital today, right now, whatever the medical advice."

"You've just been resuscitated and now you're leaving? I know what you're thinking, but believe me, this is not going to happen again."

"That's just it Ben, it will happen again. I know it will, and I know why it will, but I can't tell you. I'm getting out of bed right now. Goodbye, Ben."

She was a bit disappointed at finding the FBI listed in the telephone book. One would have expected the office to be located in a sub-basement under a shoe store. If you were in the know, you would proceed to the back room where you would pull down on the third coat hook from the end. A wall would slide back to reveal a little elevator, and after inserting your credit card in its slot, it would lower you two hundred feet to a blast-proof "war room."

Instead, she entered an ordinary looking office on Biscayne Boulevard. Sitting there was Mr. Lyle Black, somewhere between thirty and forty years old. His hair was reddish brown and close-cropped, like the college style of the 1940's. His conservative brown suit and brown tie also belonged to the same period.

"Dr. Weiss, the story is fantastic. If you weren't a physician I would have edged you out of this office after the first few minutes. We are deluged with weirdoes every day, but you have my assurance your claims will be carefully investigated, and you will get a call from me in the next couple of days."

'"Please remember, Mr. Black, the Customs people looked into this and came up with nothing. I was so embarrassed I virtually ran from their office."

"Our organization is primarily investigative. It's our meat and potatoes." Pleased with himself for using an idiomatic phrase, as the guidebook suggested during interrogational information gathering, he allowed an appropriate time interval to elapse while he smiled to simulate warmth.

"We won't make a couple of phone calls to some local sheriff and call it quits. Our field agents will be able to tell us everything that went on in those islands in the past few weeks. If there are any holes left, these will be filled in by our colleagues in the CIA. Why don't you just go home and wait for my call?"

Clara remained in her apartment the next three days. There was enough food in the refrigerator and freezer to enable her not to set foot outside. She was afraid of both missing that important phone call, and also of exposing herself to additional risk by leaving. She turned her practice over to Dr. Fishberg, and steadfastly refused to answer his questions regarding her physical and mental health. In the afternoon of the third day, she received the call she was waiting for.

"Dr. Weiss? This is Mr. Black. We have carefully investigated your story. The Bahamian authorities deny any murders or lost boats, and what is of much interest is that there is no record of any Aaron Forsythe, or Arthur Waldmann, as members of the Lyford Cay Club. Oh yes! I also looked into the death of a Mr.

Jack Stanger. He was given an assignment to do a photo story on the girls of the Orient for *Playboy Magazine*. We checked, and he is now in Kowloon, in Hong Kong, doing just that. We interviewed several of your colleagues, and find them concerned over, uh, your health. The feeling is that you have applied yourself too industriously to the practice of medicine and are having problems. To put it most kindly, it appears that the wisest move you could make is to look up one of your psychiatrist friends and put yourself in his hands."

CHAPTER XI

Attempted assassinations are the accidents of kings,

just as falling chimneys are the accidents of masons.

If we must weep,

let us weep for the masons.

Benito Mussolini

The road ahead was illuminated by the pale glow of dawn. In another hour the sun would appear on the horizon, but Clara had no interest in stopping. She was on I-75 crossing the Florida-Georgia border just South of

Valdosta and she was not going to slow down until she reached McDowell, Kentucky.

In her last year of medical school, she felt the marked deficiency in her obstetrical training. The University Hospital was one of many large teaching hospitals that suffered from the effects of the pill. OB beds first remained empty, and were then transferred to the services of surgery or medicine. OB-GYN residents, hungry for experience, hoarded their cases, while interns looked helplessly over their shoulders. The medical student was last in line, and received no practical experience at all. In desperation, the school sent its fourth-year students to outlying communities to get the training that the parent institution could not offer.

Clara had been sent to a Regional Appalachian Miners Hospital in the southeast corner of Kentucky. The hospital was located in McDowell, a town so small that it was listed only on the largest and most detailed maps. A single, mostly dirt road led to the town. This road was a dried creek bed and was flooded and impassible for much of the year. The hospital served the miners and their families who worked the coal in the surrounding hills. The nearest large city was over one hundred miles away, separated by beautiful rolling hills and dense forest. Not many physicians were willing to practice medicine in such isolation. You had better love hunting, fishing and reading because there was nothing else to do with your free time.

If you needed consultation, the phone would have to serve, as there were few specialties represented in the area. The general practitioner did internal medicine, OB-

GYN, surgery, and pediatrics. He would send only the most difficult cases the one hundred and twenty miles, much of it over poor roads, to the University Medical Center in Lexington.

Staff and the hospital administration liked her, and invited her to practice in McDowell after her internship. She never considered the offer seriously. A city girl, born in New York City, she was happy in the activity of Chicago or Miami. When her internship was completed, she received a letter repeating the offer, but the letter quickly ended up in the wastebasket.

Now, there was no choice. She needed isolation and anonymity. Clara had never had a serious accident in her life. When two life-threatening incidents followed one after the other, she could not accept Ben's explanation that they were merely accidents. The sinking of the boat and Jack's death had converted her to a cynical and suspicious woman turning on and tuning in all her mechanisms for survival. She had an overwhelming desire to confide in Ben. To face this challenge alone was appalling. However, she hesitated to tell Ben her story, as she had no wish to endanger another life. It was apparent that she held a piece of information that was an important secret for someone. That person wanted her dead. It also seemed obvious that her hunter had some sort of law enforcement sanction. Any of her friends who knew of her fears might also become targets.

For a while in Miami, she thought of changing her name and melting into the masses of a large city such as New York, but how could she practice medicine? To get hospital privileges, you must have diplomas, licenses, and letters of recommendation from your professors and colleagues. If she were to melt away, she would have to forget about medicine. She would have to get a job as a waitress, secretary, or clerk. The years of training would be an investment thrown away. McDowell was a compromise. Perhaps no one would make the effort to track her into the mountains of Kentucky.

Her city friends thought she was weird. When other physicians were driving Lincolns, Cadillacs or Mercedes, she purchased a big, boxy Jeep station wagon. It was a no-nonsense car. The seats were hard. There were no electric servomotors to change the seat position or lift the windows. It had four-wheel drive and enough traction to climb trees. The dirt road would have ripped the bottom out of a Cadillac miles back, but the jeep, with its high clearance, took the rough going in stride.

Clara had stopped in a little motel outside of Paintsville for a night's rest before tackling the last few miles of Route 122, over a road that was merely a dry creek bed. Normally, a physician cannot walk into town and announce he is opening a practice. Months of preparation involve checking credentials, filing applications to the county medical society, and records are reviewed by credential committees, then executive committees, and finally, boards of trustees of the local hospitals. But this was not true of a community desperate for the services of a physician. Go to work first, the details can be worked out later.

She had called the hospital from the motel, and they set up an interview for the following morning.

"Dr. Weiss, we are real pleased to see you again, and of course our offer still stands, but this is quite a surprise. Quite a pleasant surprise to say the least."

"I've always considered the city as my home. The pressures have just gradually mounted until one day I realized that I was surrounded by concrete and steel. I was driving for miles every weekend to get to the country where I could see some grass and trees. I guess I just had it with city life; when I finally made my decision and drove out here. Don't worry. I'm not that scatter-brained. I didn't leave Florida until I turned my practice over to a close friend of mine. I know he'll take good care of my patients."

"We have a building next to the hospital in which we rent living space to our employees. You're welcome to move in there until you get situated. Today's Friday. How about coming to work in our outpatient clinic Monday? That should hold you together until you can find your own office space."

She had spent uncountable hours frozen in the driver's seat, her mind churning. Her eye was almost constantly on the rearview mirror. Clara had limited cash, and was using credit cards. She knew she was leaving a trail that any novice could untangle. Driving for long periods were anesthetic, but left too many levels of her mind functioning. She froze with terror each time a huge semi passed. Involuntarily, her hands gripped the wheel more fiercely as her brain shrieked that this might be the vehicle to push her Jeep off the road. When the leviathan had finally passed, she would exhale and breathe normally for a time.

327

At last, lugging cartons across the threshold of her new living room was more real than the possibility of some vague shadow following her. Vigorously, she began slapping books on the shelves. She thought over her predicament again and again. How the hell could she hide? No one would hire her without checking her credentials. If she changed her name, those credentials would be invalid. The only way she could have covered her tracks was to take another name, and do something besides medicine. She'd rather be dead than not practice medicine. She shivered despite the late summer heat, as she realized that she had made a major decision regarding her safety. "Rather be dead" was more ominous than a figure of speech.

After stacking her boxes of novels in the hall closet, and arranging her medical books on the shelves, she walked out onto the small terrace leading from the combination living room and kitchen. A few soft breezes played calmly. The two-story apartment building was set on a hill, and Clara's apartment overlooked a valley. It was mostly fields with a few trees, and an isolated house here and there. You certainly could not complain about crowds in this community. Neighbors tended to be separated by at least a mile. The late afternoon sun did not sparkle on any swimming pools in this town. It was such an unruffled scene. Clara began to feel more tranquil.

As night settled, all the fears clustered about her. She crumpled onto the floor of the little balcony, and cried.

Medicine was practiced differently in the hills. Her rotating internship from years ago now demonstrated its practicality. No longer could she limit herself to the internal medicine problems with which she felt most expertise. There was no rheumatologist, neurologist, dermatologist, or gastroenterologist to which she could direct referrals. She was seeing whole families, including the infants. She was delivering babies again. The delivery room nurses were understanding, and gently and subtly reminded her of the techniques that she had forgotten. Carefully they brought her up to date on some of the advances in obstetrics.

Broken arms could not be sent to the non-existent orthopedist. After a quick run to her private study to look up the procedure, she would return to the exam room to apply the cast herself. The tension of constantly working at the edge of her knowledge and skill was nerve-wracking, but the challenge was also exciting and enjoyable. This practice would never fall into the rut of seeing the same common diseases day after day.

The weeks passed quickly. She put a down payment on a small home and moved in. She found a storefront building in Paintsville and opened her office there. She continued to practice two days a week in the hospital clinic.

This was the land of the Cumberland Gap, and the heavily forested hills and valleys were of a beauty unparalleled east of the Mississippi. The area was dotted with lakes, and on weekends Clara either went boating on Dewey Lake with new friends or hiked through the wilderness of the Daniel Boone National Forest.

"Dr. Weiss! This is Dr. Douglas Goldstein. I'm sorry to bother you this late, but I can really use some help. I'm in the Intensive Care Unit now with a patient I just admitted through the ER. He's a fifty-seven year old white male smoker who has suffered an acute myocardial infarction. In fact, he's lost his 'R' waves and has ST elevation in all of the chest leads. His blood pressure can only be palpated and it's around 75 to 80 systolic. He is in frank pulmonary edema, yet after one hundred milligrams of IV Lasix, there's no output. I thought we were pretty lucky when I found that we had added a cardiologist to the staff, but I can really appreciate you now."

"Look, Dr. Goldstein, just from what you have told me, we're going to have to know this man's pulmonary artery pressure."

"I knew you were going to want to pass a Swan Ganz Catheter. I can call the University of Kentucky Medical Center, and have one flown down here by one of fire rescue's choppers. For once we'll be bringing the equipment to the patient rather than transporting an unstable patient eighty miles. Perhaps the university can spare a transducer and a monitor. Our monitors can record cardiac rhythm, but I don't think they can be adapted to measure pulmonary artery pressures."

Clara lived only ten minutes from the hospital, and when she arrived she found the patient as she expected, in *extremis*.

"Doug, the prognosis for this man is guarded to say the least."

Clara observed that this man with an acute myocardial infarction had severe pump failure as evidenced by his pulmonary edema, hypotension, and ice-cold extremities. Because he had no perfusion to his brain and kidneys he was unconscious and had no urine flowing from his bladder catheter.

"I agree with you Doug. To try any therapeutic modality at this point would be pure guesswork. Let's get everything prepared. I like the right subclavian vein approach."

The frantic flurry of activity was a futile attempt to make the time pass quickly in the presence of a critically ill patient. There was nothing to do but to pace the floor; helplessly waiting for the invaluable equipment.

A moment after they heard the sound of a helicopter a nurse rushed in carrying several carefully wrapped sterile packages. After she used a needle to locate the vein under the clavicle, Clara passed a guide wire through the needle before removing the needle from the vein. Over this wire she slid a large bore tube into the vein, and it was through this tube that she passed the catheter.

"Let's hook up the catheter to the transducer and I'll advance the catheter as we watch the pressure. Somebody better watch the cardiac rhythm for ventricular extrasystoles, and we had better keep the defibrillator charged up."

Dr. Goldstein fixed his eyes on the fluctuating pressure curve on the cathode ray tube. "So far all I see is venous pressure. Ah! Now you're in the right atrium. Keep on going. That looks like a ventricular pressure curve now. I see PVC's! Now, three in a row."

"I've pulled out, Doug. I'm back in the right atrium. His heart is too irritable. Let's give him a bolus of one hundred milligrams of Xylocaine and start a Xylocaine drip. Then I can try again."

The drug was administered, and Clara again advanced the catheter.

"We're back in the right ventricle, and everything looks stable. Watch the pressure for me, Doug."

"You've got it past the pulmonary valve now, and it looks like you wedged the catheter. The wedge pressure is about three millimeters. Pull back a bit. Okay! The PA pressure is ten over three."

"That clinches it, Doug. This patient is terribly hypovolemic. Let's start pouring in some volume expander."

Over the next few hours, with the addition of the vital fluid, the kidneys began to make urine, the blood pressure rose, and the patient woke up.

"Listen Clara, I'm chairman of the hospital's executive committee. You come to the next meeting and tell us exactly what you need for a good ICU. We have government grants to buy almost any necessary equipment. There's no question that invasive monitoring saved my patient's life. It's just that we haven't had a physician with the expertise to use it until now."

Clara's introduction to Douglas Goldstein did not stop at the professional level. After consulting with her several times on cardiology, he invited her to spend the day on his boat. It proved to be one of those small aluminum houseboats designed to go places with a pair of hefty stern-drive engines. It was great for exploring lakes, but you wouldn't want to be caught in the open sea with this top heavy boat. It had most of the comforts of home. Except for the enclosed head, it consisted of one room that served as bridge, living room, galley and bedroom.

"Doug, I hate to seem like a nag so early in our relationship, but what in hell's name is a doctor doing with a cigarette in his mouth. And of all things, you're smoking at the same time you're filling the fuel tank."

"I know it's a bad image, but I started smoking when I was thirteen, and I'm thoroughly addicted hook, line, and sinker. If I had to give up either smoking or sex, I'd have to think the matter over with care. I try not to let a patient see me with a cigarette. I don't want them to think I condone these things. As for the gasoline, don't worry. I never let my face get that close. Never seen an accident yet."

"You have not quite convinced me, and if you're going to smoke I wish you'd switch to diesel. If you continue to smoke around gasoline, we may get an unexpected aerial view of the surrounding countryside. Just to change the subject, what's a nice doctor like you doing in the sticks like this?"

"I was born in sticks like this. I'm an old country boy from Pikesville. The University of Kentucky wanted to manufacture doctors that would stay in the hills, so getting into medical school was easy. I was accepted in spite of grades I wasn't too proud of. The school knew I'd stick around. You may think this a nothing place, but if you'll let me, I'll introduce you to beauty you'll never see in the big city."

The tank filled, Doug cast off and edged the craft stern way into the swift current.

"This river runs between Dewey and Fishtrap Lake. In a little while we'll be moving into Dewey Lake and the water will be a bit calmer. I'd like you to take the helm then. You'll see what a joy this boat is. People think a houseboat is for parking at the dock or piddling on the bay, but this one you can really take places."

They were soon in a larger expanse of water. The currents were gentle, and Clara enjoyed nosing around the edge of the lake. Gone were the choppy waters of the Caribbean. All was quiet and serene. The shore line was densely forested, but here and there she saw a beach and a small clearing. Many of the clearings were occupied with three or four people in bathing suits, a portable grill and a small tent. As they pulled near, each group in turn gave them a friendly hail.

"This is really the life. I hope I don't fall asleep at the wheel, Doug."

"Whenever I can manage coverage, I get out here. I love to explore all the little tributaries that lead into the lake. In spite of my years here, I still find new places. I've got a fishing pole in the back, and sometimes I catch dinner. I even have a small barbecue grill near the stern."

"You've been spoiled. You have no idea what seawater and barnacles do to a boat. We used to put on SCUBA and scrub away the green gunk each time we brought our boat into port."

"Well, you couldn't do that here. There's no dive shop or safe compressed air supply for miles."

"I know. One think I'll miss is my diving. You may not have a reef loaded with coral and incredibly colored fish, but I'm sure there's plenty of life in the river. One of these days I may make a major investment and buy a small compressor. You teach me the river, and I'll teach you to dive."

The hours passed quickly, and soon it was dusk and she was helping to moor the boat.

"Clara, you and I have to do this again. Let's try getting coverage two weekends from now."

Practicing medicine in the backwoods of Kentucky was not as peaceful as one would imagine. Instead of a small, plant-filled waiting room with a few patients, Clara now faced a stark anteroom to her office, constantly crammed with people. This mob was present even when her schedule listed only a few office appointments. In the hills, when an individual goes to the doctor, the whole family accompanies him. Newborns, grandparents, aunts, uncles, and an endless array of siblings are packed into the waiting room. A visit to the doctor is a real family outing

—just like a picnic. In Clara's case, the whole county was anxious to look her over, not just because she was a specialist, but a young woman physician in this area was really something to be gawked at.

The biggest difference was the ambiance of her new waiting room. In Miami, impatience hovered constantly. Although many of her patients were retired, if it was five minutes after their appointed time, the impatience in the air became palpably heavy, like cigarette smoke. If she was called away for an emergency at the hospital, or a patient was suddenly brought to her office wheezing with an asthmatic attack, the impatience turned to hostility and anger.

"He didn't wait his turn.... I was next.... So what, if his lips are blue. If I don't get to see the doctor in the next ten minutes, I'm joining an HMO."

Here in Appalachia, there was calmness in her waiting room. The doctor would see you when she had a mind to. Meanwhile, set a spell, friend.

"Have you seen the new lady doctor?"

"Nope."

"I saw one once up at the Medical Center, and you could never tell she was a doctor. Looked just like a pretty young girl."

"Yup?"

"I saw one once. ...weren't so pretty."

"Can't all be pretty."

"Nope."

"She told me I have something called a manic phase of a bipolar disorder, whatever that is. I'm supposed to have some sort of problem keeping my mouth in gear with my brain. What have you got?"

"Laryngitis."

Clara's nurse/right-hand/sometime translator/office manager, and new friend, was a middle-aged woman named Ellen, a former nurse from Cincinnati. Ellen's husband decided to retire after he sold a chain of laundries, and just relax, hunt, and fish. To Ellen, Clara's coming probably saved her marriage. Although her husband was content to fish and hunt all summer, play cards and chat with his cronies all winter, this was not a life for Ellen. As a former head nurse in a coronary care unit, she found the last two years crushingly dull. So, when Ellen heard of a cardiologist opening an office in Paintsville, she tracked Clara down. There was an immediate rapport. They spoke the same language. Ellen had the organizational abilities that Clara lacked and needed.

This was a rough time for Clara. Coming to an office, and not finding her "family" or Casey, there were many lonely nights when she almost called them to let them know she was well. Fear stopped her. Maybe that phone call would be the final link to involve them. Maybe Casey and Anne were being watched in the hope that they would lead them to Clara. "I don't know who 'them' is," Clara thought. "I don't want to know, either. Dear God, just let them not find me, and let me practice medicine in peace."

In general practice, she saw many more patients each day. All those facial lacerations that used to go to plastic surgeons, biopsies, a lot more gynecology, some obstetrics, and all the noise of pediatrics meant unusual exhaustion. This was healthy for her. Clara wanted no time to think. She needed exhaustion as a sleeping potion. Fatigue was her tranquilizer.

As she was leaving her office, Ellen stopped her in the hall. "Dr. Goldstein is outside. Shall I show him in?"

"Of course."

He covered the entire hallway distance in about six strides, beaming. "Hi!"

"Hello, Doug."

"I was coming past your office when I saw that yellow monstrosity of yours parked outside. So I thought it would be a good time to pay you a neighborly visit."

"That monstrosity is a Jeep Wagoneer, and I'm very fond of it. I want you to know that a snowplow is an optional attachment. So when you're stuck somewhere this winter, just think about my monstrosity chugging through the snow with its four-wheel drive and muscular little snowplow on its nose."

"I think you're chortling, Clara, but it's very becoming, like everything else you do." Doug held out

338

his hand to her as he said, "now that I'm here, what home folks would do is show me around the place."

"Well, it's really not much," Clara began as she walked into her consulting room. "This is where I speak to patients before examining them. I think it's crummy to be shown into a cold, clinical exam room, told to strip, handed a scratchy paper gown, and then have some stranger come in to prod at you. So I like to talk to the patient in my office first, especially if we've never seen each other before."

"Looks comfortable."

"I always have a couch in my office, so I can grab some sleep when there's a lull between patients, only there doesn't seem to be a lull here."

Clara continued talking as she walked back out into the hall and showed Doug into three small rooms. "I have three examining rooms. You really need them."

Doug stared in amazement. "They just don't look as bare and professional as mine do."

"It's the plants, Doug. They're all over. Somehow green makes people feel less hostile."

"Well, your office is certainly the nicest looking one I've seen up in this territory."

"It's just plants and my photos."

"Did you take all of them?"

Clara seemed lost for a second before she was able to answer. From somewhere, Doug's question kept echoing around her and from that somewhere else, Jack's body still lay on a wooden floor.

"No, Doug, some are mine, but a lot of them were done by a friend."

"I've never gotten into photography."

"Well, it's a much more fulfilling hobby than shooting unarmed animals. I can't see how you can reconcile that with your Hippocratic Oath."

"Now wait a minute, I thought only redheads had a temper. I don't know what I did to get under your skin, but let me make amends for it. How about going to the hospital and making evening rounds together? Then we can take a leisurely drive into Lexington for dinner."

"You're insane. That's a good three-hour drive."

"Yeah, but it's Friday. We can be there by nine, and slowly drive home. I'm sure we can get someone to cover for us tonight."

"I really couldn't, Doug. I feel a little tired."

"You'll rest in my car. A nice three-hour nap on my shoulder should appeal to you. It certainly appeals to me."

"No, I'm sorry."

"Thick, crusty, cheesy onion soup...."

"No, I really...."

"Caesar salad for two, heavy on the croutons."

"Doug, I don't want to get in...."

"Perfectly cooked Mountain Trout in a wine and mushroom sauce, like you've never had before."

"Doug, please...."

He leaned over, whispering gently in her ear, "...followed by chocolate rum mousse, and covered with whipped cream and fresh strawberries."

"Oh, damn you." She hugged him. "Let's get started. It's a long ride."

Clara remembered nothing of the ride to Lexington, Kentucky. She was too busy experiencing the only three hours of uninterrupted sleep, free of nightmares she had had in the months since Jack's death. Her subconscious had finally given her some respite, allowing her to feel safe with Dr. Goldstein.

She woke to find Doug holding her, parked in the Coach House parking lot. "This is really nice, Clara," he murmured while kissing her neck. "If our stomachs could only growl synchronously, I'd have some other plans for us besides food right now, but food first."

"You think you can buy me with food?"

"Of course. All Jewish girls with big boobs can be bought with food."

"I never heard that before."

"I learned it in medical school. Page 412 of *Harrison's Principles of Internal Medicine.*"

Seated at a comfortable table, with the usual dim lights, white napery, candles, and with Dr. Goldstein for a companion, Clara's feeling of serenity remained. She could almost imagine that she had endured some long nightmare and would return to Miami to find Jack straightening up their bedroom.

A dream quality flickered with the candles. She knew she would soon awaken to find Jack quietly hanging up the clothing she had scattered on the floor the night before. When she'd stretch and begin to yawn herself awake, Jack would be at her side gently kissing her closed eyes. She'd put her arms around him and murmur into his shoulder, "I'll hang them up. Just a few more minutes."

"Honey, rest. I'll do it. Get a little more sleep."

"If you knew how messy I was, would you still have fallen in love with me?" She'd huskily ask.

He'd answer, "I knew how messy you were the first second I saw your desk. Takes more than that to frighten me off."

She'd pull him down on top of her as she'd sigh, "Tomorrow, I'm going to clean my closet out."

"Tomorrow," he'd answer."

Doug's hand closed around hers, bringing her back to Kentucky. She smiled at his nice face, enhanced by the candlelight. At least for now, she could pretend to be a medical student again, returning to the scenes of her childhood.

A succession of dishes with appropriate wine accompaniment began slowly to appear, and more quickly disappear. Clara, who normally put a one-drink limit on herself, felt various emotional barriers crumbling as the aperitif gave way to the sherried soup, to the alcohol in the main course, to the heavily flamed dessert; and all those wines along the way culminated in the brandied haze in her coffee. So, when Doug suggested staying overnight in Lexington, her head could only nod vertically.

They found their way to a lovely inn, surrounded by gardens, and bordered by the rolling pastures and stately mansion of a prominent horse farm. How they got from the restaurant to their room was a mystery to her, but she now found herself slightly awake, with Doug trying to ease her onto a bed. "My God, how did we get here?"

He lay beside her, cradling her in his arms. "We took a cab." He kissed her neck, and then worked up to her ear, as he whispered, "You think I'd drive with anyone in my condition?"

As Doug made love to her, Clara felt as if she were floating in some comfortable limbo, where none of her memories could follow. If only she could stop time now, pressed against Doug's warmth, his hands soothing her, feeling him inside her, warm, safe, alive; she would never have to live again with fear.

The next couple of months were idyllic. Her practice grew with patients who respected her, and her love life was more than satisfactory. Their relationship had progressed from a simple affair to where Doug was hinting at marriage. Her feelings for him were such that marriage was beginning to sound very natural.

They made plans for a more extended vacation rather than the quick weekends away on his boat. When Clara had seen her last patient that day, she was to grab a suitcase and meet him at the dock. They would leave Dewey Lake and explore the Levisa Fork as far as they cold go in three days out, three days back.

The sun was setting as Clara anxiously drove her jeep toward the dock. The scene was not at all familiar. The usually quiet river edge was congested with people. Debris was floating on the water.

"I'm sorry, Miss. I must try to keep this area clear."

"What happened, sheriff?"

"Some damn fool was smoking while he was loading gas. Blew himself to kingdom-come."

CHAPTER XII

Under the spreading chestnut tree

I sold you and you sold me:

There lie they, and here lie we

Under the spreading chestnut tree.

Orwell

Aaron Forsythe ambled into a small shoe store located at the far end of Bay Street. Tourists didn't wander to this end of the street. It was a bit far from the cruise ships, and there were only a few dingy stores, selling dingy fabrics to the natives. Dingy fabric shops, dingy cotton clothing shops, and this little dingy shoe store.

The clerk was busy behind the counter doing what clerks do. What does a clerk do in a store that sees perhaps two customers a day? At any rate, the clerk appeared to be busy and didn't raise his eyes to welcome this potential customer. Perhaps there were other reasons for the clerk's lack of interest.

Aaron showed the same regard toward the clerk, and without speaking, he parted a curtain of beads leading to the back room. They jangled together behind him as he slipped off his jacket and carefully hung it on the third hook from the end. Removing his American Express Card from his wallet, he did something very strange with the card. It was particularly strange because it was a Platinum American Express Card, and should be treated with the respect that such a card deserves. He slid this shiny card into a rather dirty crack in the wall. Certainly one would expect the coarsely granular plaster to scratch this emblem of wealth and status. Instead, a bookcase against one wall rotated toward him. In the dim light one could barely make out the presence of a small elevator behind the bookcase. This was a small elevator indeed. Big enough for one man, although two very close friends could squeeze in.

Aaron Forsythe stepped into the elevator. There was no elevator door — most certainly below code even for Nassau. The elevator descended.

A familiar place: the wall with the fine collection of books on war and other forms of killing, with other three walls holding the instruments of death which man has used to maim and destroy his fellows over the centuries.

346

Draco was the first to speak. "Gentlemen, part of our task has been accomplished. The crate containing the weapons grade Plutonium has been wrested from the grasp of an unstable and hostile African nation. It is now in the hands of the NATO Alliance. The world has been spared the addition of another nuclear power, at least for a while. Our inventory of fissionable material has been increased, while that of the other side has been diminished. A minor and almost insignificant change in this day and age, perhaps, but nevertheless a change toward world survival. There remain, however, some loose strings which must be trimmed. Draco?"

"Aaron Forsyth" — Draco — painfully shifted his weight to the other foot. It was obviously going to be a long dissertation. Damn these hard floors.

"Our loose end, so to speak, has fled into the back country of Kentucky. This is the final result of our futile attempts to get cooperation from the authorities. I am concerned over all the "civilians" that had to be sacrificed. Enough is enough."

" However, on the bright side, she is thoroughly cowed, and I'm sure will never attempt to expose her, uh, escapade again. She is convinced her dear Jack is dead. Blowing away that dead derelict's face worked. Dressing him in Jack's clothing must have been a bloody, stinking job, however. I'm happy that I was able to delegate that. Oh well, rank does have its privileges."

"I trust Jack is doing well?" Draco retorted. "When I invited Jack to join our club, he was extremely resistant, and I was afraid he would actually become

347

combative. Then I made an offer he could not refuse. We would allow him to live. He was not completely untrained. His stint in Special Forces will be useful. For now we got him out of the way. He's not real happy with his Alaska station, but he's grateful to be alive. He will have no further contact with the doctor. After our plastic surgeon finishes up with him, we can give him a new identity. It was her life, or some uncomfortable surgery and a new identity for him. In the end, he understood that Jack Stanger would have to die if Clara Weiss was to live. He signed the official secrets contract, and he knows what will happen to him if he ever breathes a word."

Arthur Waldman said, "Maybe we can run down the Russian bastard who snatched the Plutonium in the first place. I wish we knew who he was. He really needs to be completely disassembled down to his component parts."

The director scrutinized both men for several seconds, his mouth drawn up grimly. Then, he leaned back, pushing the massive oak chair as he arose. Walking slowly to his left, he stopped at a large black and white photo above his fireplace. It was a photo of Wild Bill Donovan, and Dulles. The great movers and shakers of the old OSS group. His thick hands, the index finger with its missing joint, made tight fists behind his back as he allowed himself a minute of reverie.

Turning slowly, hands still clasped behind him, he said, "Gentlemen, allow me a projection. Permit me to place us nearly a decade in the future. Although I am not possessed of psychic abilities, I can well see addressing you with a question: 'Do you remember an organization called the NSA? I'm being facetious of course,'" he continued sarcastically, his stubby hands describing small but graceful arcs in the air. "They have not accomplished a thing in years, so why should you remember them? Our parent company was an efficient organization, which, like us, used a large assortment of extra-legal means to protect the United States. Their computers assured the destruction of any citizen's privacy. In partnership with the CIA they assisted juntas to overthrow communist regimes. They assisted democracies in their struggle against dictatorships. Much of their work necessitated the use of secret agents in so-called friendly countries such as France and Great Britain. They did not play by the rules out of necessity. If your opponent cheats and you don't, well you know who wins. In short, gentleman, we were created because the NSA and CIA were too visible to continue covert activity. Out of necessity we must remain invisible."

Draco began to shift restlessly in his chair.

The Director focused ferret-like eyes on him as he resumed. "My impatient young colleague, you will have to give me your forbearance as I continue my futuristic allegory. Now, there was another group, which went by the initials 'FBI.' It stood for the Federal Bureau of Investigation. To accomplish their very valuable work, they found it necessary to use phone and mail taps, sometimes without the red tape of judicial orders. It was necessary to do some private work for various presidents, and also to break into certain depositories to gather evidence. To make a long story short, their activities, as well as the NSA's were leaked to the public. The public does not understand these things. The public believes that its government's organizations must follow the letter of the law scrupulously. The public does not realize that it and its precious law will be destroyed if it plays by Queensbury rules when the enemy plays without rules. In short, the CIA and NSA were so paralyzed and so demoralized that they could not give sound advice when such advice was desperately needed. We lost South Vietnam because of its weakness. The FBI's lack of presence is a bit more subtle, and being primarily a national rather than an international organization, not quite so far-reaching. Its essential demise in the United States has given organized crime what amounts to free reign.

It makes me a bit uncomfortable to say this, but I believe that killing Clara now would be needlessly destroying an innocent, and a productive person. One who will never do us any harm. Additionally, if we pursue this matter, we expose ourselves to a risk of discovery that outweighs the need.

However, gentlemen, this organization will not suffer the same fate. We will not risk leaks, and we will not risk going public — however slight the risk. Is that clear? If the good doctor climbs out of her shell, and starts making waves, I will rescind this parole. I don't want any more accidents planned in this matter. We have the habit of occasionally killing the wrong people. So, if it comes to that, we will kill her. Another apparently senseless murder in the United States will hardly make news. It saddens me that so-called innocents must be sacrificed, but we all know that the tree of liberty must be watered with the blood of free men. This is a small price to pay for the security and even survival of the free world.

If you ask, as someone always does, who is to decide the matter of life and death, the answer is simple. We will. This organization's mission is clear. If there is a doubt about the survival of the free world, we are to eliminate the doubt; if there is a risk, we are to erase the risk. It is that simple."

."

—TO BE CONTINUED

www.ingramcontent.com/pod-product-compliance
Lightning Source LLC
Chambersburg PA
CBHW020327180626
46812CB00001B/86